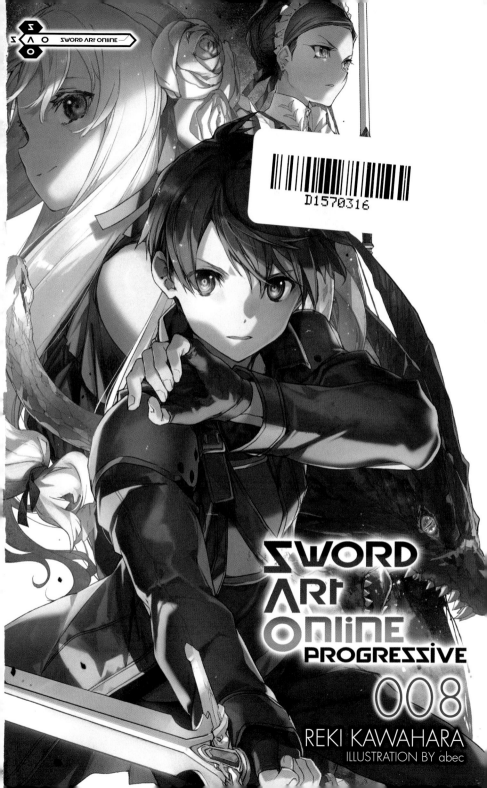

"Shut up;
this is
just what
you do."

Asuna

A girl trapped inside the
game of *SAO*. She used
to be self-destructive but
now works hard to help
beat the game.

"Um...what is this?"

Kirito

A swordsman striving to reach the top floor of Aincrad. He's a solo player by nature but working with Asuna for now.

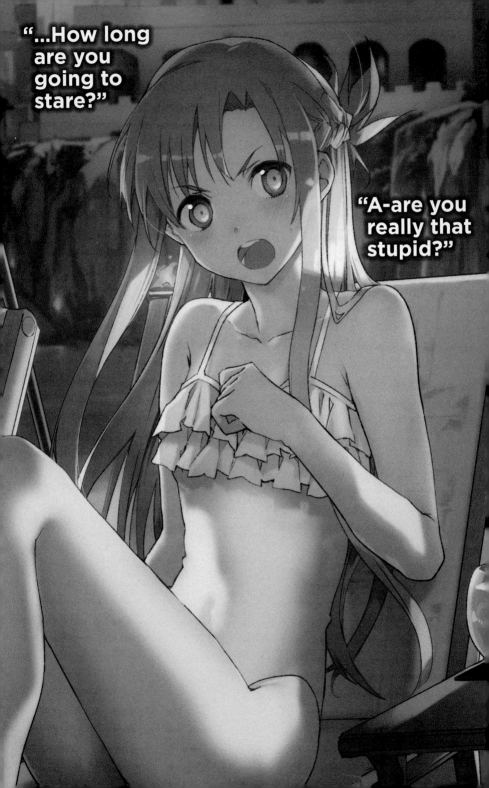

"Goaaahhhh!"

Aghyellr the Igneous Wyrm
Boss of the seventh floor of Aincrad.

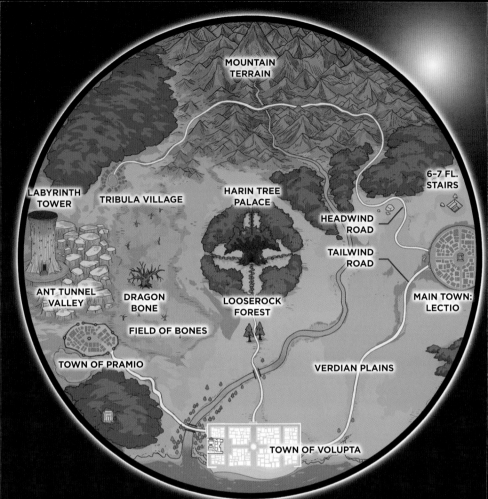

Map labels:
- MOUNTAIN TERRAIN
- 6-7 FL. STAIRS
- LABYRINTH TOWER
- TRIBULA VILLAGE
- HARIN TREE PALACE
- HEADWIND ROAD
- TAILWIND ROAD
- ANT TUNNEL VALLEY
- DRAGON BONE
- LOOSEROCK FOREST
- MAIN TOWN: LECTIO
- FIELD OF BONES
- TOWN OF PRAMIO
- VERDIAN PLAINS
- TOWN OF VOLUPTA

FLOATING CASTLE AINCRAD FLOOR DATA ΛIΠCRΛϽ

SEVENTH FLOOR

The seventh floor has two main features. The first is its eternal summer climate. Kirito and the other players arrive in January, right in the middle of winter in the real world. But the blazing sun and humidity of midsummer blanket the entire floor.

The other feature is the casino. The starting point of the seventh floor, the town of Lectio, is on the eastern end, while the labyrinth tower is on the western end. There are two roads leading there. One is Headwind Road, where treacherous terrain and numerous monsters await. The other is Tailwind Road, where the path is gentle and few threats exist. Traveling down Tailwind Road leads to Volupta, a town with a very large casino.

Volupta's casino offers all sorts of gambling, including plenty of card games, dice, and roulette wheels. The biggest draw of them all, however, is the Battle Arena—a monster coliseum.

All the monsters there are from the seventh floor, and battles are one-on-one. There are five battles during the day and five at night. Many players went broke here during the beta test.

Map Illustration: Tatsuya Kurusu

SWORD ART ONLINE PROGRESSIVE

VOLUME 8

Reki Kawahara

abec

bee-pee

YEN ON

New York

SWORD ART ONLINE PROGRESSIVE Volume 8
REKI KAWAHARA

Translation by Stephen Paul
Cover art by abec

SWORD ART ONLINE PROGRESSIVE Volume 8
© Reki Kawahara 2021
Edited by Dengeki Bunko
First published in Japan in 2021 by KADOKAWA CORPORATION, Tokyo.
English translation rights arranged with KADOKAWA CORPORATION, Tokyo, through Tuttle-Mori Agency, Inc., Tokyo.

English translation © 2022 by Yen Press, LLC

Yen On
150 30th Street, 19th Floor
New York, NY 10001

Visit us at yenpress.com
facebook.com/yenpress
twitter.com/yenpress
yenpress.tumblr.com
instagram.com/yenpress

First Yen On Edition: May 2022

Yen On is an imprint of Yen Press, LLC.
The Yen On name and logo are trademarks of Yen Press, LLC.

Library of Congress Cataloging-in-Publication Data

Names: Kawahara, Reki, author. | Paul, Stephen (Translator), translator.
Title: Sword art online progressive / Reki Kawahara; translation by Stephen Paul.
Description: First Yen On edition. | New York, NY : Yen On, 2016–
Identifiers: LCCN 2016029472 | ISBN 9780316259361 (v. 1 : pbk) |
    ISBN 9780316342179 (v. 2 : pbk) | ISBN 9780316348836 (v. 3 : pbk) |
    ISBN 9780316545426 (v. 4 : pbk) | ISBN 9781975328146 (v. 5 : pbk) |
    ISBN 9781975383336 (v. 6 : pbk) | ISBN 9781975339913 (v. 7 : pbk) |
    ISBN 9781975343385 (v. 8 : pbk)
Subjects: | CYAC: Virtual reality—Fiction. | Science fiction.
Classification: LCC PZ7.K1755 Swr 2016 | DDC [Fic]—dc23
LC record available at https://lccn.loc.gov/2016029472

ISBNs: 978-1-9753-4338-5 (paperback)
        978-1-9753-4339-2 (ebook)

10 9 8 7 6 5 4 3 2 1

LSC-C

Printed in the United States of America

"THIS MIGHT BE A GAME, BUT IT'S NOT SOMETHING YOU PLAY."

—Akihiko Kayaba, *Sword Art Online* programmer

SWORD ART ONLINE PROGRESSIVE

RHAPSODY OF CRIMSON HEAT (PART TWO)

SEVENTH FLOOR OF AINCRAD, JANUARY 2023

14

SHE KNEW FROM A BOOK IN THE REAL WORLD THAT the word *spa*, as used in Japan to refer to an all-in-one bathing and beauty complex, came from the name of an actual hot spring area in Belgium.

So when Nirrnir, the overseer of the Volupta Grand Casino, suggested that they "go to the spa," she was briefly taken aback. But then she adjusted her perception—these people were residents of an unfamiliar world, and yet they spoke Japanese. It was simply part of the conveniences of the game. It was all a VRM-MORPG being run in virtual reality, and the people in it were merely NPCs being operated by the program itself—she supposed.

"I'll scrub your back for you, Asuna," said Kizmel, the dark elf washing her hair directly to Asuna's left.

Asuna was startled but came to her senses with a smile. "Really? Well, if it's not too much trouble."

"No trouble at all."

Kizmel grabbed a thin sponge that looked to have been fashioned out of some kind of plant, poured some bottled liquid onto it, and frothed it up, then moved her wooden stool to sit behind Asuna. The girl rounded her back, waiting for the touch of the sponge, but was startled by a finger that slid down her spine instead, causing her to jump.

"Hya! Hey…! What was that for?!"

"Ha-ha-ha, I'm sorry. I was just recalling how many times Tilnel played tricks like that on me when we were bathing together. It made me want to have a little fun myself."

"Well, it doesn't make sense to get back at *me*…but I forgive you."

"Ha-ha. Sorry again," Kizmel repeated, this time beginning to rub the sponge on Asuna's back. It was just the right amount of pressure, not too strong and not too weak. She didn't think anyone had done this since the early days of elementary school, when her family actually bathed together.

She doubted Kizmel had been programmed with instructions to wash a player's back if they bathed together, and the idea of "getting back at a player for the pranks her little sister played" was something that few people would think of in real life—and certainly not inflict on another person. Kizmel wasn't just some program; she was something very different from artificial intelligence as Asuna understood it in the real world.

At this point in time, Asuna viewed Kizmel, and many of the other NPCs she'd met, as real people who lived in a real world called Aincrad. She was certain that her temporary partner, Kirito, shared that view.

As Kizmel went to work, the principal representative of "other NPCs," Nirrnir, watched the activity with envy from their right.

"That looks very pleasant. Will you do that to my back, too, Kizmel?"

"Gladly. Just give me a moment." Kizmel finished scrubbing Asuna's back, then used the basin full of hot water to carefully wash the suds off.

"Thank you, Kizmel."

"You're welcome," she said, smiling at Asuna, then moved her seat over to the right.

Nirrnir was seated on another wooden stool. She had her luxurious golden hair parted in two, hanging in front over her shoulders. Her exposed back looked like it belonged to a doll. Kizmel sponged it very gently.

Asuna smiled to herself as the girl closed her eyes in bliss. Then she looked around the rest of the bathing area.

The bath in the luxury hotel on the third floor of the Volupta Grand Casino was certainly deluxe enough to be called a spa. Upon passing through the door in the hallway, they entered a lounge with reclining chairs, then a pristine changing room, followed by the bath at last. It was reminiscent of a real resort hotel, hot spring grand bath, a local public bathhouse, or a neighborhood health spa—and yet also unlike those things.

For one thing, there were no windows. It was one o'clock in the afternoon, and if there had been a big window pointing south, they'd be able to bring in all kinds of sunlight, but the only light came from the lanterns on the wall. The natural black rock interior made the bath very dim, if not as dim as Nirrnir's room. On the other hand, there was a great variety of plants around the place that made it feel like a greenhouse—and not so cramped and stuffy.

Half of the bathing room, which was a good thirty feet to a side in total, was dedicated to a washing area built in direct facsimile of the Japanese style. Pipes pumped in fresh water at all times, while wooden bath stools sat in front of shelves with sponges, shampoo, and body soap. As a matter of fact, you could say that this entire facility was Japanese style; there weren't many group baths like this in America or Europe.

In a sense, given that Aincrad was based on classical fantasy themed after medieval Europe, this place might be inappropriate for the setting. But to Asuna, any realism-based design philosophy that would eliminate a spacious, luxurious bath was worth less than the bloodsucking slugs in Looserock Forest.

Between the tented bath in the dark elf camp on the third floor, Yofel Castle on the fourth floor, the village bath in Shiyaya on the fifth floor, and the underground bath in Castle Galey on the sixth, Asuna had received an immeasurable amount of refreshment and vitality. Even the bath in the room above the farmhouse that Kirito was renting on the first floor…If she hadn't been able to bathe to her heart's content that day, Asuna might have lost her will to fight against this game of death forever.

She recalled that the bath was where she first met Argo the info dealer. When the girl strode right into the bath, Asuna had screamed her lungs out, but now Argo was a friend she could confide in without reservation.

Speaking of Argo, she had quickly washed her hair and body and was now monopolizing the spacious bath. When Asuna spotted her in a state of utter relaxation with her limbs splayed wide, she couldn't wait any longer.

"I'm going into the bath," Asuna told Kizmel.

"Yes, I will join you soon."

Asuna stood up and crossed the stone floor to the bath. She used her bucket to rinse off first, then slid into the crystal-clear water.

"Auuuuh…"

She couldn't stop the sound from escaping her throat. The numbing, throbbing sensation extended to the tips of her fingers and toes, and she sank down to her mouth and closed her eyes.

SAO's VR system had trouble re-creating the sensation of liquid, Kirito had said once. It was true that when she bathed on the first floor, something felt off about the way the water pressed against her bare skin, the sense of overall pressure, the reflection of light on the water surface, and the way individual droplets worked. But the more opportunities she found to bathe, the less she minded these things. Either she was getting used to VR bathing, or the system itself was evolving. If Kirito were here, she could ask him his thoughts…and then she had to scold herself: *No, he's not supposed to be here!*

As though reading her mind, Argo lazily murmured, "Gosh, if only Kii-boy could be here, too…"

Asuna very nearly swallowed some water. She had to lift her mouth back above the bath. "Wh-why would you say something like that…? There's no men's bath here."

"Just give him a blindfold, and he'll be fine."

"That would be kind of mean." Asuna chuckled, but then she realized something. "Wait…Argo, was there a sign that this was a women-only bath…?"

"Nope."

"……"

She glanced back at the entrance. That meant this was a mixed bath, and a male NPC—or worse, player—could walk through at any moment.

"You're safe," said a voice from behind her, once again reading Asuna's thoughts. She spun around and saw Nirrnir, her face and body washed, standing with her hands on her hips. "The hotel's guests can only use the bath between three and nine o'clock. It's all ours at the moment. That means we can even do this."

She crouched briefly, then sprang high into the air, did a pike flip, and landed bottom-first into the bath. Despite her tiny size, the sheer momentum of her maneuver splashed water everywhere. It rained down over Asuna's and Argo's heads.

They sat there, unmoving, as water dripped down their bangs. Kizmel, meanwhile, silently slipped into the water and said, "If Miss Kio were here, she would have scolded you."

"She certainly would have," admitted Nirrnir as she floated up to the surface. "Almost every bath I take is accompanied by Kio, so on the few occasions this is not the case, I get to do things I'm not normally allowed to do. Why don't you try jumping in, too?"

"Um, I'll pass," Asuna said, doing her best to smile. On the inside, she was thinking, *There's no way this girl is just a program.*

She slicked back her wet hair, then relaxed once again. The bath was a bit on the hot side, but the good thing was that you couldn't get light-headed or dehydrated in the virtual world. Even better, her waist-length hair didn't need to be tied up before it hit the water. There were no loose hairs floating in the water or clinging to her skin.

If I get too used to the conveniences of this world, I'm going to have a hard time when I get back to reality. She chuckled to herself—until her smile turned bitter. She was acting like they'd come so far since the first floor, but they were only on the seventh. There were ninety-three unconquered floors of Aincrad above their heads. Even if they took a week to complete each one, that would take nearly two years. And that was an optimistic view; the difficulty was only likely to rise as they went upward.

Strangely, however, thinking about the future didn't fill her with the same sense of despair as before. She had to banish the idea that she might be getting used to this wild scenario: a virtual game world that would kill her if her HP dropped to zero even once. Maybe she was getting a tiny bit used to it, but that wasn't all.

Most likely, there was something building up within her that was neutralizing that despair. The beauty of the scenery, the taste of the food, the pleasure of the bath, the satisfaction of solving riddles, the socialization with Argo and Kizmel...and her ever-present black-haired temporary partner. It was a little galling to admit it, but for every time he angered her, or annoyed her, or surprised her, or delighted her, some tiny bit of the built-up silt of fear and panic at the bottom of her core blew away.

If she kept going on adventures with him, would all that darkness within her eventually disappear? Would she feel like there was a meaning one day, a benefit to having been trapped in this place?

She couldn't be sure yet. Maybe some massive, unseen misery was going to beat her down, leaving her unable to get back up again. But even still...

On her right, Kizmel's eyes were closed. On her left, Argo was watching with a smile on her face. Across from her, Nirrnir floated on the water, limbs outstretched. Asuna decided that if she had the chance later tonight, she'd invite Kizmel to join her in the bath again.

With swimsuits, of course.

15

SHEESH, IT'S HOT.

After some thought, I opened my menu window and unequipped my main armor, the Coat of Midnight. After another few seconds of consideration, I also returned my Fortified Breastplate to storage.

That left my only clothing, aside from underwear, as a black long-sleeved shirt and black pants. Both were tight-fitting, but the pants were made of a fantastical material called Shadow-thread, which gave them a substantial bonus to Hiding and also a small amount of temperature regulation. I sighed and took a look around.

My current location was in the middle of a narrow, dark path between the north wall of the Volupta Grand Casino and the tall wall surrounding it. A heavy iron gate separated this pathway from the front garden of the casino, so it was clear that guests were not meant to come back here. But because *SAO* didn't have those invisible walls from classic 3D action RPGs, you could always cross any fence or wall—provided you had the strength or agility. And the game did not automatically turn you into an orange criminal player for doing so.

But NPC town guards were a different story. I didn't think they'd just attack me without warning, but after what happened at Harin Tree Palace, it was quite possible I'd be apprehended, taken to jail, and held for questioning. On my left was the wall of the four-story casino building, and on my right was a ten-foot wall. If I got trapped on both sides—front and rear—there would be no escape. Tonight was our plan to expose the wrongdoing of the Korloy family for Nirrnir, and tomorrow was our crucial mission to take back the sacred keys and restore Kizmel's reputation. I couldn't afford to be arrested for even a single night.

Should I turn back and play it safe...? I wondered. But there was a vague worry deep in my gut that I'd been missing some crucial detail. We'd all but confirmed that the Korloys were dyeing the fur of a higher species of lykaon to pass it off as a Rusty Lykaon in the Battle Arena. Kio the maid was mixing the decoloring agent at this very moment, and once sprinkled on the creature in view of the betting public, the Korloys would have no excuse. In my head, I knew Nirrnir's plan was foolproof, but the gamer part of me always suspected a trap when things were going *too* smoothly.

I'll just take a quick peek at the monster stables behind the casino, and if nothing sets off my intuition radar, I'll leave at once, I told myself, then resumed walking down the path.

Fortunately, I reached the northwest corner of the building without encountering any guards, so I pressed my back against the white surface of the casino and listened closely. I could hear the faint sound of talking, but no one seemed to be coming closer. Leaning just barely around the corner, I took a quick peek.

There was a space behind the casino lined with stones that was much more expansive than the front garden. Three carriages without any horses were parked there. The doors on the rear of the carriage were made with iron bars that slid sideways, making it seem like these carriages were for transporting monsters captured in the wilderness.

On the northern end of the space was a warehouse-like structure, but I heard sounds like whinnying now and then, which suggested it was the horse stable. I leaned out farther so I could look along the wall of the casino itself; there was a massive gate large enough for the carriages to pass through, with smaller doors on either side. Inside had to be the monster stables I was after.

I'd assumed that would be a separate building, but they kept the space inside the casino. My initial plan was to sneak up and peek through the window, but that was now impossible. Sneaking inside would be much too dangerous—and yet one of those two small doors was half-open, beckoning me closer.

Fine, fine, I'll go! I growled to the *SAO* game system—or just my own goddess of fate. Once again, I examined the whole space beyond the corner. From the horse stable, which was no more than twenty feet from my current hiding spot, I could hear the faint sound of a mop being used and a voice singing a rather silly song, but there wasn't any other sign of humanity. My guess was that the capturing teams for the Nachtoys and Korloys were still out doing their jobs.

I steeled myself for the task ahead, rounded the corner, and rushed along the wall in a hunched position. I paused before the open door, listening for sounds, then slipped inside once I was sure the coast was clear.

The first thing I noticed was a faint, unpleasant odor. It reminded me of the zoo: a combination of straw, soil, and animal smell.

The place was dark and spacious, not unlike a garage. The walls and floor were made of stone and had two large square holes on the back wall. Seeing this confused me at first, until I realized they were doorways for loading monsters. Most likely, the carriages backed into the garage until they were flush with the holes, then they slid the metal grates open so the monsters could pass through the holes on their own.

Listening carefully, I felt like I could hear low growling from behind the holes. I certainly didn't want to go in there, but I couldn't see any other— No, there: plain gray doors on both the right and left walls. If I squinted, I could make out crests on the doors—a red dragon on the left and a black flower on the right, most likely a lily.

Red dragon and black lily. One was probably the Korloy family crest, while the other presumably belonged to the Nachtoys. I tried to remember the past day's events but could not recall seeing the same symbols in either Nirrnir's room or the casino itself. If I sent a message to Asuna or Argo, they might be able to ask Nirrnir directly, but then I'd have to explain where I was and what I was doing, and if I was honest, they'd command me to call off my mission at once.

Well, I told myself, *what else do you do at a casino but rely on your hunches?*

But then I remembered the monster arena last night. The Korloys' Rusty Lykaon and the Nachtoys' Bouncy Slater had appeared from different entrances into the cage, left and right. If the monster stables were separated into left and right areas farther within, then the side the lykaon appeared from was the Korloy stable, and the one the pill bug came from was the Nachtoy stable.

Playing back the visual memory of which was which, I had my answer. The pill bug appeared first from the left, and the lykaon came out second from the right. That meant the Korloy stable, the one I wanted to investigate, was...*not* the black lily door on the right. I was facing the stable from the opposite side as the arena last night, so the directions should be switched. That meant the Korloy door was the left one, with the red dragon.

Sneaking closer, I reached for the knob, turned it, and pulled. It opened easily, so I waited for a moment, then snuck inside when I heard nothing. I quietly closed the door and turned around.

Much like the cells beneath Harin Tree Palace, there was a gloomy corridor that extended to the left and right. But here, the floors, walls, and ceiling were hard stone. The doors were wooden—but reinforced with iron. There would be no burning through locks with a torch if I got caught and held here.

I thought about equipping my sword from my inventory but rejected the idea. I was the one trespassing here. If the guards spotted me, I didn't want to make things worse by getting violent. If spotted, I'd run away at top speed, and if I failed, then I failed.

The hallway ended shortly to the left, so I followed it right instead. There were a few doors on the wall; I tried opening one of them, but it was just a dusty storage room, so I ignored the rest.

On the wall at the end of the hallway was an open passage with no door; beyond was a spiral staircase heading downward. I listened carefully, then quietly snuck down the stairs. The lantern-lit steps were natural stone that had been worn smooth with use, speaking to the long history of the two families at the coliseum.

The temperature dropped as I descended, and the animal smell increased. Presumably, all the monsters in the Battle Arena were tamed through the hero Falhari's secret technique to command monsters, but Nirrnir said their obedience didn't last indefinitely and unconditionally. So there was no guarantee that being in the presence of an outsider like me wouldn't cause the monsters to go feral again. As I reached the bottom step of the stairs, I kept my senses as attuned to danger as I possibly could, ready to flee at the first sign of trouble.

Beyond the arched doorway was another hallway, this one wider than upstairs. But lining the walls was a series of steel cages, not doors. I didn't see any humans in the hallway, but I could hear muffled voices in the distance.

I listened as hard as I could, but I couldn't even tell how many people were speaking, much less the content of their conversation. Once again, I told myself, *Just gotta go find out*, and proceeded down the hall.

After a few yards, I peered into the cage on the right and saw a squat animal lying on dirty straw, something like a cross between a pig and a capybara. I recognized it as a Giant Pincer Rat, a creature that lived near Lectio, the main town of this floor. It moved slowly and had no special attacks, but the pincer-like teeth that gave the rat its name were extremely powerful. If they bit down on your weapon, it was essentially impossible to pry it loose. You'd have to beat the rat with another weapon or get a party member to help—or else it would break your weapon. Even a huge two-handed ax wouldn't withstand the pressure.

But as long as you were aware of that, they were easy to defeat, so they'd been a big source of experience points in the beta. I'd beaten far more than just fifty or a hundred, but looking at it now in this setting, I felt pity for the creature.

Don't be a hypocrite, I scolded myself, backing away from the bars and deciding not to peer into any of the other cages. I passed the second through fourth, but as soon as I reached the fifth cage, my eyes found themselves automatically drawn to it.

This cage was not bound with vertical bars like the others, but it was surrounded by a fine iron lattice pattern that ran vertically and horizontally. The gaps between the bars were barely an inch wide, suggesting that quite a small monster was being held inside. But once I saw the shadow huddled in the corner, I could see that it was no smaller than a capybara. Interested, I stared at it until its cursor appeared. The monster's name was ARGENT SERPENT. I couldn't recall such a monster from the beta, but it was clearly a snake of some kind. Unfortunately, my mental dictionary did not contain the adjective that described it.

In any case, the cage now made sense to me; a narrow serpent would be able to slip its way through spaces that a larger mammal could not. Yet the gaps between the bars in the actual arena within the casino were more like three or four inches. If they unleashed the snake there, wouldn't it slip through and threaten the guests watching the battle?

Just then, an angry voice echoed through the corridor. "Dammit, behave!"

I spun around on reflex, but there was no one around. Whatever the voice was yelling at, it wasn't me.

Facing forward again, I could see a cage on the left and one on the right—and then a rather small doorway on the far wall, which did not seem to be a monster's chambers. If I focused, I could hear something like an animal growl from the back-right cell.

I snuck forward slowly, pressing myself against the wall, and peered carefully into the sixth cage.

The little chamber was maybe eight feet to a side, and two men stood inside, their backs to me. In the corner, resting atop a pittance of straw, was a dog-type monster with red fur. I didn't need to see the cursor to know it was the Rusty Lykaon from yesterday. There were spots where the red color was coming off its body, revealing white fur instead.

The lykaon bared its fangs at the men, growling softly. If that was a higher version of lykaon with its fur dyed, it would be dangerous enough that even the most advanced players would be wary of it, but these two were totally unconcerned—because the lykaon had a collar made of heavy iron that chained it to the wall.

The men were solidly built themselves and wore deep red shirts, leather vests, and long gloves that went up to the elbow. Both of their cursors said HANDLER OF THE KORLOY FAMILY, meaning that their job was to deal with the monsters.

The man on the right lifted a short whip and shouted, "Damn mutt! Do what we say, or you'll get a taste of this!"

The lykaon instantly backed down further but did not stop growling. The man on the left muttered with irritation, "We gotta paint this thing quick, otherwise it won't take to the fur by the match, and it'll still smell. It wasn't totally dry last night, either."

I noticed he had a large brush in one hand and a ceramic jar in the other. The brush was covered with red from the jar—the fur dye.

Concentrating on the lingering smells, I picked up a sweet, sharp scent among the animal odor. It was definitely the same smell as the red stain we wiped off the bars of the arena. I didn't like it the first time, so it had to be overwhelming to a dog-type monster's sensitive nose.

But the Rusty Lykaon—or whatever the proper species name was—was supposedly under the control of Bardun Korloy's power of Employment. There was a food dish and water bucket in the corner, so I assumed it hadn't lost its tamed status from hunger. So why was it continually baring its fangs at these handlers?

Obviously, they couldn't have sensed my thoughts, but all the same, the man on the right scratched the back of his neck with the handle of his whip and grumbled, "We're gonna need Master Bardun to redo the trick on it."

The burly shoulders of the man on the left bobbed up and down. "But the plan is to dispose of it today, right?"

"Yeah. Even those foolish Nachtoys are bound to notice something's wrong by now. Once it's performed its last shift tonight, this doggy's going off to the farm."

"So if we ask him to apply his trick again, he's just going to order us to make it last one more fight instead. It ain't cheap to do."

"That's true…"

What did they mean when they said the technique to tame monsters wasn't cheap? According to Nirrnir and Kio, it was a special power inherited from their ancestor, the hero Falhari. That sounded like an Extra Skill to me. Whatever it was, something wasn't adding up.

The man with the whip clicked his tongue. "Tsk, fine. I'll whip it until it can't move anymore. Then you apply the dye. As long as we feed it healing potions throughout the afternoon, it should be ready for that last fight tonight."

"All right. Go ahead," said the man on the left, stepping back.

The one on the right swung his arm back. The corded leather whip made a whistling sound and cracked firmly on the lykaon's back.

The creature yelped and fell onto its side, red damage effects streaming from its back. It got up and resumed growling again, but just that one attack had taken its health bar from about 60 percent down under half.

The whip whistled through the air again. The lykaon tried to jump away, but the short chain jangled and held taut, keeping it within the whip's range. It cracked against the lykaon's ribs, hurtling it backward and onto the ground again. Another 10 percent was gone from its HP, and it was now under a stun effect.

For a third time, the man lifted his whip.

"Stop!!" I shouted before I even knew what I was doing. I clamped my mouth shut, but it was too late.

"Huh?!"

"Who said that?!"

I pulled my head back just before they could spin around to see. If I ran away now—but no, if they shouted, their companions were likely to trap me on the spiral stairs. On a snap judgment, I opened my window and equipped a Tattered Burlap Sack over my head.

With a whoosh, the sack appeared and fit right over my head. There were no eyeholes, but the fibers were woven so wide that I could actually see much better than I expected. The moment I closed my window, the door of the cell hurtled open, and the men leaped out into the hallway. Their eyes went wide the moment they saw me standing there with the impromptu mask over my face, but they quickly recovered and shouted, "Who the hell are you?!"

"Are you with the Nachtoys?!"

The second accusation was perfectly accurate, but I wasn't going to admit to it. Instead, I said nothing. The handler with the brush and jar, who also sported the perfectly villainous combination of a bald head and goatee, scowled and spat, "Whoever you are, we can't let you leave. Let's rough him up and toss him in one of the empty cells."

"Sounds good. I've always wanted to try hitting a person with this thing," said the other handler, smacking the whip against the ground. That was the signal to turn their color cursors from yellow to red.

But the shade of red was quite pale; that meant their level was far below mine. However, not only was it the first time I'd fought a person using a whip, I was also the trespasser here. Just because fighting them wouldn't turn me orange didn't mean I could just *kill* them. Perhaps I could neutralize them without taking too much HP, so I could escape the place before the real guards rushed in.

The whipmaster had no beard, but his hair was long, and his brows were thick and angled with fury and concentration as he pulled his arm back.

While it was my first time fighting against a whip, I'd seen its ideal range and attack timing after watching him punish the lykaon. By the time the whistle echoed off the walls, I was already charging forward.

The weapon came from the upper left, which I ducked to avoid, the enlarged tip brushing the top of my head as I rushed past. I held my left fist at waist height, then thrust it forward.

The glowing red fist struck the whip handler right between his impressive eyebrows. That was the basic Martial Arts skill, Flash Blow—not so powerful but with a much higher chance of inflicting a stun on a clean hit than a slashing sword did.

As I hoped, the whip handler flew off his feet and splayed out on the ground, motionless. Over 70 percent of his HP was left, but there was a yellow ring of light rotating around his head. That was the stun effect I wanted—and not the weakest kind that wore off in just three seconds, but a powerful stun that would immobilize him for nearly a minute. It didn't work that well against players, but it seemed to me that ordinary NPCs who weren't soldiers or warriors were more likely to fall victim to negative status effects.

"Wha…?!"

The other handler gasped with shock, then sucked in a deep breath. He was going to shout for the guards. I leaped forward again, determined to stop him.

This time, I threw a Flash Blow with my right fist, directly into his temple. The handler left his feet, smacked the back of his head against the metal bars of the cell, then fell to the floor, covered with visual effects indicating damage and a stunned effect. The jar came loose from his hand and fell—I caught it just before it could smash noisily against the floor.

Just as I'd hoped, I was able to neutralize my adversaries without killing them, but at best, they were only going to be stunned for another fifty seconds. I had to escape the Korloy stable and return to the front of the casino within that span.

I was just pivoting around on the ball of my foot when I caught sight of the Rusty Lykaon, lying limply on its side in the back of the cell.

On pure instinct, I tensed my foot, then tried to run again, but my avatar would not obey me. What would those handlers do to the lykaon if I ran out on it now? They'd assume that their fur-dyeing scheme had been leaked to the Nachtoys—and eliminate their "evidence" sooner.

Even still, so what? It was going to be destroyed later tonight anyway, so it was just a difference in timing. And the lykaon wasn't someone's beloved pet; it was just a monster like all the lancer beetles and poison wasps and hematomelibe we'd already killed on this floor. A simple mob, the likes of which I wouldn't hesitate to fight with my sword in the wilderness.

All of these facts I knew perfectly well. And yet...

"...Dammit!"

I leaped through the open door into the cell.

The prone beast craned its neck and growled—but its voice was weak and unintimidating. The yellow color cursor showed that its HP bar was only a third full.

I opened my window and tossed the jar into my inventory, then hit the QUICK CHANGE button to equip my sword. Once I'd drawn it from my back, I took one swing and severed the chain that connected the lykaon's collar to the wall.

The lykaon barked, feeling the vibration of the blow. I quickly put my sword away and whispered to the injured beast, "Just stay calm."

"Grrrl..."

I couldn't tell if that growl was a yes or a no. But the cursor was still yellow, so at the very least, it wasn't targeting me for attacks. I approached carefully and put my arms around the creature, which was the size of a German shepherd, lifting it up. Its frame was sturdy, but because of my strength stat, it didn't feel very heavy to me.

"*Grar!*" the lykaon barked, struggling a bit before giving up and hanging its head. It hadn't accepted my control; it just didn't have the strength left to fight me.

Out in the field, monsters would battle it out to the very last pixel of health. It should have been true for this lykaon, too, so why couldn't it move? Maybe it was inflicted with some kind of negative status.

But I could figure that out later. At this moment, I had to get out of the underground stable.

I leaped out of the little cell, holding the lykaon. The handlers were still stunned, but the yellow visual effect encircling their heads was much fainter than before. They'd probably be up and moving in less than twenty seconds.

At full speed, I dashed down the hall, using the loose weave of the burlap for visibility. In less than three seconds, I was through, into the corridor without slowing. Within five steps, I was past the curving wall and into the stairwell, where I bounced up three steps at a time.

At last, I could hear their shouts behind me. But the building wasn't built with security against intruders in mind; I didn't hear any alarm trumpets or bells. It was going to take longer for the guards to hear from the handlers.

Once I was on the ground floor again, I hustled through the short hallway into the loading garage. Fortunately, it was still empty in here—though I was sure the open yard in the back would not be the same.

I stopped briefly in front of the door I used to get inside, peering out carefully. As I suspected, in the middle of the loading yard, the two employees had finished cleaning the horse stables and were in conversation with two fully armed guards.

If a stranger wearing a sack over his head tried to leave now carrying a lykaon, it was going to cause an uproar—and in another twenty seconds, the handlers from below were going to be up here. Perhaps I had something that might help me in my inventory, but there was no time to go scrolling through the huge list.

...My inventory.

"___!"

My eyes bulged. I slipped the lykaon under my left arm and opened my window with my free hand. At the top of my inventory, which was ordered by most recent pickup, was an item called Rubrabium Flower Dye. I tapped the name and materialized it, grabbing the jar and pulling back as far as I could.

I could really use the Throwing Knives skill right about now, but this distance should be close enough. *Please hit them!* I prayed, hurling the jar at full strength through the half-open door.

The jar flew straight and smacked off the sturdy breastplate of the guard facing this direction. It burst, spraying red liquid like mortar. Instantly, all four of the faces in conversation were splattered with the same color as the lykaon's fur.

"Aaaah!"

"Wh-what's this?!"

"My eyes! My eyes!!"

The instant the men hunched over, hands over their faces, I bolted out into the courtyard. At that very moment, voices behind me wailed.

"Guards! Guards!"

"There's an intruder!"

But the guards and stable hands were preoccupied. I rushed past the four of them, and rather than using the side path I took around the casino building, I headed for the double gates at the back of the rear yard. Obviously, I couldn't go running past the front door holding an actual monster in my hands. But this route wasn't going to be easy, either.

The gates were the sliding kind, thick panels reinforced with steel. Not even a two-handed hammer could break through these, much less a sword. The two latches on the top and bottom might break if I used a sword skill, but with the handlers on my tail, I didn't have any time to waste dealing with this gate.

That left just one method of escape: to jump over the eight-foot wall while carrying the lykaon.

It was the same height as the iron gate blocking the side path winding around to the rear of the casino, but this time, there was no perpendicular wall right next to it I could climb up. The stone walls on either side of the gates were taller and completely smooth. The only things I could even potentially use as footholds were the two latches holding the connecting parts of the gates in place.

The latches were the kind that had metal rods with a hook on the end that you dropped into the receiver, but they were so large that the toes of my boots could just manage to find purchase on top of them. My chances of success while holding the lykaon, however, were fifty-fifty at best—and I had to do it twice in a row, so that made it 25 percent.

Within three seconds of sprinting, I confirmed the circumstances, and in a fourth, I made up my mind. As I rushed toward the gates, I shouted to myself, "*Go!*"

If any amount of fear or hesitation made its way from my mind to my avatar, I would fail. Attempting to use every last mental signal for the NerveGear on my real-life head, I willed all my strength into my right foot and launched myself off the cobblestones.

Like a long jumper, I bounded nearly fifteen feet and caught the toe of my left foot on the lower latch. Trusting in the firmness of the sensation coming through the tack in the sole of my Spiked Short Boots, I jumped vertically this time.

My right foot just barely reached the top latch. But this was the end of my run-up momentum. The only thing left that could carry the lykaon and me another three feet was pure strength.

"Yaaaah!!"

Shouting wasn't a good idea, given the possibility that guards might be waiting on the other side of the gate, and it wasn't clear that shouting in a virtual setting would have any effect on your actions, but regardless, I converted that yell strength into my second vertical jump. My left leg reached up high enough to cause a creak in my groin, and it just...barely...*failed* to reach the top of the gate. I could reach out with my right hand to grab it, but if I did that, I would drop the lykaon.

If only my legs were one inch longer!

I dispelled my lament and instantly changed plans. Before I could start to fall, I kicked off the gate with my left foot and did a hundred-and-eighty-degree turn, facing the courtyard. The guards and stable workers were still clutching their faces, but the two handlers were already in the middle of the yard. If I did nothing, I would fall back to the ground, but even assuming I suffered no damage, I didn't have time to jump up again.

I did, however, have one last trick up my sleeve.

As I fell, I folded my legs and bent my top half over. A high-pitched whine arose, and yellow light glowed in my right leg.

That foot stepped onto empty air, then shot into the air. A propulsive force that completely ignored all the laws of physics catapulted me directly up.

This was the Martial Arts backflip kick skill, Crescent Moon. It left a yellow arc of light in the air.

Because I was relying on the game to push me upward, it wasn't as powerful of a lift as if I'd actually jumped off of solid ground, but it was just enough for my upside-down head to clear the top of the gate. The tuckered-out lykaon barked softly, alarmed by the flip, but luckily, it didn't panic. It probably didn't have enough strength to do that anyway.

I did another two flips and a twist before my feet hit the ground. I looked around rapidly in a crouch—as I feared, there were fully armed guards on either side of the gate. Their eyes bulged within their helmets.

"Wh-what?!"

"Where did you…?"

But while they wasted time talking, I was already upright and running. The stone wall that surrounded the rear of the casino was also the wall of Volupta itself; a graphic reading OUT OF TOWN appeared before my eyes and vanished. I could hear the howls of the handlers behind me, but they rapidly dwindled.

Up ahead was grassland in blazing midsummer sun, as well as an unpaved path scarred with countless wagon wheel marks. It curved ahead to the right and would surely lead back to the road that went through the west gate of Volupta, which I'd passed through with the rest of the group just hours earlier. But I couldn't run into the town with the monster, and on the open road, I was visible to anyone who came chasing me.

I looked over my shoulder as I ran and saw the two armed guards and the handlers starting to run after me. I'd gotten a lead of at least a hundred feet on them, but I was also carrying a creature the size of a large dog, so I wasn't sure I could outrun them on flat, open ground. I needed to break their sight line to escape.

As soon as I faced forward again, I remembered something: If I continued straight where the path curved, I would reach the riverbed where we searched for the wurtz stones earlier, less than five hundred yards ahead. And on either side of the river were patches of overgrowth that would be a perfect place to hide.

"Hang on a bit longer!" I urged the exhausted lykaon, shifting my feet into a higher gear.

I was running like a ninja, keeping my body inclined as far forward as it could go and keeping my stride as even as possible. The shouts grew quieter in the distance, but if I got too desperate in my escape, I could trip and lose my balance. I focused on the ground ahead, evading any stones hidden in the grass or dead branches.

After reaching the top of a gentle hill, the green bush patches came into view, framing the silver gleam of the water between them. That was the largest river of the seventh floor, starting from the mountains in the north and flowing across the plains into the sea to the south. I was curious where so much water actually *went* once it reached that small sliver of sea, but that was not a mystery to wonder about at this moment.

There was a spot of about five or six bushes clumped together that I eyed as I hurtled down the hill. The game tended to generate denser bushes near trees, and that would offer me adequate hiding space. The only question was if I'd get in position before my pursuers reached the top of the hill and saw me.

I practically toppled down the last hundred yards of the slope. It felt like the game was rolling whether or not I fell with every step; I could only trust my stats and true luck. My focus was on the edge of the rapidly approaching brush, and once I was just fifteen feet away, I leaned backward and slid on my back, holding the lykaon tight with both arms as my foot led the way into the mass of leaves.

Nearly all trees and bushes in *SAO* could be lumbered—i.e., destroyed—but some trees had a basic core that was indestructible. If the system had designated this particular bush as having one of those impenetrable walls, it might bounce me off. Fortunately, the bush merely sprayed loose leaves as it welcomed me inside. Even luckier, the interior was a kind of hollow surrounded by several bushes, making it a good hiding spot.

I ripped off the burlap sack I'd been wearing this whole time and peered through the branches at the slope I'd just run down. After about five seconds, my pursuers appeared at the top. The two guards and two handlers looked around, searching for any sight of me. If they were players, or advanced AIs, they'd probably realize I was hiding in the brush, but these ones had typical NPC or monster-pursuit algorithms.

The four men stared all over the open field, and their faces swept over my hiding spot several times, but they weren't coming down the hill. Eventually, they stopped searching and traded a few words. Immediately after, their red color cursors turned back to yellow.

After they had turned around and descended the hill toward the town, I finally let the air escape from my lungs. That was when I recalled, at last, that I was still holding the Rusty Lykaon.

The lykaon rested its head on my arm and panted rapidly. I checked its HP bar quickly and saw that the remainder was under 20 percent—and decreasing slowly but surely. Maybe the handler's whip had poison on it? But then there should have been a debuff icon, and there was no reason for them to weaken a monster that was supposed to fight in a match for them.

That meant the DoT (damage over time) effect was from some kind of hidden negative status effect. And in most cases, such things were hidden because they were part of a quest. Which meant...

"...It's the dye!" I snarled, sitting upright.

Minutes earlier, I'd escaped by throwing the Rubrabium Dye at the guards. I was hoping just to confuse them for a few seconds, but the NPCs had collapsed and clawed at their eyes. That suggested that the dye was poisonous and would probably cause continual damage if it went into your eyes or a wound.

Meaning that the lykaon was losing HP because it was struck with a whip while the dye was thick in its fur. Maybe I could take it over to the river and wash out the dye...But no: If simple water could wash out the dye, Nirrnir wouldn't have bothered to make a bleaching agent.

If I couldn't get the dye out, then if I healed its wounds, recovering HP, the damage *should* stop.

I quickly opened my inventory, grabbed the burlap sack I'd dropped, then materialized a healing potion, which I opened and held out to the lykaon's mouth.

"Here. Drink this."

But the lykaon just panted, its tongue lolling out of its mouth. It did not try to drink. I tried dripping some of the red liquid on its tongue, but it just dripped off onto the ground. In an older

MMORPG I'd played before, healing a tamed monster's HP required the appropriate skill, so perhaps it worked that way in *SAO*, too. That would mean I had no way to heal the lykaon now. A healing crystal might do the job, but the only crystal we'd found on this floor was in Asuna's possession, and I didn't want to use what could be our lifeline on a monster.

It was a sudden impulse that led me to save the lykaon and escape; was that gesture pointless? No, I would also be eliminating a chance to reveal the Korloy family's wrongdoing, so it wasn't just pointless, it was a setback. How could I apologize to Argo, who took on the quest; Nirrnir and Kio, the clients for the quest; and Asuna, who worked so hard to help gather the materials for the decolorant...?

"......Ah," I gasped.

There was perhaps one other way to save the lykaon. The chance of it actually coming to be was low, but if I gave up now, I'd never forgive myself.

I went back to my open player window and wrote a quick message to another player. Then I cradled and stroked the dying lykaon's neck, until a response arrived two minutes later. I gave it a quick read, exhaled, then put the potion back in my inventory and pulled out a leather waterskin instead.

"You might not like the potion, but I bet you'll drink water."

I poured out some liquid into my palm and held it up to the beast's snout. The lykaon lifted its head a tiny bit and lapped at the water. Of course, that alone wasn't going to heal its HP, nor stop the damage. At the very least, I wanted to take off the iron collar with the dangling chain, but it was fastened very tight, and I couldn't loosen the nut with my fingers.

Instead, I let the lykaon's head rest on my lap, and I waited patiently.

16

I THOUGHT THERE WAS NO WAY IT COULD BE SOONER than thirty minutes, but it only took fifteen before I heard the sounds of feet approaching through the grass.

Through the branches of the bush, I could see two figures descending the hill toward me. They couldn't see me inside the bush—they were just following the location marker on their map—but just in case, I stared until their cursors appeared, so I could read their names.

The green cursor in the front belonged to ARGO. But the yellow one behind it was KIO.

"Huh...?"

I checked the lykaon's remaining HP, then rushed out of the undergrowth.

"Argo, over here!" I waved. The info dealer trotted closer, wearing her usual hood.

"Kii-boy, I gotta tell ya..." she started, looking exasperated.

But I cut her off. "Thanks, sorry, talk more later." Then I turned to Kio.

The tall maid strode smoothly down the hill, dressed for battle with her breastplate, armored skirt, and estoc. Her hair was parted to the side, and the look in her eyes was the most dangerous I'd seen from her yet.

I came to a sudden standstill, feeling slightly intimidated. Kio said, "Kirito, why have you snuck into the Korloy family stables and removed the Rusty Lykaon from their possession?"

"I'll give you a full explanation later; there's no time now. Did you bring what I asked for?"

"...Right here."

From a large leather sack on her belt, Kio removed a container shaped like a wine bottle. In fact, it *was* a used wine bottle. A milky white liquid filled it to the stopper, shining like a pearl in the sunlight. Based on the size of the bottle, there had to be at least a pint in there.

"Is that the decolorant...? I thought you said there was only going to be a tiny bottle of it."

"If it had sat for three hours as planned, it would have condensed down to a third of this size. If we use all of this, the effect should still be the same," Kio explained. She looked from the bottle to me and asked the natural follow-up. "I have brought the solution as Lady Nirrnir bade me...but why do you need it if you have already removed the lykaon from the stable? What would be the point of returning its fur to normal now?"

"That's a good question," I admitted, pausing to consider how to answer her. I told the two, "Uh, give me a moment."

Then I glanced around, ensuring nobody else was nearby, and snuck back into the bush. The lykaon was still lying on its side under the branches. Its HP bar was down to 15 percent. It felt as though the rate of decrease was speeding up as it got closer to the end.

"I'm going to save you now," I said, an encouragement I couldn't guarantee, and crawled over, sliding my hands under the lykaon so I could flip it onto its other side with my elbows and knees. Then I crawled backward, holding the creature, and stood up.

"*Nwa!*" yelped Argo, leaping backward. It seemed like an overreaction to a dying dog, but it *was* a proper monster, I supposed. Maybe her reaction was the correct one.

Kio seemed unaffected by the sight, so I approached her and

quickly explained, "It seems like the Rubrabium Dye they used to color its fur has toxic properties, and it got inside a wound. It's going to die soon. If we don't bleach out the dye right now..."

Kio's brows knit. But it wasn't because she was especially concerned for the lykaon.

"Rubrabium...Yes, that flower is poisonous. I assume they could not find a better dye to match the proper color. It is a very dangerous substance, however."

"Right, so use that decolorant to..."

"Why?"

"Huh?" I gaped.

She snapped, "Why would you try to save that lykaon? It is not some dog or cat like people keep as pets—or a beast of burden like cattle and horses. It is a true monster. It might be under the effect of Bardun Korloy's ability for now, but when that wears off, it will attempt to tear out your throat. And even if the ability stays in place, it cannot be returned to the Korloy stables, and because they will suspect Lady Nirrnir's involvement, it cannot be given to her for retraining and entered into the arena. What is the purpose of using our valuable bleach on its fur now?"

That was the same question I'd been asking myself—as I jumped into the cage, as I fled here, and as I waited for Argo in the bushes. Ultimately, there was no logical reason for what I had done. The best thing I could say was...

"...If Asuna were here, she would have done the same thing," I muttered. Kio's eyes narrowed, and she gave me a piercing stare.

"How can you insult her profession like that? She is an adventurer like you; she must have killed countless monsters on her journey to Volupta. What makes that lykaon you're carrying any different from those beasts?"

"Its pride. Its dignity," I offered.

Kio's brow furrowed again. "Dignity...?"

"The monsters that Asuna and I have defeated have come to us in top condition, not under anyone's orders, fighting for their lives. Yes, I've killed many monsters, but they had the possibility of killing me, too, and I've nearly died on many occasions. But this creature is different. It was chained up inside an underground cell, painted with poisonous dye, and whipped by handlers. Fighting an enemy under equal conditions isn't the same thing as leaving a tortured animal to slowly die," I explained as earnestly as I could.

There was one big hypocrisy behind my words, however. In truth, not all monsters attacked players of their own accord. The *SAO* system merely instructed them to—in fact, most likely they did not have any individual will of their own. Unlike the independent AIs of Kio, Nirrnir, and Kizmel, they were merely a part of a much larger system, and this lykaon was no exception. What I was doing was not fundamentally different from pulling a flower off a tree with one hand and then caressing it with the other.

But even then...

"...I see," said Kio. She glanced down at the apron dress, then at me again. "I serve Lady Nirrnir with ultimate loyalty, but I am not under the sway of violence, bondage, or unique abilities. I suppose that is what you mean."

"Um...yeah, more or less."

"So if you heal that lykaon, and it follows its 'monster's dignity,' as you call it, to attack you—would you draw your sword and kill it?"

It was a tough question, but I had to answer it.

"...Yes. Although it might kill *me* instead."

"......Ha." To my surprise, Kio actually chuckled at my answer. "Ha-ha. You are a strange one. Are all adventuring men like this one, Argo?"

From ten feet away, Argo replied, "Nope, he's crazier than the rest."

"That is a relief to hear...Very well. There is no other use for the bleach at this point. You might as well use it," Kio said, handing me the glass bottle.

I laid down the lykaon on the grass at my feet, then took the bottle with both hands. Perhaps the liquid itself was heavy, because it felt much bigger than a regular wine bottle of the same size.

"Um...don't I need a brush or something?"

"No. Simply sprinkle the liquid onto it from head to tail, nice and slow."

"......All right," I said, pulling out the cork.

I gave it a sniff out of sheer habit. The peculiar, peppery-lychee scent of the narsos fruit was almost entirely gone. I crouched over the lykaon and carefully tilted the bottle.

The pearl-colored liquid, which was just slightly viscous, glooped out onto the lykaon's head. Its round ears twitched, but it did not react otherwise. I moved the bottle to the right, allowing the liquid to fall onto its neck and body.

Once I'd finished applying the mixture to the end of its long, thin tail, the bottle was empty. The red-dyed fur was shining where the liquid touched it, but it didn't seem to be washing out the color. In fact, there wasn't nearly enough of it to finish the job...

But the thought had only just crossed my mind when the liquid suddenly and violently began to bubble. The fine white suds bubbled up rapidly until they covered the lykaon's entire body.

"H-hey, is this supposed to happen?" I asked Kio in a panic.

The armed maid barely lifted an eyebrow. "Shut up and watch."

"...Yes, ma'am," I said, hunching my neck.

The suds rose higher than my knees, sizzling and fizzing, growing and writhing like a living creature. It made me worry that the lykaon underneath might suffocate, but I could see its HP bar through the bubbles, and it was not decreasing at all.

"Oh?!" Argo suddenly exclaimed from her position of distance. My eyes widened, too.

The mound of suds was turning red, starting from the bottom. At first, I thought it was the lykaon's blood, but when the smell in the air turned sharp and sweet, I realized it was the Rubrabium Dye melting off.

Once the entire mound of suds was dyed red, it began to sink back down, seemingly evaporating into thin air. In just seconds, 70 percent of it was gone, revealing the monster it had initially swallowed.

"Ooh..."

Now it was my turn to exclaim in wonder.

The signature mottled spots on the lykaon's pelt were still the same, but the muddy-red rusted color was gone. The metal collar still circled its neck, but even the fur underneath had been leached of its dye. The creature's original color shone silver, a light gray in the sunlight.

After all the dyed suds bubbled and popped away, the lykaon remained prone on the grass, eyes closed. But its labored breathing had calmed. The steady decrease of its HP bar had stopped, too.

I let out the breath I'd been holding, and the front part of the name RUSTY LYKAON melted away from the label under its HP bar, revealing a different descriptor.

STORM LYKAON. Fortunately, this word was within my middle-school-education English level.

"Storm Lykaon...You know anything about these, Argo?" I asked, glancing to my right.

The informant shook her head. "Nope. Never seen one, never heard o' one."

"Neither have I...Are you familiar with this creature, Kio?" I continued, turning to her next. The maid shot me a look.

"I am not."

"What...? I thought the Nachtoy family had a list that ranked all the monsters of the seventh floor."

"I did not say it was *all* the monsters," Kio corrected me, glaring. "What is listed on the rank sheet are merely those monsters of the proper size to fight in the arena's cage—and that have no special attack methods that might pose a danger to the audience or building."

"Oh, right…But wouldn't this Storm Lykaon fit the requirements? The rotating attack it used to beat the Bouncy Slater was surprising, but it didn't seem likely to destroy the cage."

"I did not witness this rotating attack you speak of. But…I very much doubt the Korloys would bring out a monster that would destroy the cage itself. Which *does* make it strange that this Storm Lykaon would not be on the list…" Kio murmured, looking down at the doglike creature.

The HP bar had stopped decreasing, but its health was not recovering from its low position. The lykaon's eyes remained closed, and it lay still on the ground.

Normally, after a monster took damage from a player in battle, and either side ran away to put an end to the fight, those HP would recover rapidly. Perhaps that would happen for this Storm Lykaon if we left, but the situation was too irregular for me to be certain of that. If it stayed in this condition, a player busy leveling around Volupta would eventually find it and kill it, even if its cursor was only yellow.

Perhaps the only option would be to take it farther away from town, somewhere no player was likely to come anytime soon, I thought—when Kio pulled another bottle out of her pouch.

This one was much smaller than the wine bottle in my hand and had multifaceted cuts in its surface, like gemstone faces. It contained a pink liquid with an orange tint.

"Use this," she said, holding it out. "It is a healing draft for monsters."

I stared at the bottle. "Uh…Wh-why do you have this? I thought you were against saving the lykaon…"

"I am. But Lady Nirrnir instructed me to take it. If you won't use it, I'll take it back with me."

"N-no, I will! Thank you!" I said earnestly, bowing my head. I took the bottle and handed back the empty one. Then I leaned over the lykaon and asked, "Um…Will this still have an effect if *I* give it?"

I was trying to suss out if I needed some kind of monster-healing skill to make it work, without actually saying so, but Kio looked as though I was being ridiculous.

"Why would the person holding the bottle make its contents change? Although, from what I hear, it does take some skill to give medicine to a monster so weakened that it cannot move."

Earlier, I tried to give the lykaon a potion, but the creature just let the drops trickle off its tongue. If the same thing happened here, I'd feel bad for Nirrnir, who gave me not just the bleach but also this curative potion, whatever her reason.

"...By the way, Kio, do you have that particular skill?" I asked politely.

The maid promptly snapped, "Of course I do not. Do I look like a stable worker or beast handler to you?"

"N-no, you don't," I said meekly. Just in case, I glanced at Argo, but she only shook her head sadly. This one was going to be up to me.

I knelt by the head of the prone lykaon. Its eyes opened just barely, and it made a brief, quiet growl, but nothing more after that.

I suspected that if I tried to drip the liquid into the corner of its mouth, the result would be the same as before. There had to be a way to get it to properly swallow. What if there was something like an eyedropper to stick in its mouth? It would probably just crush it with its powerful jaws.

After some rapid thought, I knew what I would have to do. I popped the cork off with my thumb, then cupped my left hand and poured a bit into my palm.

The sunset-colored liquid was chilly and nearly odorless. Careful not to let it spill, I lifted it toward the lykaon's snout. But it did not react at all. Perhaps I would need a special skill to do this, after all, I thought.

Just then, the lykaon's muzzle, which was slightly shorter than a wolf's, rose just a little. The black nose stretched for my hand and sniffed a few times. I almost spoke to it but held my tongue just in time.

Eventually, the lykaon lifted its head just an inch or two, then extended its tongue toward the liquid in my palm. It lapped at it once, just to check that it wasn't bad, then tried again a few seconds later, then again.

"Oh...its HP!" Argo exclaimed. I glanced at its cursor and saw that the HP bar was slowly increasing from 10 percent.

Meanwhile, the liquid cupped in my palm was empty, so I quickly added more from the bottle. The lykaon unsteadily lifted itself up, spreading its front paws out. Its nose stuck into my palm from above and noisily lapped at the liquid. It was gone in moments, so I added more.

After three sets of this, the bottle was empty.

I stood up and checked the lykaon's HP bar; it was all the way full again. I felt relief, but this didn't mean the problem was entirely solved. Deep in my mind, I heard Kio's words repeat themselves. *So if you heal that lykaon, and it follows its 'monster's dignity,' as you call it, to attack you—would you draw your sword and kill it?*

There was no sword at my side right now, but if I opened my window and hit the QUICK CHANGE button, the Sword of Eventide would instantly appear there. The dog—no, monster—in arm's reach was not a Rusty Lykaon, of which I'd killed dozens in the beta test, but an unfamiliar higher version, a Storm Lykaon. From what I could tell after witnessing its fight against the Bouncy Slater, it wasn't dangerous enough to be a major threat to us. But I couldn't be careless: If it showed even the slightest inclination of attacking, I had to equip my sword and demonstrate my answer to Kio's question.

The fully healed Storm Lykaon stood up, its powerful limbs tensing on the ground, and shook itself. The silver-gray pelt, mottled with black spots, shone in the sunlight like snow. There was no longer any trace of rusty red, and I couldn't see the wounds where it had been struck with the whip, either.

The lykaon walked in a large curve, the short chain dangling and clanking from its collar. Once it was at a distance of ten feet, it turned toward us. Those brown eyes, the one part of it that was unchanged from before, looked me right in the face.

Its head slowly lowered. The silver fur stood up. Wrinkles appeared on its snout, and I caught a glimpse of sharp teeth.

"...*Grrrr...*"

The cursor over the growling Storm Lykaon began to flicker, switching back and forth between yellow and a pale shade of red. Bardun Korloy's taming technique was wearing off.

"*Growr!*" it barked, right as the cursor turned permanently red.

It wasn't very deep, but it was certainly a darker shade than I expected. For me to see the cursor this red at level 22, it would have to be the very strongest of all the regular monsters on the seventh floor. At the very least, it had to be much stronger than the Bouncy Slater it fought last night. So why had it struggled so much in the arena?

Then again, Nirrnir said that the lykaon had won four straight battles leading into last night. It would've required that poisonous dye to be painted on its fur each of those days, sapping its strength and agility. That would mean the lykaon had just now recovered its true, original power.

And now, following its sense of dignity—or the *SAO* system's commands—it was preparing to attack me.

"Kirito."

"Kii-boy!"

Both women reacted together, Kio behind me and Argo to the right.

I understood their message. They wanted me to draw my sword. It was the right choice to make. Most of my armor was unequipped now, and my Martial Arts skill alone would not be enough to handle the lykaon's attack, I suspected.

However...

"Hey," I called out to the growling monster. "You just got your freedom again. And now you're gonna waste it fighting me and dying? Is that really what you want?"

It was a meaningless question. There wasn't a single monster in Aincrad that possessed its own independent thought-process program. They only looked like individual creatures; in truth, they were just one part of a massive algorithmic system.

If this situation lasted another five seconds, I would close my window and equip my sword. Decision made, I stared back at the fierce eyes of the majestic creature and slowly counted the seconds in my mind.

One, two, three, four...

"Grr......"

Suddenly, the lykaon stopped growling.

It kept its head low in battle mode but backed away. Once it was a good six or seven yards away, the creature spun on its heels like lightning and ran toward the river.

Its speed was astonishing. It was at least twice as fast as the Rusty Lykaons I'd fought in the beta test. The silvery beast dwindled as it sped away, jumped into the undergrowth along the river, and vanished from sight.

The red cursor was still there for a few seconds, and then that vanished, too. It wasn't hiding along the riverside but had kept running beyond it—most likely to the northwest.

"......"

I let the tension out of my shoulders, gazing in the direction the Storm Lykaon went.

On my right side, Argo said, "Did it understand what ya said, Kii-boy?"

If only, I thought, shaking my head. "No...Among animal-type monsters, some of the smarter ones like monkeys and dogs will run away when the difference in strength is too great. You know that, of course. I bet it realized it couldn't beat us."

"Its cursor was pretty red, though. I was thinkin' it might be bad news if it turned into a fight."

"Yeah, I thought the same thing...But if the lykaon was scared enough to run away..."

...That just tells you how dangerous that battle maid behind us is, I thought, finishing the sentence.

For her part, Kio watched the lykaon run off, then noticed my glance and said, "Are you satisfied now, Kirito?"

"Er…well, at the very least, I suppose I don't regret it…"

It wasn't the most forceful response, and I thought I caught a hint of exasperation in her eyes, but she was soon as stone-faced as ever. She took the wine bottle back from me, putting it away in her pouch, and announced, "Now you will return with me to Lady Nirrnir's chamber, where you will explain why you snuck into the Korloy stable and what happened while you were there."

"Y-yes, of course. I owe you that much," I said, nodding. I picked up the stopper for the restorative; it was not simply glass but had the weight and density of natural crystal, so I carefully plugged it back into the little bottle and returned it to Kio.

The fact that they brought not only the bleach I asked Argo for but also the healing potion was because Nirrnir ordered Kio to take it, she said. That was what allowed me to save the lykaon, but how had Nirrnir known we would need the healing item? There were other questions I wanted to ask, but first I needed to apologize for my actions and explain them.

"Let's go, then," Kio said, and she spun around, apron swaying, as she climbed the green hill behind us.

Argo and I rushed after the trailing white ribbon adorning her black armored skirt. After thirty steps, the Rat whispered to me at a low enough volume that Kio couldn't hear.

"Hey, Kii-boy. You know how, when you fight the same individual monster for long enough, they start to react to your weapon and sword skills and stuff?"

"Huh? Oh yeah…It happens more often with the humanoid types."

"Meaning that monsters have the ability to learn, too, just not as much as NPCs. So the longer it lives, and the more battles it experiences, the more customized it becomes as an individual, ya know? So maybe that lykaon didn't run off on the standard algorithm but made the decision on its own ta stop fighting."

"Um...Y-yeah, I suppose..." I muttered, contemplating the suggestion. I glanced over at her.

"...Wh-what?"

"Oh...I just realized you were trying to cheer me up..."

Argo made a strange face, lifting her eyebrows and puckering her mouth. The whiskered face paint made it look like she was imitating an actual rat face, and it made me burst out laughing.

"What? Am I not allowed ta cheer you up?" She pouted.

"S-sorry, it's fine. Thanks...I'll go with the Argo theory, then."

"Hmph. Shoulda just done that."

Up ahead, Kio turned around and arched a questioning eyebrow.

17

ONCE THE WEST GATE OF VOLUPTA CAME INTO VIEW,
Kio took a gray hooded cloak out of her leather satchel and put
it on. It wasn't the largest bag, which made me wonder how the
thing actually fit inside. Upon a closer look, the cloak was so thin
that it was almost see-through. Or it should have been—but it
blocked the light and didn't even flip up with a breeze from the
shore, meaning it must have been made with a special material.

Asuna and I wore hooded cloaks often on our more clandestine
activities, so I couldn't help but wish I had one—as did Argo, no
doubt—but I couldn't just ask her for it. All I could do was pray it
would be offered as a quest reward. Kio passed through the gate, her
maid outfit entirely hidden now, and we followed closely behind.

The present time was just a bit before two o'clock in the afternoon. The monster arena's daytime run started at three, so people
would be starting to gather in the space in front of the casino
about now. Most of them would be NPCs, I assumed, but if Kibaou
and Lind intended to win back those thousands and thousands
of chips, the ALS and DKB would be heavily represented, too.
And enough time had passed that more of the midlevel players
would be arriving at the casino from Lectio, I guessed.

On top of that, there were fully armed guards at the casino
entrance. While it was true that I wished for a hood to hide my
face like my companions, if all three of us were bundled up like

that in this heat, it was bound to draw attention. But the guards were probably hired by the casino, not the Korloy family directly, and I'd been wearing that sack over my head when I caused that scene in the stables, so they didn't know who I was...I hoped.

For now, Kio walked down the street with great certainty, so I could only obey and follow. The space in front of the casino was just as busy as I expected—there were even people dressed in full battle gear, whom I assumed were players. I followed the gray cloak, keeping my head down. But Kio did not turn toward the casino. She walked directly into an inn along the main street.

It wasn't quite the deluxe hotel on the third floor of the casino, but the entrance lobby here was plenty nice. I looked around and leaned closer to ask Kio, "Is Lady Nirrnir here, instead of at the casino?"

"Just follow me," she said, so I had no choice but to follow. Kio passed by the counter and a concierge in a black vest, walking briskly down a dim hallway.

She came to a stop in front of one of the doors, then removed a ring of at least a dozen keys from her cloak, selected one, and unlocked the door. The room was a single, quite nice but small, and there was no one inside, not even Nirrnir.

"...?"

If I were an NPC, you'd see a question mark over my head so big you'd think I had a quest to offer. Kio shrugged off her gray cloak and folded it up until it was no bigger than a wallet, tucking it away again. Then she exhaled and walked to the closet in the corner.

I watched over her shoulder as she pulled open the doors. Inside was neither Nirrnir nor a single piece of clothing. But Kio reached into the empty closet, grabbed the silver hanger bar, and rotated it forward.

It ground, then clicked. The back panel of the closet creaked and swung backward.

"Whua—?!" I yelped, shocked. But a few blinks later, I noticed that Argo was very quiet. In fact, she was grinning rather smugly.

"You knew about this?"

"I went through this room on the way in, the first time," she replied. That cleared it up for me.

"Oh, I see…"

Over Kio's shoulder, I saw a dark passage through the back of the closet, leading somewhere else. Actually, there was only one place it could be going.

"Kirito, Argo, you first," said the battle maid, turning back to us.

"Sure." Argo shrugged and headed right into the closet. I followed her without a word. It wasn't large enough to be a walk-in, but without any drawers below, I didn't have to raise my feet much.

Beyond the back panel, which swung open ninety degrees like a door, the surfaces were all stone, just the way you'd expect a secret passage to look. It was less than two feet wide, which was just enough for Argo and me to walk straight through if we hunched our shoulders, but a larger player like Agil would have to crab-walk sideways.

That thought made me wonder where the friendly ax warrior and his fellows in the Bro Squad were right about now. Meanwhile, Argo came to a stop about six feet down the passage.

I turned back, careful not to scrape my shoulders, and saw Kio coming into the closet. She pulled the double closet doors shut from the inside, stepped backward into the passage, then pushed the panel back to its original position. It clicked into place, then she pulled down a lever located high along the wall, engaging a lock with a metallic scraping sound. It seemed like tedious work if you didn't know all the steps, and there was no way to squeeze past another person in the cramped space, which is why she made sure Argo and I went in first.

When the closet panel closed, the passage was briefly dark, but a faint light from farther down lit the way. There was clearly some kind of light source set up here, but it wasn't orange from flames; rather, it was a mysterious pale green hue. I wondered what it was.

"Continue forward, Argo," said Kio.

"You got it."

I hurried after the info dealer, who went thirty feet down the passage before turning right at a spot where a mysterious object was set into the wall. There was a hole about four inches to a side in the stone, out of which stuck a thick, short branch that was emitting the faint green light. Actually, it wasn't the branch that was glowing, but a narrow mushroom at the end. It was...

"A bonfire shroom...?" I murmured, coming to a stop.

Behind me, Kio commented, "You know them? I suppose your friendship with the Lyusulans isn't just for show."

"W-well, it isn't *just* not for show," I murmured, which was more confusing than I meant it to be. I hunched my shoulders in embarrassment, then turned my head to ask, "Anyway, why is there a bonfire shroom here? I thought they died as soon as you plucked them from Looserock Forest..."

The light itself wasn't bright, but it made for an excellent emergency light source. More than a few players in the beta tried to collect the mushrooms as a tool, myself included. But no matter how carefully you did it, or what container you put them in, the mushrooms would wilt away and melt into nothingness within just ten seconds.

I can't believe they'd make them harvestable in the full release. I should've filled a bottle full of them...

"That is correct," Kio said, dashing my hopes immediately. She instructed me to take two steps farther inward so she could inspect the pale glow of the mushroom. "If you pulled this bonfire shroom from the branch, it would die immediately. But to explain why this one still lives...would require you to swear an oath to Lady Nirrnir and enter service to House Nachtoy."

Under her solemn stare, I withdrew my neck into my shoulders as far as it could go. "I'll, uh...think about it."

The armed maid chuckled, which took me so much by surprise that I stared at her in the green light. Then her smile vanished, and she was cold and stern once more.

"We don't have time. Onward."

"You got it," said Argo, continuing down the tunnel. I hastily turned myself back around and followed her small figure.

There were bonfire shroom branches every thirty feet or so in the passage, and I had counted five of them when the end finally came into sight.

This time, we didn't pass through a closet; the passage turned directly into a set of stairs. It reminded me of the spiral staircase at the Korloy stable, but half as wide. After Argo, I climbed up the stairs, which proved to be nearly endless.

I had lost all perception of how many steps or how many floors we'd risen when they finally came to a stop. From there, it was another cramped corridor. We turned right, then left, then right again, and we were finally at our destination.

The passageway was blocked by a heavy-looking panel, with a small lever high on the wall to the right. It was just tall enough that I might be able to reach it if I stretched for all I was worth. But that meant...

"Uh-oh...Dang it, I can't reach up there," said Argo, reaching for the lever. But even on tiptoe, she was six inches short. She could reach it by jumping, of course, but it was so delicate it would likely break under an entire person's weight at once—even a small person like Argo. Assuming it was breakable to begin with.

Speaking of which, I feel like this has happened a number of times before...

Thinking of old memories caused me to act subconsciously, grabbing Argo under the armpits and lifting her up.

"*Nnowuh?!*" she yelped bizarrely, which made me realize how strange my action was. But I couldn't just drop her now. I hoisted up the struggling woman and said, as calmly as I could, "There, pull it down."

"Don't treat me like a child!" she protested, but she pulled down the lever anyway. It made a sharp *click*, and the panel blocking the end of the passage swung open.

Satisfied, I lowered my hands. As soon as Argo's feet hit the floor, she rounded on me and jabbed a finger in my face. "Kii-boy, who taught you it was acceptable ta grab a lady like that?!"

"S-sorry, sorry. It just seemed like the thing to do."

"The thing ta do? You don't pull stunts like that with A-chan, do ya?"

"N-no, I don't, I don't!" I insisted, shaking my head.

I wasn't thinking of Asuna, but a memory of my sister, Suguha. When she was young, and we were leaving the house, she always wanted to be the one to turn out the light in the entryway herself, so I'd have to lift her up. It seemed hard to believe now, given that we were only a year apart—technically, half a year—but until she was in kindergarten, I recalled that Suguha was actually much smaller and weaker than the kids her age.

Only once she started elementary school and was doing kendo training did she grow like a weed, tall and healthy. It was an example of how you never knew how kids were going to grow—but this was all just a mental diversion from what was coming to me.

Argo finally lowered her hand and said, "The next time you try a stunt like that, I'm chargin' ya money."

"M-money? For what?"

"It's the side-squeeze tax!" she snapped, turning around in a huff. I exhaled weakly. I thought I heard suppressed chuckles over my shoulder, but the only person behind me was Miss Kio, who was battling with the dark elf blacksmith from the third floor for Most Unfriendly NPC, so I was sure my ears were playing tricks on me.

Beyond the panel Argo opened was a simple set of doors, which she pushed open. A faint bit of light entered the passage. It was not green, but orange—light from a classic lantern.

I followed her through and found myself in a cramped chamber with small metal rods fixed into the walls on either side, upon which hung women's clothes. If it were any larger, I might have thought we'd exited into a clothing store. All the clothes were fine-looking party gowns, dresses, and camisoles. Every one of them seemed to be quite small.

After going a bit farther and turning around, I saw that the exit I'd just walked through was a brilliant red-brown closet from this side. Like the entrance in the inn, the exit was also disguised. Then again, considering the way it was used, perhaps *this* side was the entrance.

Kio came out last of all, then rotated the pole at the top of the closet inward, which caused the rear panel to creak shut and click into place. She shut the closet doors and turned around.

"...Are all of those Lady Nirrnir's clothes?" I whispered.

"That's right. Don't touch them with your dirty hands."

I gave her an awkward smile, then examined the dresses on the walls again. In a new light, I could see that some were red, blue, and purple, but most of them were black. Nirrnir might like black clothing, or maybe all the black gave her a bonus to Hiding...Nah.

"Wow...This is gonna be tough, huh? When Lady Nirr gets bigger soon, she'll have to buy a whole new wardrobe, I bet..."

It was just the first thought that came to mind, but Kio merely gave me an odd look and said nothing. After further thought, I realized that child NPCs in Aincrad might not actually grow up. In fact, while it wasn't true of *every* RPG, it was the very rare exception that actually modeled that sort of thing. No wonder my question stumped even the advanced AI of the NPC.

I decided this probably wasn't a topic worth drawing out, so I headed for the door that exited the dressing room. But the moment my hand was about to make contact with the golden knob, it rattled on its own, sending me jumping backward.

Standing on the other side of the door as it opened was not a town guard or an assassin, but my temporary partner, wearing a white dress.

"How long were you going to stand around chatting in the closet?" Asuna asked with familiar exasperation.

All I could muster was an awkward smile. "Uh...I'm back."

Outside the changing room with the secret passageway was a darkened room that featured a large canopy bed placed smack in the middle. It was clearly Lady Nirrnir's bedroom, so I crossed it to the far door, taking care not to look around too much.

At last, we were in a familiar place: the main area of Room 17 at the Grand Casino Hotel. But before I could enjoy a moment of relief, a figure stood up from the three-seat sofa, rushed over, and grabbed my shoulders.

"Kirito! I should have expected this...You always find a way to get into trouble."

"Sorry to worry you, Kizmel," I said to the dark elf knight, patting her awkwardly on the back and turning to the five-seat sofa.

The owner of this room and manager of the Volupta Grand Casino overall, Lady Nirrnir Nachtoy, rested on the pile of cushions there, reading an old, faded book. Her eyes drifted up off the page and onto me.

"Welcome back, Kirito."

Her expression and tone of voice were relaxed—sluggish, even—which made it impossible to decipher what she thought about my solo adventure. One thing was certain: I caused Nirrnir's bleach-sprinkling quest for Argo to fail. I could tell, because the glowing question mark over Nirrnir's head when we left this room hours ago was gone.

I knew I'd have to give Argo an apology later. For now, I waited for Kio to take her usual place next to the sofa. As soon as the armed maid was in position, I straightened my back and announced to the young mistress, "I have returned."

"...And?"

"Um...I'm afraid I have c-caused you great offense..." I stammered, trying my best at a formal apology. But Nirrnir scowled and waved me off.

"We don't need to go through all that. Just explain what you saw and what happened in the stables."

"A-all right."

Kizmel handed me a glass of water, so I thanked her with a glance and drank it all down. It wasn't as cold as the ice water Argo fixed last night, but after a big adventure like ours, it was good enough.

Refreshed, I cleared my throat, then explained everything as politely as I could: what happened in the stable, how the Rusty Lykaon was actually a Storm Lykaon, and how it ran away after I healed it. The only thing I didn't mention was my discussion with Kio about the dignity of monsters.

I finished by saying, "And that's everything." Nirrnir remained seated, saying nothing for the time being. She did not speak for a full fifteen seconds.

"Just to confirm, absolutely *no one* in the stable saw your face?"

"Yes," I said at once. That much, I was sure of. "No one saw me slip inside, and I was wearing the sack over my head the entire time the handlers could see me."

"Put it on again."

"I'm sorry?" I asked, but it was clear there wasn't a single yoctometer of possibility that I'd misheard her, and I certainly didn't have the standing to refuse.

I opened my window, tapped the head of my equipment mannequin, and set it to the Tattered Burlap Sack. With a little swish, the sack appeared, the rough fibers covering my sight.

"...This is what it looks like..."

I could tell my voice was a bit muffled, but the room was almost totally silent, so I was sure Nirrnir heard me. Yet there was no response at all.

"Um..."

I looked over at Kio next to the sofa, unsure of what to do. For some reason, she looked away from me. I looked at Argo, Asuna, and Kizmel on the other side of the low table, but they had the same reaction.

I just stood there, hoping someone would say something, when Nirrnir abruptly shoved her face into the cushions, her shoulders trembling. Was she crying? It looked more like she was holding back laughter.

In a chain reaction, Kio's head dropped, her hand covered her mouth, and the girls turned their back to me. It was the exact same reaction they'd had when I'd squeezed that narsos fruit with my bare hands. That time, I felt honored to have brought laughter to the group, but doing it twice in one day was a little too much debasement for me. I could be forgiven for fighting back.

I inched to the left until I was standing directly in front of Kio. The battle maid sensed my presence and looked up. In that very moment, I extended my arms up and to the sides, letting my fingers dangle and lifting my left knee to stand on one leg: the crane pose.

"*Bfftp!*"

A bizarre sound escaped from the hand covering Kio's mouth, and underneath the sack, I grinned with satisfaction. But then her hand left her mouth and zipped with lightning speed to the hilt of the estoc at her side.

"Aaah! Wait, wait, no!" I yelped, sticking my hands out forward and shaking my head.

Nirrnir had recovered from her giggle fit and said hoarsely, "Kio, I have more to ask of him, so I need him alive a bit longer."

"...Yes, Lady Nirrnir. As you wish," Kio replied smoothly, taking her hand off the weapon and returning to her usual standing position. I exhaled with relief...but didn't know if I *should* yet. I took Nirrnir's comment to be a joke and wanted to believe that Kio did, too. But if the NPCs could use dark humor this effectively, then Argus's—or Akihiko Kayaba's—AI development was even more advanced than I'd given them credit for.

In any case, I seemed to have avoided giving offense, so I lowered my hands and asked Nirrnir, "Um…can I take this off now?"

"I wish I could say no, but it would be better if I didn't burst into laughter every time I saw you."

With her permission, I pulled the sack off my head, then put it back into my inventory, praying I'd never need to wear it again. Nirrnir gestured toward one of the three-seat sofas, so I sat down. Argo sat next to me, while Asuna and Kizmel took the other one.

Kio prepared some tea—today's tea was cinnamon-flavored—so I had a sip, then returned the conversation to the topic at hand.

"…Anyway, as you saw, my face was completely covered."

"Indeed. The Korloys would not have been able to identify you…I think…" said Nirrnir, albeit with hesitation. She gazed at my upper chest, then added, "But just in case, I would not wear that all-black clothing. Do you have any other colors?"

"…I don't," I admitted sheepishly.

Asuna added, rather unnecessarily, "Not only does he not have any other colors, he doesn't have any other clothes, *period*."

"Really…? Just that one outfit? That you wear every single day?" said the girl, her seemingly twelve-year-old face full of revulsion and pity. It was withering.

"N-no, I wear something else when I go to bed…"

The thing was that clothing stains in this world were simple graphical effects that faded with time, and clothes never got stinky with sweat, but I decided not to bring up these facts. There were baths in this world, but I couldn't recall ever seeing any kind of laundry implements. If there was no concept of laundry, then what was the problem with wearing the same clothes without ever changing?

But no amount of self-absolving arguments would stop Nirrnir from scowling at me.

"If you had said you didn't even have nightclothes, I would tell you to sleep on the floor next time. Well, if that's all you have, that's all you have. Kio, I'm sure some of Father's clothes are still around here. Find something for him that *isn't* black." She waved, prompting the maid to give her a concerned look.

"Are you sure?"

"Yes. They're only clogging up the wardrobes anyway."

Asuna assumed a pensive look after hearing the two talk this way, and I realized what she was thinking. If Nirrnir had a father and mother, one of them would be the leader of the Nachtoy family, of course. But if young Nirrnir was the one currently in charge, her parents were most likely already...

I wasn't sure if I should really ask to confirm the answer to that question. So Kizmel did it instead.

"Lady Nirrnir, do you not have any parents or siblings?"

"No," Nirrnir confirmed, her sluggish expression unchanging. "My mother and father passed away long ago. I did not have any siblings, so I run the house now. What about your family, Kizmel?"

The knight looked down. "My parents live in the city on the ninth floor. But my sister was called to the Holy Tree during a battle with the forest elves just fifty days ago."

"I see...You have my condolences."

Nirrnir had switched from her teacup to a glass of red wine, which she lifted in honor, then closed her eyes and drank. She lowered the empty glass, twirling it in her fingers, and said to no one in particular, "Lyusulans and Kalessians cannot help but continue their fight, even after centuries. Well, I have no room to criticize. I've been squabbling with the Korloys for years."

"...I have no hatred for the forest elves, either, but perhaps......"

Kizmel slowed and allowed the words to hang in the air before she closed her mouth. When she continued, it was in a suppressed whisper.

"Perhaps, if a babe was born again to Lyusula and Kales'Oh, bearing the blood of the two priestesses who gave their lives to the Holy Tree to stop the ancient war, we might finally see an end to this long, long battle...Or so Her Majesty once said to me."

"Wuh?" blurted out not Nirrnir, not Kio, not Asuna, not Argo—but me. I immediately regretted it, but I couldn't take it back now, so I cleared my throat and asked what was on my mind.

"This baby with the blood of the priestesses. Didn't you say the Holy Tree priestesses died ages ago, during the Great Separation? So how can there be…Oh! Unless their family lines are still alive today?"

"That is not the case," the knight said, shaking her head. "For one thing, the priestesses who served the black-and-white Holy Tree are not a hereditary position in either Lyusula or Kales'Oh. When the priestess reaches the end of her years, and her power of prayer wanes, a baby born somewhere in the kingdom will contain that power and become the next priestess. But after the miraculous feat of the Great Separation, there has not been a single babe who carries the priestess's power, even after these many years. Not in Lyusula—and I suspect not in Kales'Oh, either…"

"…I see…"

It was a story archetype you saw often in both Western and Eastern fantasy—but looking at Kizmel's melancholy expression, it felt callous to sum it up that way. The elves of Aincrad had no choice but to grow up with an exile's identity, cast away from their beautiful home.

So it made sense that the forest elves wished to collect the six sacred keys to open the Sanctuary and return the floating fortress to the earth. The problem was that, according to the dark elven legends, opening the Sanctuary's doors would lead Aincrad to catastrophic ruin. And as claimed by the fallen elves, opening the Sanctuary would cause "even the greatest magic left to humankind to vanish without a trace."

It wasn't clear exactly what this catastrophe entailed, but there was a greater-than-zero chance that it meant Aincrad would not gently glide down but slam into the earth like a meteorite in a vast explosion, obliterating all the NPCs and monsters and players alike—meaning that Asuna and Argo and I would *actually* die. And if the "greatest magic left to humankind" that General N'ltzahh of the Fallen mentioned was our art of Mystic Scribing, meaning the player's menu window, then we wouldn't be able to change equipment, earn skills, or hold items in our virtual storage. It would make reaching the hundredth floor an impossible task.

It felt improbable that the status of a quest that only Asuna and I were following could decide the fate of eight thousand other surviving *SAO* players, but after what happened in Stachion on the sixth floor, I couldn't rule out the possibility. Because the PK guild killed the lord of Stachion, no one who came after could start the "Curse of Stachion" quest. If a single player's malice could ruin the main quest of an entire floor, I couldn't categorically rule out the downfall of Aincrad itself.

We had to do whatever it took to retrieve the four keys that Kysarah the Ransacker stole from us, I thought with renewed determination. Nirrnir clapped her hands to cut through the gloomy air.

"Now, Kio, bring out all of Father's clothes that we have. We shall work together to choose one that will suit Kirito," she said.

When I saw it, I inwardly yelped with dismay, but there was no escape now.

Ten minutes later, the changing room's period of terror and chills was over at last, and I sank into the sofa, reeling from a kind of mental exhaustion I'd rarely experienced before in my life.

Ultimately, the women selected a light blue half-sleeve linen shirt, a pair of off-white cotton three-quarter pants, and brown leather braided sandals, a very resort-y combination. Among the clothes that Kio brought out were white tuxedos, crimson silk, and frilled shirts—the kinds of things French noblemen wore. So at least I didn't have to wear *those*, although up close, the linen shirt had very fine flower patterns, and the pants were cool and smooth to the touch. I didn't know much about fashion in *any* world, but it was clear just from wearing them that buying these clothes in an NPC shop would cost a total of at least five thousand col.

"Ha. Well, you look better just not wearing black," said Nirrnir, sipping on her second glass of wine.

I straightened my back and bowed formally. "M-my thanks. I will endeavor to return them as clean as when you gave them to me."

"You don't have to give them back. I have no use for them anyway."

"Uh...but..."

I couldn't bring myself to say, *These are a memento of your father, aren't they?* Normally, Asuna would help me out of an awkward social situation, but she had gone with Kizmel and Argo to the changing room.

Nirrnir could sense what I was thinking, however, and shrugged, her bare shoulders visible above her summer dress.

"You saw the wardrobe when you came through the hidden door. I've got a ton of Father's clothes left behind."

"Th-that's true...He was quite a fashionable fellow, wasn't he?"

"I suppose. He would go to the upper floors to spend money on them, since there aren't any great shops on the seventh floor. I believe that's how he got the shirt you're wearing now, Kirito."

"From the upper floors...?" I repeated, looking at the ceiling. "But to go between floors requires going through the labyrinth tower...er, the Pillar of the Heavens, where a guardian beast lurks, right? He didn't *beat* them, did he?"

If that were true, we wouldn't need to fight the floor boss here, I thought optimistically. It took barely a second to have that idea shot down:

"Hardly. Only reckless, death-defying adventurers like yourselves would dare attempt that tower. The monster-capturing teams that the Korloys and we employ are veteran fighters, but even they're forbidden from approaching the tower."

"Oh, I see. In that case, how did he...?"

"You know there are some who travel between floors without using the towers for passage."

"Without using the towers...?" I wondered, until realization struck. There was a teleportation system on each floor that humans could not utilize. "Oh...do you mean, el...?"

Just then, the door to the bedroom opened forcefully, and Asuna came in, her cheeks flushed.

"Oh, wow, that was incredible! You should have seen it, Kirito!"

"I saw it earlier..."

"Then you should be more enthusiastic," Asuna scolded. She turned to Nirrnir and said, "Thank you for showing us your clothes, my lady! I've never seen such a lovely wardrobe in this world...or even in the place I came from!"

"I'm glad you enjoyed it," replied Nirrnir with a smile. "If the sizes had matched, I would have loved to gift you some of them, but..."

Asuna waved her off. "No, I couldn't! I had the time of my life just looking at them...So..."

She trailed off awkwardly at the end, which suggested to me that she hit upon the same question I had a moment earlier.

Clothing and armor in this world had no concept of "sizing." It would always stretch or shrink to fit the person equipping it. But that did not apply to Lady Nirr's wardrobe, apparently. In that sense, I supposed it was my good fortune that her father's clothes were in my size. Though perhaps it was just the case that all clothes were split between "adult" and "child" specifications, and the auto-sizing function only worked within the boundaries of each.

In any case, Asuna quickly regained her smile, thanked our host again, and sat down on the sofa. Argo and Kizmel followed her in, so we sipped on Kio's fresh pot of tea as I returned to the report that had been interrupted earlier.

"Once again, please allow me to apologize for going off on my own. I don't know how I can make it up to you for wasting the decolorant you went to the trouble of making..." I apologized, racking my vocabulary for the best possible words to describe my contrition.

But Nirrnir cut me off again. "I told you, enough of that. There's nothing we can do about what's already been done. I'd rather talk about what comes next."

"What comes...next...?"

Nirrnir's initial plan was to sprinkle the decolorant on the Rusty Lykaon in the monster arena, thus revealing its true fur color to the betting guests and making plain the Korloys' gratuitous rule-breaking behavior. But I used up the only bottle of the bleaching agent, and the Rusty (Storm) Lykaon had run off across the map. There was no way to repair our strategy, it seemed to me...

When I couldn't come up with a new comment, Argo crossed her arms and legs and said, "The lykaon that Kii-boy freed has run off, but that just means there's a blank slot in the fights tonight. Lady Nirr, how do y'all decide to cover for something like that?"

"We have no rules for it," said the young head of the house, shaking her wineglass back and forth rather than her head. "As I told you, a monster that is registered for a fight must appear... That is the rule of the Grand Casino."

"But you said that rule has been broken before," noted Asuna. "Twice, in fact..."

Nirrnir nodded. "Yes. In both cases, the house that could not fulfill the rule had to apologize directly to the other and plead for the right to substitute a different monster. It involves a great amount of shame and expensive reparations."

"And that will happen here, too?" asked Kizmel, who was sitting next to me. Nirrnir looked at the elf, her dark reddish eyes blinking several times first.

"I'm not sure. Bardun Korloy might decide it was the fault of the mystery dog thief that he could not submit his lykaon for battle—and refuse to admit his family's error."

"Ah, I see...Much as it pains me to admit, similar squabbles have arisen between the three knighthoods of Lyusula, from what I hear—losing equipment during group training sessions, getting the meeting time of cooperative missions wrong. When such things occurred, the different groups always resisted taking responsibility."

"In that sense, humans and elves are much the same," said Nirrnir, smiling wryly. "Which means that Bardun might claim it was a Nachtoy member who absconded with the lykaon—and blame us for the loss…which would be true, of course."

She shot me a keen glance, and I shrank my head as far down into my shoulders as I could. But Nirrnir wasn't angry; she seemed to be holding back laughter, if anything.

"However, they can't possibly track your identity from the clothes you wore, so all we have to do is insist we have no idea about that. Ultimately, they will have to plead with us to allow them to replace their monster with another one."

"…And will you accept that substitution?" prompted Kio from the side of the sofa. Nirrnir murmured thoughtfully to herself, a mannerism that was actually rather adorable.

Behind the eyes staring at her wineglass, her mind seemed to be working hard. Nirrnir was an NPC, advanced AI or not, so her actual "brain" was not her own, but it was located somewhere in the real world—most likely the processor of the *SAO* server in Argus's headquarters. Yet it was impossible to see her avatar as just some visual cypher and nothing more.

But by that token, Asuna, Argo, and I were just empty avatars without real brains in them, too. The only difference between us was whether the avatar was connected to a biological brain or integrated circuits.

After a few seconds of consideration, Nirrnir stated, "Because the match cannot be canceled, we will have to accept it in the end. However, following past precedent, we will be able to demand some kind of compensation. Rather than simple goods or money, I would prefer something that might expose the Korloys' ill deeds."

"What kind of thing would that be?"

"The right to inspect the Korloy stable unannounced," she said, to my open-mouthed surprise.

But Asuna, who was sitting across from me, understood Nirrnir's meaning with her usual sharp insight. "Of course. If we inspect the stable, we might find traces of the red dye or some other evidence of their scheme. And if they were to refuse, it would essentially be admitting they're hiding something..."

"But what if they refuse that in the first place, knowin' they'll be suspected anyway? What'll happen next if the Korloys refuse an inspection, Miss Nirr?" Argo asked.

Nirrnir wore a cold smile that did not at all suit her preteen appearance. "Then we will refuse their request for a replacement, and they will have to either produce a new Rusty Lykaon or cancel the evening matches. The final match is at ten thirty, so they have over seven hours to act, but there is no way they can dispatch a capturing party to the lykaons' habitat far to the west and bring it back in time for the fight, even with all those hours. So practically speaking, they must choose to cancel."

"But...earlier, you said that the match *can't* be canceled," I interjected at last.

It was her maid who replied. "That is correct. The battles at the casino each night are a five-part *test* to determine who should be the rightful heir, in accordance with the last will of Falhari the Founder. According to our customary rules, if a single bout should be canceled, the tests will be considered concluded, and the next best-of-five series will determine the official head of the house. Bardun Korloy is motivated by making money; he would not pursue such a risk."

Nirrnir bobbed her head and added, "That is correct. So I believe Bardun will accept an inspection of his stables. If we find evidence of wrongdoing, it will give me the means to make the Korloys pay—if not quite as effectively as if the fur-bleaching strategy had worked."

"H-hold on…I mean, please wait, my lady," I interrupted, leaning forward. I intended to ask the question I was sure Asuna, Argo, and Kizmel were wondering as well. "If canceling the match is against the rules, shouldn't cheating also be illegal…? Wouldn't that be the end of the test matches, too, and send it straight to the official battle to determine the rightful leader?"

"………"

Nirrnir did not reply at once. She swirled the bit of red wine at the bottom of her glass, then finished it off. She handed the empty glass to Kio and stared at me.

"I did not want to draw you into the stir that would ensue, which is why I did not mention this…The law states that if one side is accused of cheating, the matter will be judged by Falhari's spirit."

"Falhari's spiriiiiit?" screeched Argo incredulously. She unfolded her arms and made a grand gesture with her hands. "Meaning, yer gonna summon yer ancestor's spirit through a ritual and whatnot?"

"And whatnot," agreed Nirrnir. Next to Argo, Asuna's shoulders hunched. She hated anything to do with ghosts. While it would be nice to reassure her, sadly, there were plenty of astral-type monsters in this world, like wraiths and wights and specters. I couldn't rule out the possibility of Falhari's spirit appearing.

But despite bringing up the topic of ghosts, Nirrnir just waved it away. "No one has ever seen him, though, myself included. For one thing, not once since the founding of the Grand Casino have we ever required Falhari's judgment."

"In that case…if you go to inspect their stable and find some dye or other evidence, is it even going to mean anything?" asked Kizmel in a measured tone. "If Falhari's spirit does not appear with the ritual, how will it deliver its judgment? Do the rules state what happens then?"

"Nothing of the sort. But that's not your concern," Nirrnir said rather brusquely as she turned from Kizmel to me. "Kirito,

I am not criticizing you for taking the Rusty Lykaon out of the Korloy stables, saving its life, and letting it go free. But if you feel apologetic for what you've done, will you undertake another job for me?"

As soon as the words had finished, a golden *!* appeared over the girl's head. Apparently, the series of quests was not over.

Gamer instincts aside, my morality did not allow me to refuse this request. I wanted to say yes at once, but I wasn't the one who started Lady Nirr's quest in the first place; that was Argo. I looked across to the info agent to get her thoughts—her large eyes blinked with purpose.

I could practically hear her voice telepathically telling me, *Don't just sit there like a dunce, accept it!* so I quickly turned back to Nirrnir and said, "Of course. Whatever you need."

"I'm glad to hear that," she said, grinning, as the *!* mark turned into a *?* overhead. She leaned back against the cushions and entered explanation mode. "Don't worry; this job will not be difficult or dangerous."

"Meaning…?"

"I want you to accompany me on the inspection of the Korloy monster cells."

"……Ah, I s-see," I said, while on the inside, I thought, *Awww, do I have to go back there?!* But to her, I merely nodded and said, "That will be easy. I don't know if it will help you, however."

"As long as you remember the layout, that is fine. None of my people have ever been inside Korloy stables. My expectation is that the time we have to go inside and look will fall in the two-hour period between the end of the daytime matches and the start of the nighttime preparations. I will need a guide to help me spot any signs of wrongdoing."

"Okay…Well, I'd be happy to show you around, but I don't recall it being that complex on the inside," I muttered, picturing my mental map of the Korloy stables.

To the left of the sofa, Kio said, "Then, do you remember how many monster cells there were?"

"Huh? Of course," I said, then realized that while I counted the number of cells on the right side of the basement hallway, I didn't pay any attention to the left side. So I couldn't actually be certain. "There were, uh, eight or nine or ten or eleven or so…"

"That is not what *remembering* means," she snapped. Asuna and the others all shook their heads.

18

NIRRNIR SAID SHE WOULD WAIT IN HER ROOM FOR the Korloys to make contact, so Asuna, Kizmel, Argo, and I left the hotel room on the third floor of the casino. We walked down the extravagant staircase to the ground floor and crossed directly toward the entrance, where Argo theatrically clutched her stomach and wailed, "Oh, I'm so hungry! We gotta get somethin' to eat!"

"Agreed," said Asuna.

"That's a good idea," added Kizmel.

Nirrnir had instructed us to return before the end of the daytime arena matches, but we probably had time to eat, I supposed.

Argo, however, lowered her head to gaze up at me and asked, "What's up, Kii-boy, aren'tcha hungry?"

I took a step back and replied, "N-no, I *am* hungry...but I had a sandwich at the casino after we split up this morning..."

"You traitor!"

"L-look, you guys were enjoying the bath!" I protested, glancing at Asuna. "Didn't you eat anything after you got out?"

"Not a bite. In fact, we were just taking a breather after getting out of the bath when you sent your message, so we didn't have time to eat, even if we wanted to."

"Oh, sorry about that...Well, let's go and grab a bite, then," I urged, until I remembered that our party had an extra member now. Asuna and Argo and I would enjoy just about anything, of course, but I still didn't know much about a dark elf's typical diet. During our time at Yofel and Galey Castles, the food they served us was healthy, with plenty of vegetables, and the only animal protein I got was grilled white fish and poultry. Surely she would eat other things than that, though?

"Uh, Kizmel, is there anything you'd rather avoid…? Or actually, what do you *like*?" I asked.

The knight inclined her head as she considered. "Hmm. I do not consider myself a picky eater…but if I had to give you an answer, I'd say I do not much like rare meat dripping with blood and fat—or dishes with strong spices."

"Or narsos fruit, huh?" I teased with a grin.

She shot me a smug look and quipped back, "No, but that is medicinal. You do not eat it for the taste."

"No kidding. Okay, so we're avoiding steaks and kebabs…Any recommendations outside of those, Argo?"

"Hmm, let's see," Argo murmured, her whisker-painted cheeks puckering briefly. She snapped her fingers. "That's it! I know where we'll go."

"Where is that?"

"You'll have to look forward to the surprise."

Argo's "surprises" could be total bull's-eyes, or they could be too avant-garde for their own good, so I wasn't sure how to feel about this development. Ultimately, I just had to hope it would be the former.

"Well, lead the way."

"That's the spirit! Follow me," she said, marching off. Asuna, Kizmel, and I followed her in order.

It was like a good old-school 2D pixel RPG, the four of us walking in a line down a side street that headed into the southwest block of Volupta. Normally, the streets in this town were supposed to be aligned in the four cardinal directions—if not quite as precisely as in Stachion—but because of the chaotic ways the buildings themselves bulged and leaned, the alley actually twisted left and right as it went.

Decaying barrels and boxes and such were strewn about the alley, and the paving stones were cracked here and there, which pushed this area over the line of working class into slums. If you weren't careful, it looked like you could get held up at gunpoint at any moment. It almost made me paranoid that Argo *knew* our elite NPC party member would help us clear up a few stray quests for her...but then she came to a stop.

"Here we are," Argo said.

On the left side of the alley was a building that smelled of food, with an aged iron sign hanging on the door. The design of it was a pointed leaf, almost like the one on the Canadian flag. At a glance, it looked more like an herb seller than a restaurant.

Since our guest of honor was not familiar with human cooking, I figured (ungratefully) that if we were going to stretch her boundaries, we could just go back to Pots 'n' Pots again. But Argo was already pushing the faded wooden door open.

A deep voice greeted us as soon as the tinkling doorbell announced our entrance. Asuna and Kizmel followed Argo right through the entrance, so I brought up the rear.

On the inside, the place was cramped and built to look like a grotto. But it went back much further than Pots 'n' Pots, which just had a counter. At the very end, there was a four-seat table. On the left side was a counter that could seat about five people, behind which stood a figure like a small mountain.

This would be the man who welcomed us in, and he was both taller and wider than Agil. My first thought was that he could be an ogre trying to pass himself off as human. But the women headed straight for the table without any sign of intimidation, so I had to hurry after them.

Asuna and Kizmel took the far seats, leaving Argo and me to sit next to each other. There were two ancient-looking menus resting on the shining black table surface. The reddish-brown front cover had the name written in a simple style: *Menon's*. That would presumably be the owner's name, but I was having trouble associating the cute writing with the muscular, towering man behind the counter.

"Uh...who's Menon?" I whispered. Argo jabbed a thumb at the counter to her left.

My instincts to peek were too strong for me to ignore the voice in my head saying, *Don't look!* Perhaps the lamp hanging from the ceiling over the counter was too low, because he just looked like a massive shadow. But there was no one else back there, so that man had to be Menon. I decided I had to get over the stubborn idea that a menacing man must have a menacing name—to me, Menon sounded rather cute—and turned back to the table and the menu.

There were only two pages. On the left, it said simply *Dolma 20c* and *Moussaka 30c*, and on the right, *Ouzo 10c* and *Coffee 5c* in rough script. I checked the back cover, just in case, but it was blank. After the hundred-plus varieties of bread bowl stews in Pots 'n' Pots, the limited options here were stifling. But more importantly...

"Um, Argo...? I have no idea what any of these are, aside from the coffee...What are dolma and *mow-saka* and *oh-zo*?" I asked, doing my best to pronounce the unfamiliar words.

The information agent stifled a chuckle. "That's exactly the reaction I was countin' on, Kii-boy."

"What? I'm sure Asuna's thinking the same thing..." I argued, but on the other side of the table, my temporary partner was *also* grinning widely at my ignorance.

"I'm sorry, Kirito, I know what these are. You got dolma right, but the other ones are *mu-saka* and *oo-zo*."

"So I'm guessing that means you know what these dishes are?"

"Of course. It's the perfect menu for this town in particular. Good choice, Argo."

"You bet it is. And my tip about this place is on the house, my friends."

Their smug superiority was making me feel a bit sulky. I looked at Asuna's seating partner and asked, "Do *you* know what dolma and moussaka are, too, Kizmel?"

"No, I have never heard of them," said the knight, shaking her head. "But since I am here in this human town, I would enjoy the chance to eat a new kind of dish. I am looking forward to these delicacies."

"Oh...okay."

Kizmel's beaming smile was so brilliant I had to shield my eyes from her radiance. Argo stifled another chuckle in her throat and snapped the menu shut.

"Well, since there ain't much room to choose, I'll just do the ordering. Hey, boss! We'll have four dolmas, four moussakas, and four ouzos!"

"You got it," said the deep voice from the counter. After ten seconds of clanking tools and knives, I started to smell a delectable scent. *Hmmm, maybe this will be tasty, after all,* I thought.

Then a voice said, "Hey, buddy."

"Y-yes?!" I answered automatically. I was the only person at the table who could possibly be referred to as buddy.

Thankfully, the huge cook had not read my mind. He said apologetically, "Would you mind carrying this stuff to the table? I run this place all on my own, so I don't have anyone to serve ya."

"O-of course, I'd be happy to," I said, getting to my feet. When I approached, his enormous hands set down a ceramic bottle, a pitcher of water, and four wineglasses.

After careful consideration, I cradled the bottle in my left arm, the pitcher in my right, and gingerly held two glasses in each hand, then carried them over to the table. The moment everything was safely to the tabletop, and I'd let go, Asuna clucked, "You could have just brought them over in two or three trips! What if you got tripped up and dropped them?"

"W-well, I didn't."

"Yes, but you *could* have!"

"Well, if you're going to blame me for things that didn't happen, then...uh..."

I tried and failed to think of what the antonym for "All's well that ends well" would be, and a burst of laughter erupted from behind the counter.

"You got style, buddy, carrying all that over in one go. Try this next, then."

"What? Again?" I complained, thinking this was a rather abusive restaurant toward its customers. Back at the counter, there were four steaming dishes and one basket of cutlery.

The plates each contained a mysterious dark green object covered in a milky white sauce, which I found very intriguing, but I had my pride to live up to. I ran a mental simulation, then made full use of my left fingers to hold two plates. I carefully placed another one on my forearm, so I had three on one arm.

The rest was easy. Three fingers on my right hand held the last plate, and I hooked the cutlery basket with my pinky. Then I turned back to the table and put them all down in reverse order.

"There, see?"

"See what? I'm telling you, that's not going to end well..."

"Then you could get up and help me, Asuna."

"Then you could ask me for help."

Once again, the cook interrupted our argument.

"Hey, buddy, here's the last one."

"All right!"

I turned back, excited to see what was next. On the counter were four sizzling gratin dishes.

"Urgh..." I swallowed and considered this development gravely.

Even ignoring the sizzling heat of the gratin dishes, they were lipped in a way that rose vertically around the edge, which made it impossible to hold two in one hand with different fingers. I could hold one with my left hand and place another on my arm, but then I couldn't do the same on the other side with only one open hand.

I've just got to lift it with sheer willpower! I told myself, honing my mind, but I could not psychically lift the dish. Swearing to myself that I'd learn the Psychokinesis skill one day, I turned back to Asuna and said, "I'm sorry; please help me..."

"You should have just started with that," she said, rolling her eyes. Asuna stood up and promptly pushed down Kizmel, who tried to rise with her—Argo did not budge from her seat—before coming to the counter.

We each took two dishes and carried them to the table. Now we had the mystery dolmas, moussaka, and ouzo for each person. The only thing I'd learned so far was that ouzo was the beverage.

"Well, shall we share a toast?"

Argo picked up the ceramic bottle and poured two fingers of liquid into each of the wineglasses. Then she added the same amount of water from the pitcher, instantly turning the clear liquid cloudy and white. It reminded me of the dye being washed out of the lykaon's fur, so I asked her quietly, "Uh, this is safe to drink, right?"

"Yeah, no worries," she said, which was not all that reassuring. She passed out the glasses, and I lifted mine with trepidation.

"To meeting Kizmel!" Argo announced. We clinked glasses, and I took a little sip of the cloudy liquid.

Immediately, a powerfully herbal scent stung my nose, and the alcohol burned my throat. If it was this harsh when cut with water, how strong was the liquid straight from the bottle? I grimaced and looked across the table, where Asuna's brows were slightly knit. Kizmel looked totally unaffected. She drank it down in one go and placed her glass on the table.

"Ah, this drink is good. It uses a good variety of herbs and plants."

"I figured an elf would like it," Argo replied. I wanted to ask, *Really? You did?* But if Kizmel was happy, that was all that mattered.

I promptly poured another drink of ouzo in the knight's glass. I was about to pour in the water, but she requested "a little less," so I gave her half as much water as alcohol.

Somehow, I managed to finish my own ouzo, then placed my glass at the edge of the table to make it clear I didn't need more. Instead, I picked up my knife and fork to try out the food.

The small round plate featured two elliptical dark green objects slathered in a milky white sauce. Whatever they were, they seemed to be steamed inside of large leaves. The exterior reminded me of *kashiwa mochi*, rice cakes wrapped in an oak leaf. Based on that, I assumed you were supposed to peel the leaf off without eating it, but the whole thing was wrapped so tightly that I couldn't tell where I was supposed to start removing it.

At this point, I decided to copy Asuna or Argo and snuck a quick glance at them, but both were sipping their ouzo and watching my hands very carefully. Not because they were ignorant of how to eat this, but because they wanted to watch my attempt.

Fine. You want to laugh at me? Go ahead.

I stabbed my fork into one of the elliptical things. Then I lifted it to my mouth and bit down. The leaf split with a nice crisp texture, and as I chewed, the texture turned much thicker. The inside was probably...rice and meat? It was kind of like a Western-style sticky rice dumpling but with a lemony cream sauce that matched the flavor and a fun, crispy leaf texture on the outside.

I popped the other half on my fork into my mouth and said, "It's good."

"Of course," replied Argo, stabbing one of her Western dumplings with her fork and taking a bite. Asuna and Kizmel politely cut theirs into pieces with a knife first.

I finished off the other dumpling quickly, then pulled my glass back toward me and poured a bit of ouzo. I added extra water and gave it a taste. At a more diluted level like this, the eccentric flavor and scent didn't bother me so much; in fact, it was kind of refreshing.

At this point, I wanted to get right into the gratin, but it seemed politer to wait for the others. For whatever reason, Asuna started to unroll the leaf of her second dumpling. Using her fork and knife, she carefully peeled off the leaf and laid it out atop the plate.

"Look."

"Look at what...? Oh!"

The leaf, which was a bit larger than my palm, had jagged edges and two large clefts—much like the Canadian flag—the same shape as what was on the iron sign on the door.

"So the sign outside was this leaf? Maple leaf...?"

"*Bzzt!* It looks like it, though. No, this is a grape leaf."

"Ohhh," I murmured as Kizmel said, "Ahhh. There are vine-yards on the ninth floor, but I did not know the leaves could be used for cooking. Which is this, the dolma or moussaka?"

"Dolma," said Asuna at once. Then she added, less decisively, "I'm pretty sure it means *stuffed*."

Based on the way she said it, I had to assume that these dolmas, and probably the moussaka and ouzo, too, were real-world dishes, just like the *khao man gai* from Lectio. But I couldn't begin to guess which country they were from.

"Hmm, interesting. Seems more 'wrapped' to me...but anyway, it's good. I'm looking forward to the moussaka, then," said Kizmel, pulling the rectangular gratin dish toward her. I followed her lead. The material must have been very good at insulation, because the outside surface was only warm, but the contents were still bubbling and steaming. It wasn't exactly cool inside the restaurant, so it was the kind of dish I'd prefer to eat on a win-ter floor. Still, the way the heaping white sauce browned up was boosting my appetite.

It might be the first gratin I'd had so far in Aincrad, I thought. Argo passed over the cutlery basket, so I pulled out a spoon with a flat end and scooped up a bite from the very bottom of the dish.

Beneath the sauce, it was neither rice nor macaroni but lay-ers of ground meat, mashed potatoes, and sliced eggplant. After blowing on the spoonful, I stuffed it into my mouth.

"*Hwuf, hffh...*It'fh good!"

It was like a scene from a comic book. But of course it was good. Tomato-flavored ground meat, steaming potatoes, and soft eggplant mixed with rice white sauce? It was a perfect mixture, and the flavor was so satisfying it was hard to believe this was virtual food in a virtual world.

Asuna and Kizmel moved their spoons in silence, as did Argo, who had presumably tried this dish before. In just two or three minutes, we had all emptied our servings.

A little swig of ouzo cooled down my overheated mouth and tongue, and I rapped the glass down on the table. We'd eaten delicious food all over on the seventh floor, and the dolmas and moussaka together might be the most satisfying yet. The gruff excuse for customer service here was a small price to pay for flavor like this.

Kizmel was just as satisfied as I was. She finished off her glass of ouzo, which had barely any water in it, and exhaled. "Ahhh...Both food and drink were very good. Asuna, what does *moussaka* mean?"

"Um...from what I remember, it's like *something juicy* or *something chilled...*"

"Huh?" "Wha—?"

Argo and I craned our necks in the same direction. It was served in an oven-baked dish so hot it could burn your tongue. That name couldn't be any *less* accurate. Asuna looked our way and pursed her lips with frustration.

"Look, it's not like I have an entire dictionary in my brain. But I'm pretty sure that in the place where moussaka was first developed, it was a chilled appetizer. Then in Gree...in a different area, it turned into a hot dish."

"Ah yes. Such things do happen," Kizmel agreed. "In Lyusula, we have a dish called ponnecorkle that came over from Kales'Oh. It is like a lightly cooked pancake. While the forest elves eat theirs with only a sprinkle of sugar and cinnamon, we dark elves prefer a healthy serving of jam and cream on top. I hardly think I need point out which is tastier."

The sight of her culinary pride made me smile. I promptly commented, "That sounds very good, indeed. I'd like to eat it someday."

"Of course. When you come to the city on the ninth floor, you can eat all that you like," Kizmel replied generously, but her smile did not last long, presumably remembering her personal situation.

After escaping from the cells at Harin Tree Palace, Kizmel could not return to the castle on the ninth floor, or any of the other strongholds, unless she brought back the four sacred keys with her. At the moment, my proposal to track the Fallen Elves was our only hope, but we didn't even know that all four keys would be kept at the Fallen's base, should we succeed. And if Kysarah the Ransacker happened to be there, we would be wiped out at our current strength.

On top of that, we didn't even know how the Fallen were traveling from floor to floor, given that they couldn't use the spirit trees. Until we solved that mystery, another attack from Kysarah would always be possible, even if we took the keys back.

I sighed, thinking about the challenges ahead of us. Asuna put a hand on Kizmel's back and said, "It's all right. My premonitions always come true. We're *going* to get the sacred keys back."

"Yes…of course we are," she replied, smiling again. She poured back the last of the ouzo in her glass and turned to the other person at the table. "Thank you for bringing me to this wonderful place, Argo."

"Glad ya like it. But you oughtta thank Kii-boy instead."

"Huh? Why me?"

It didn't seem like carrying the dishes to the table was worthy of such a display of gratitude, but before I could say as much, Argo flashed a smirk at me.

"Because Kii-boy's payin' for the meal, obviously."

It wasn't until recently that I'd learned that the timing for payment at NPC restaurants depended on the establishment.

Most places would bring up a small payment window upon each individual order, which would subtract the requisite col when you hit the OK button. If you didn't pay, the food would not appear, no matter how many hours you waited. In other words, you paid separately and up front.

But in fancy restaurants that weren't my style, and in some tiny locations, an individual person could pay the entire bill after the meal. In the case of the former, it was to avoid ruining the atmosphere with a cheap demand for payment, and in the latter, I suspected it was to tempt the player with an eat-and-run challenge. From what I'd heard, there were bold players who ate all they could, then sprinted out of the building and succeeded in escaping both the cook and guards, thus enjoying a free meal without suffering the cost of a prison stay in Blackiron Palace.

Of course, I did not run out on the bill. I thanked Menon for the meal, then paid the cost of 420 col for the four of us. For excellent food and alcohol to boot, the price was quite reasonable. But if Argo chose this place specifically because she knew she could force the bill onto me, I had to give her a piece of my mind.

I headed out the door, resolute, only to be met by the three women outside, smiling and saying, "Thanks for the meal!" I made a face like I'd been sucking on a lemon for ten years.

"Um, you're quite welcome."

"Well, shall we get goin'?" said Argo, back in her usual mode, and she turned and strolled north down the street before I could give her any lip. Kizmel followed after her, and I lined up next to Asuna in the back.

"...So which country are dolmas and moussaka from?" I whispered after we'd gotten to the end of the building.

Just as quietly, she replied, "Greece."

"Ah...just like how Volupta reminded you of Sa...Santorini?"

"Yes."

"Interesting. So that's why you said it was the perfect meal to have in a town like this," I remarked, watching Argo's back as she took the lead.

It seemed that the Rat hadn't chosen that restaurant to make me pay for it but because she understood that the style of Volupta was reminiscent of the island of Santorini—and that the dolmas and moussaka were Greek food. Asuna was quite the source of real-world information and customs, but Argo seemed to have all of that *on top of* a vast knowledge of Aincrad and the systems of *SAO*.

I couldn't really tell what her age was—she seemed to be our age, but she also called herself Big Sis a lot, so she could be older. Where had she gotten this encyclopedia of knowledge and experience? And why did she pursue the job of selling information in this deadly game—an act that was in some ways more dangerous than being a player trying to beat the game?

Of course, if you're that curious about something, it's best to just ask directly—but that wouldn't work with Argo. I could just see her smirking and saying something like, "That'll be ten thousand col, bub." If I ever owned ten million col, I told myself that I'd buy up every last personal fact that Argo sold about herself. I was pretty sure I'd made that decision before.

The side street took us back to the open space in front of the casino. It was about ten minutes after four o'clock in the afternoon. The final battle of the daytime monster arena was scheduled for four thirty, so we still had time to get back to Nirrnir's room. But I was also worried about the possibility that the ALS and DKB might be attempting to double their chips with each battle to get to a hundred thousand.

Argo must have been thinking the same thing, because she leaned in and said under her breath, "I'm gonna go check on the monster coliseum. You go back to Lady Nirr first. It's not like I'll have any role in the inspection of the stables."

"Sure, if you say so...But you're the one who accepted the quest from her, right? Sure you shouldn't be with us?"

Since forming my temporary partnership with Asuna, we had almost never worked separately, so my knowledge of how quests and parties interacted wasn't all that solid.

Argo just tilted her head, though, and said, "No worries. If we're in a party, we share quest status. Just make sure ya don't accidentally kick me out."

"Got it."

"Just shoot me a message when yer done with the inspection."

Argo headed off, so I rejoined Asuna and Kizmel, who were chatting and looking around the plaza. After a few words, we walked toward the casino.

The pure white building was glowing golden in the slanted sunlight. Since coming to Volupta, Asuna and I had spent about twenty-four hours in and around the city. It was on the southern edge of the floor, so in terms of simple distance, we had crossed half the floor so far, but the Tailwind Road that connected the main town to Volupta was a long, plain road with no dungeon or bosses along the route. But the route to Pramio northwest of here—and the route from Pramio to the labyrinth tower—was full of challenges. In terms of the actual work to conquer the floor, we were 30 percent of the way through at best.

Of course, if either the ALS or DKB gained the completely game-breaking Sword of Volupta, the pace of our advancement might speed up significantly. However, they were relying on cheat sheets to win that were certainly a trap created by the Korloys to sucker high rollers into losing big money.

Still, if Kibaou and Lind were sharp enough to detect the trap and bet on the opposite card in the final match of the night...But maybe the Korloys had a plan in place for that, too. In the end, they were just an individual facet of the massive *SAO* game system, and unlike the real world with its immutable laws of physics, Aincrad was a virtual place where the system could do anything it wanted, if it had reason to. Much like the pattern with the color of the roulette dealer's bow tie and the odds of landing on that color.

Maybe the seventh floor is going to take a lot longer than I'm thinking, I wondered.

Suddenly, Asuna was at my side and prodding my elbow. "Come on, let's go back to Lady Nirrnir."

"R-right. Are you full now, Kizmel?" I asked, without thinking much.

The knight narrowed her eyes with part exasperation, part outrage. "I am fine. Kirito, how much of a glutton do you take me for?"

"I—I was just checking…Shall we go back?"

I did a ninety-degree turn to the left and quickly marched off toward the entrance of the Grand Casino. Behind my back, I heard the women quietly giggling.

19

WE GOT THROUGH THE SECURITY CHECKPOINT WITH Kio's pass, climbed the huge spiral staircase to the third floor, then informed the check-in counter where we were going, and made our way to Room 17 on the south side of the floor.

It occurred to me that we were paying many more visits to Nirrnir's chamber than the platinum suite we'd coughed up so much money on at the Ambermoon Inn, but that would only last until the end of this quest series. And according to my instincts, the climax was near. Things had taken a big detour when I freed the lykaon, but going by the pattern of proper storytelling, an inspection of the stable should turn up undeniable evidence of wrongdoing. Then the judgment of Falhari the Founder would kick in, something unexpected would happen, a major story event would occur, and we'd launch into some kind of huge battle, which, if won, would spell the end of the quest. At least, that was my assumption.

If there was any concern on my end, it was that the "Curse of Stachion" quest on the previous floor had completely ignored typical story logic, but I wanted to say that was only because the PKers had interfered permanently by killing the lord of the town. They hadn't shown up at all in Lady Nirr's quest, so I could only pray that this story ended safely.

Contemplating all this as I marched down the dark hallway to

Room 17, I knocked and answered the replying voice with, "Kirito and Asuna and Kizmel." A fancy, heavy lock clicked loose.

Kio the battle maid opened the door, then frowned as soon as she saw me. "Kirito, have you been drinking during the day?"

"Huh...? Y-yes...but not enough to smell bad..."

For one thing, drinks in this world only tasted like alcohol; they didn't produce acetaldehyde in the body. If the game was simulating alcohol effects, too, then it made no sense that Nirrnir, who looked no more than twelve years old, was chugging glasses of wine like water with no visible effect.

But my guess was completely wrong.

"It is not the spirits I smell, but the anise. Have you been drinking ouzo down in town?"

Anise? I wondered, until I realized that must be the name of the particular herbal flavor in that strong drink.

There was a mixture of fictional plants in this world, like narsos and Celusian, and real plants, like juniper and aspen. I couldn't tell in the moment if anise was one or the other, but either way, she was right that I'd been drinking ouzo at Menon's, so I fessed up.

"Y-yes, I have."

"I knew it. I won't tell you to avoid it, but it is strong and best saved for the evening."

"Y-yes, ma'am."

I bowed and glanced sidelong at my companions. Asuna had twice as much as I did—and Kizmel at least three times, but they both looked as stoic as though they had no idea what I'd done.

I felt like the fact that I could resist telling Kio, "They were drinking, too!" was a sign of how mature I'd become as a person. But before I could think on it more, from the back of the large room, a young voice hailed, "Welcome back, Kirito, Asuna, Kizmel."

Kio held out her right hand, motioning us toward the enormous couch. As usual, Nirrnir was slumped on the cushions with a sluggish demeanor. When she saw me, her nostrils perked up adorably.

"Yes, you *do* smell like ouzo. That takes me back. I haven't had ouzo in a long time," she said.

That one surprised me. Ouzo was a drink several times harsher than wine, and she said it had been a "long time." How old could she have been when she drank it? Aincrad might not have any laws against underage drinking, but that seemed like something her parents should be aware of. Then I remembered that Nirrnir's father and mother were already out of the picture. Kio might be acting as her protector, but a maid was not the same thing as a guardian. And who was I to act like her parent? I was just an errand boy.

I glanced at the floating *?* over Nirrnir's head and asked, "So... how did negotiations with the Korloy family go?"

"We argued somewhat, but as I expected, they ultimately agreed to allow an emergency inspection. It will start ten minutes after the end of the final daytime arena match, so it will be five o'clock regardless of how long the fight drags on. Are you ready, Kirito?"

"R-ready whenever you are...But I'm not inspecting the stables all by myself, am I?"

"Of course not. In fact," Nirrnir acknowledged, making a face, "they added the condition that I must be present as well. So the entire inspection party will be two of our handlers, two armed soldiers, you, Kio, and me."

"Uh-huh..."

I felt better about having more people around, but I couldn't guess what the Korloys were doing here.

"Why would they make that demand, though? The more people inspecting their stables, the higher chance we might find some evidence of wrongdoing, right?" I wondered.

Back in her usual standing spot, Kio scowled and said, "They intended it as a mean-spirited hassle."

"Huh…? But the stables are in the basement of this very building, right? It can't be that far that it's a hassle for you…"

Nirrnir might have been a refined young lady, but she was still strong enough to walk up and down stairs, I thought. But Kio fixed me with a fierce glare.

"That is not what I mean."

"Then what…?"

"It is nothing you need to concern yourself with, Kirito," said Nirrnir herself, putting an end to the discussion. I clammed up, and she asked me a different question.

"With that said, where is Argo?"

"Oh, she said she was going to see the monster arena," I replied. Asuna quickly added, "If we need more people for the inspection, I will go in her place."

"No, the inspection will be fine. I have a different job for you to do, Asuna and Kizmel."

"Yes? Anything."

Whoa, don't promise too much! I thought with trepidation, but Nirrnir's request was actually exceedingly simple.

"I want you to watch this room for me. Typically, both Kio and I almost never leave this place unattended, but not long ago, when we left together, someone poisoned my wine."

"P-poisoned?!" I squawked, but then I remembered that Kio had said the Korloys were attempting to kill Nirrnir. She herself bravely said she'd welcome a direct attempt over a bunch of trickery and poison. Apparently, it was more literal than I realized.

"B-but you were all right?"

"Well, I'm alive right now, aren't I?" Nirrnir said, then bobbed her shoulders and added, "But if Kio hadn't noticed the needle hole in the cork, I might have gulped the poison right down. I put a nice ribbon on the bottle and gave it to Bardun as a present." She giggled at the thought of it.

Asuna told her, "Very well. Kizmel and I will stand guard at your room while you are gone."

"I appreciate it," said the girl. She then looked at Kizmel.

Normally, in this situation, the dark elf would give one of her elven salutes. Instead, she said with concern, "Meaning...that their request for you to personally join the inspection party was for a plot of that kind? And now that they will corner you in the underground stables, where you cannot escape?"

"I did consider that possibility as well," Kio said, briefly downcast, and shook her head, "but there is no point for the Korloys to do such a thing. Their assassination must come at unidentifiable hands. If they attack Lady Nirrnir, and everyone knows it, then by the laws of the Grand Casino, the Korloy family would be forever stripped of their claim."

"I see...but you will still be venturing into enemy territory. You oughtta be cautious."

"That is exactly what we intend to be."

Kizmel and Kio traded firm, determined nods. It shouldn't have taken me this long to notice how alike they were.

Just then, there was a knock at the door and a man's muffled voice. "Miss Kio, it is Huazo. The daytime matches have just finished."

"Understood. We'll be right out," she answered crisply, checking that her estoc was in place on her left hip. She turned to me and asked, "Kirito, do you only have that shortsword?"

"No, not at all," I said, looking down at myself in the bright blue shirt and white pants. I opened my equipment mannequin and quickly adjusted it.

With a little whoosh, my trusty sword appeared on my belt. It was woefully mismatched with my resort wear, but it was better there than on my back, I supposed.

Nirrnir straightened up on the sofa the moment she saw the Sword of Eventide on my person. "Oooh. That's a sword for Lyusulan nobility. Did you steal it?"

"Wha...?"

What an accusation! I thought, feeling as outraged as Kibaou was on a regular basis—but I held it in.

"C-certainly not. It was a que...er, a reward for doing a job."

"Hmm. Well, be ready, if it should come to that," Nirrnir said. She lifted up her feet, then swung them down to stand with alacrity. Kio had prepared a thick cloak that she put over the girl. The black velvet looked stifling for such a hot floor, but I had to admit that the oversize hood looked very cute on her.

I hurried after the two as they headed for the door. Asuna and Kizmel sent me gazes that said, *Be careful.* The mission was guiding her around the basement stables, so there shouldn't be danger, but as Nirrnir warned earlier, there was no guarantee that things wouldn't go south.

I gave them a thumbs-up and proceeded out of the chamber.

Waiting in the hallway was a young man with a bold face, a full head taller than me. He didn't look like an animal handler, so I presumed he was one of the guards who was accompanying the investigation. Unlike the guards at the entrance to the casino, he wore just a dark gray uniform and breastplate, rather than shining, ostentatious plate armor. The emblem of the Nachtoy family, a black lily on a white field, was sewn to either shoulder, and the weapon on his belt was a thin sword that seemed like the midpoint between rapier and longsword.

"Thank you, Huazo," Nirrnir said. "Where is Lunnze?"

He straightened up and answered, "Waiting before the stables, with the others."

"Ah. Then, let's go."

She turned, flipping her cloak, and started walking down the hall, followed by Kio and Huazo. I brought up the rear, attracting the attention of the soldier, who leaned forward and whispered to Kio.

"Sister, who is he?"

"Call me by my name while on duty."

"Yes, Miss Kio. I'm sorry."

Huh? They're siblings?! I was stunned. But now I could see that Huazo's short-cropped hair and Kio's were the same shade of dark brown. I inched just a bit closer so I could hear Kio's response.

"That is Kirito. He is an adventurer Lady Nirrnir hired to help us solve this matter."

"...Even though we are more than capable of dealing with it ourselves, without needing to rely on an outsider."

"We must find evidence of wrongdoing in the short span of an inspection. An outsider is *more* likely to find certain things we take for granted."

From what Kio was saying, she hadn't told Huazo about my infiltration of the Korloy stables or that I had freed the lykaon that was living proof of their cheating. I told myself anew that I really needed to perform this next task properly in order to make it up to them.

Nirrnir took us down the darkened hallway, not to the spiral stairs down to the entrance of the casino, but farther into the hotel. We passed a space where it smelled very mildly of bathwater, then took a right turn, followed by a left, stopping at a door at the end of the hall.

The hotel owner pulled an old key out of her cloak, stuck it into the lock, and turned. It made a heavy *click* that sounded loud in my ears. Beyond the door was a dimly lit spiral stairwell. This one was far more cramped than the one at the front of the building. Nirrnir proceeded down it with assured steps.

Kio and Huazo followed their master, so I brought up the rear and waited for the door to close behind me before timidly heading down the steps. There was no central pillar in the stairwell; the steps just stuck out from the walls, and there was no handrail. I peered down the middle and saw nothing but darkness below. If it was empty from the third floor of the Grand Casino down to the first, there had to be a drop of at least thirty feet. A missed step and a headfirst landing on the stone floor meant certain death.

This is still better than climbing down the outside of Harin Tree Palace! I told myself, keeping my hand firmly on the side wall as I followed the others down. I was losing track of how many circulations we'd done when the floor finally came into sight, and I could breathe a sigh of relief.

There was a similar door on the first floor, which Nirrnir again unlocked. She turned the doorknob and pushed it open, revealing a hallway that looked similar to one I'd seen before. There were four doors on the right-hand wall and one on the left.

"I will go first, my lady," said Kio, passing her master and standing before a door on the right wall. She paused, listening carefully, before opening the door.

A small amount of reddish light came through the crack. Kio passed through the frame, followed by Nirrnir, who had her hood pulled low, and then Huazo.

As I followed, the last to leave the hallway, I murmured, "Oh, it's here..."

It was a space that looked suited for storage, wide enough for a carriage to fit inside. In fact, it *was* meant for a carriage. This was the monster-loading entrance that I saw before breaking into the Korloy stables. The reason the hallway looked familiar was because it was built to the same specifications as the one on the Korloy side.

The loading bay, which had been so dark four hours ago, was currently wide open, letting in a nearly blinding amount of orange light. The open door was facing west, so it was directly in the line of the setting sun, coming through the outer aperture of Aincrad.

In the center of the huge loading bay, two groups were facing off, outlined in the sunlight.

The three closer to us were wearing the same dark gray uniform as Huazo. One carried a sword, while the other two had coiled whips.

Beyond them were ten figures in deep red uniforms with golden breastplates. All of them had swords. The shoulder emblems they bore were of a red dragon on a black field. So the three closer to us were the Nachtoy soldier and handlers taking part in the surprise inspection, while the other ten were Korloy soldiers.

Suddenly, there was a whip crack, and the soldiers in red parted, allowing yet another silhouette to stride forward, back to the sun.

"It's been a while, Miss Nirr," said the crisp, baritone voice of a tall, thin man with white hair and whiskers. The elderly gentleman wore a perfect three-piece suit of dark brown, and his mustache and beard were immaculately trimmed. He looked about five feet eleven, nearly as tall as Huazo. In all honesty, he was a good 50 percent more impressive than Cylon, the lord of Stachion.

"And I see you are looking healthy, too, Bardun," Nirrnir replied. She stepped forward but stopped about six feet before the crisp line of sunlight that fell onto the floor.

So the older man was the master of the Nachtoys' rival clan, Bardun Korloy. Just in case, I kept my eyes focused on him, which brought up a yellow color cursor with the name BARDUN on it.

Of Bardun, Nirrnir had said, "He is obsessed with gathering all the gold he can to buy scant moments of life, and he's lost sight of everything else." But based on the image he cut here, he did not seem to be close to death or in any desperate need for gold.

Bardun took another step forward and spoke in that rich, flavorful voice. "You have my deepest apologies for my family's impropriety. It has caused a monster registered to compete in today's matches to be unable to appear. I certainly did not expect that anyone lurking in this town would be bold and wicked enough to sneak into my stables and free the monster."

The bold and wicked person himself wanted to hunch his neck with guilt, but I had to play it cool right now. As usual, Nirrnir was unfazed and spoke with maturity beyond her years.

"That little pooch of yours was winning so many matches that I suppose some wealthy merchant wanted him as a guard dog. But if you withdrew him to sell him off in secret, that might have offered you one last chance to strike it rich."

"How dare you suggest such a thing!" came a shout—but not from Bardun nor any of his soldiers. Behind the elderly leader, a short, portly, middle-aged man in a black tailcoat leaped forward. He screeched, "You make it sound as if the Korloy family only engages in the coliseum in order to make money! Retract that comment at once!"

Above the little man's head, his cursor said *Menden*. Based on his clothes, he appeared to be a butler, but there was a fancy-looking rapier on his left side, and if anything, he seemed more like a mansion owner than his counterpart. Kio strode up to her master's side and shot back, "Lady Nirrnir said nothing of the sort, Mr. Menden. Let us proceed with the inspection, please."

"*Inspection*, she says! Menial maid! You are being allowed to *examine* the stables by Master Bardun's generosity!"

"Enough, Menden," commanded Bardun, raising his hand, and the butler fell silent at once. "We bear the fault in this instance, for allowing the brigand to infiltrate and flee. If they are willing to see the stable as the price for allowing us to substitute a different monster, we would be happy to allow them."

"Yes, sir," said Menden, raising his hand in a theatrical gesture and prompting the Korloy soldiers, who had parted five to a side, to make a ninety-degree turn and march to line up beside the door on the far wall.

Bardun gestured toward the door, which was carved with the same red dragon insignia. His attitude seemed to say, *Go on in, if you can*. But there was nothing on the stone floor that blocked our way.

He isn't going to order his soldiers to attack, is he? I wondered.

Kio moved her hand. Instantly, Huazo and his three followers lined up directly behind her. I rushed over to take up the rear, and the gray-uniformed animal handler right in front of me whispered, "Scoot closer."

From the side, the five of us were so close we looked like we were pressed chest to back. That would make it hard to walk, but this was how it had to be, apparently. I took a big step forward and filled the gap between the handler and me.

The six of us lined up as tight as a human wall, and at Kio's second signal, we began to move forward. We took small, frequent steps, inching forward. On our right, Nirrnir walked at the same slow speed, wearing her black cloak.

After six feet or so, I passed out of the shadow of the loading bay wall, and red sunlight hit my left cheek. I turned my face in that direction, where the massive sun was visible through the outer aperture of Aincrad, far in the distance. Even as it was setting, the heat was intense; I had to assume that was the effect of the eternal-summer floor.

"Last one; get closer!" hissed the handler in front of me again, and I looked back in alarm. But I could barely do as he said—the front of my shirt was brushing the handler's back every now and then. I completely sealed the gap, preparing myself for the possibility of a tumble.

You couldn't walk in this position unless everyone marched in step. I tried my best to match them, counting off *One, two, one, two* inside my head. It was like a centipede race from sports day in elementary school.

Up ahead, the Korloy soldiers were stifling mocking chuckles. Their master, Bardun, was stone-faced, but even his butler, Menden, couldn't hide the smirk behind his tiny, groomed mustache.

What kind of quest is this anyway? I wondered, continuing the tight march, until we crossed the sun from the loading bay entrance and entered the shadow again. Again, the handler hissed, "You can back away now."

This time, I could hear the voice a little clearer, and my first surprised thought was, *It's a woman?* I inched backward and looked at the cursor over the handler's head, which said LUNNZE, but I couldn't be sure based on that. On the other hand, I seemed to recall Kio saying the name Lunnze earlier…

Just then, Nirrnir stumbled on my right. On pure reaction, I leaped forward and held up her tiny body. Lunnze cried, "Lady Nirrnir!" That drew Kio's attention.

But Nirrnir just clutched at my shirt and rasped, "I'm fine. Go."

"……Yes, my lady," said Kio, proceeding quickly for the door.

Behind her, surrounded by Huazo and Lunnze, I followed with Nirrnir.

I glanced at the lines of soldiers in dark red as we passed. Some of them were still smirking, but others were glaring with outright hatred. Surely they weren't going to attack, but there were only seven of us to twelve of them. I kept my eyes moving to either side, making sure I was ready for anything.

Standing behind the soldiers lined up on the right was Bardun Korloy. My eyes met his.

Seen up close, his three-piece suit was spotless, and his coif and facial hair were immaculate. But there were many deep wrinkles around his forehead and mouth, making him look older than my first impression of him.

Even still, the power in the gaze coming from those sunken eye sockets was sharper than a steel harpoon. Nirrnir was so much younger, she could be his granddaughter or even *great*-granddaughter. What was the emotion in his gray eyes when he stared at her...Hatred? Or envy...?

"Hurry, Kirito," said Kio, sharpening my focus. The battle maid stood to the side of the wide-open red dragon door, watching me. I nodded and picked up my pace.

Past Kio and the doorway, I found myself in a familiar darkened hallway. After walking six feet to the right, I stopped and asked Nirrnir, who was still propped up on my arm, "Are you all right? If you're feeling sick, you should leave the inspection to us and return to your..."

"I'm fine now."

Nirrnir slipped away from my arm and leaned against the wall instead. But from what I could see through her hood, her face was noticeably paler than usual, and the HP bar over her head was about 10 percent lower. An unfamiliar debuff icon below the bar was presumably the source of the damage, but what did a black circle surrounded by thornlike triangles mean...?

While I puzzled over that one, Kio followed us through the hallway and strode up to Nirrnir, giving her something.

"Here, my lady."

It was a black bottle, small enough to fit in your palm. There was no label or identification, so I didn't know what was inside. Nirrnir just shook her head and straightened up, stepping away from the wall.

"I'm fine. I will be better soon. Let us hurry with the inspection."

".......Of course."

She inclined her head and put the bottle away, but I could see the concerned look on Kio's face. I was worried, too, of course. It was clear that Nirrnir was suffering from some kind of illness, and that was presumably why she did not regularly leave her hotel room. Belatedly, I realized why Kio described the Korloys' demand that Nirrnir be present as a "mean-spirited hassle."

The black debuff icon was not going away, and her HP continued to fall, very slowly. I wanted her to go back to her room right away, in all honesty, but she wouldn't listen to me, I knew. We just had to follow her instructions and find evidence of wrongdoing as soon as possible.

"Take the lead, Kirito," whispered Kio. I did as she said and looked around the hallway.

There were four doors side by side on the opposite wall from the entrance, but anything that might serve as evidence—such as a jar holding Rubrabium Dye—wouldn't be left right out in the open in a place like this. If we were going to find anything, it had to be underground.

I gave Kio and Nirrnir a knowing look, then moved farther down the hall. Through a door carved right into the stone hall, there was a dingy spiral staircase. There was no handrail here, either, but I'd already used it once, and unlike the other, this one was no more than fifteen feet. I swiftly made my way down the steps, wary of a sneak attack, and reached the floor of the basement.

From what I could see, the cell-lined hallway was empty. I proceeded in a ways before turning back to see Kio, Nirrnir, Huazo, Lunnze, and the other two follow me inside.

"...Mmm. So these are the Korloy stables," Nirrnir murmured, flipping back her hood and surveying the area, then sniffing the air. Her little face scowled. "Their cleanliness and ventilation leave much to be desired. They are looking after their monsters poorly."

"Y-you can tell these things?" I asked, stunned. Nirrnir made an unpleasant face and replied, "It smells like blood." Before I could say something else, a rich baritone voice issued from behind us.

"You'll have to pardon me, Lady Nirr. If you'd given me another day, I would have seen them cleaned out."

Bardun Korloy and his butler, Menden, came into the hallway behind us, along with five of their soldiers. They'd left the majority of their force upstairs, thankfully, but it meant there were fourteen people in the stables in all. The walkway itself was reasonably wide, but I couldn't help but feel like we were cramped.

If it wasn't coincidence that there were seven members each of the Nachtoy and Korloy sides, we might be set up for a battle event. Setting aside Nirrnir and Bardun, we had two handlers with whips, so they had more combat ability than us. If it turned into a fight, I'd have to neutralize two, or hopefully three, of their soldiers right at the start.

While my mind worked on calculations, Bardun spoke again. "Because we must prepare for the night schedule of the monster arena at seven o'clock, I can only give you two hours to inspect, Lady Nirr. Go ahead, sniff around my stables all you like. But my skill of 'Employment' has already worn off on some of these monsters. I cannot guarantee your safety if you go into their cells, and if you harm any of them, I will have to seek damages for violation of our laws."

"Very well," Nirrnir said, shrugging off Bardun's threat. "And if any one of your men interferes with our inspection, we will consider that to be a violation of our deal, and I will retract my permission to use a substitute monster. That means you will need to prepare a new Rusty Lykaon before the final match tonight. If this is understood, would you please return to the entrance of the stairs?"

"Rrrrgh..." grumbled Menden the butler. But Bardun gave a little signal, and the five soldiers retreated to the very edge of the hallway.

Once Nirrnir was satisfied, she turned back and looked at me with dark red eyes. Despite being only an NPC, I could practically sense her unspoken message: *I'm counting on you to take it from here.*

Part of me thought, *You sure you wanna do that?* But the situation turned out the way it did because of my actions, and I had a responsibility to fix it. Fortunately, the time limit was quite long for an investigation-type quest. I just had to find some evidence of wrongdoing within the next two hours—most likely more Rubrabium Dye.

Once again, I examined the area.

The hallway was a good fifty feet long. There were six cells on each side, for twelve in total, each containing one of the monsters for the daytime and nighttime fights. The end was a simple stone wall, and I couldn't see any storage or a break room area. So any evidence would be hidden within the cells. Bardun's warning about being attacked by monsters was apt, but at this point, I'd just have to go in and test my luck...

But...no.

The situation might have been unplanned, but upon further reflection, it would have turned out this way even if I'd done nothing. The original plan was to sprinkle the decolorant on the Rusty Lykaon during the arena fight, revealing that its fur had been dyed. But in that scenario, the Korloys would not have admitted fault, either. Most likely, we would have needed to come down here to look for evidence of rule breaking anyway. I ought to assume I was back on the main path of Lady Nirr's questline.

In that case, it was highly likely that entering the monster cages was the path to failing the quest. There was no way I could avoid being attacked by a monster whose "Employment" (taming) had worn off, after all. The Rusty Lykaon, actually a Storm Lykaon, had only escaped because it was outdoors. Trapped in the cage, it would certainly have attacked me.

The key evidence was not inside a cell, but outside. In that case, it was probably the first-floor storeroom I'd passed—or maybe behind the spiral staircase. And that meant that the way the Korloy soldiers blocked the doorway to the stairs was very suspicious, indeed.

"I'm sorry, Lady Nirrnir, but I think the evidence might be on the ground flo..."

I paused there, quite unnaturally.

"...What?" said my client, raising a skeptical eyebrow. I apologized to her again, then spun on my heel.

At the end of the long hallway was a wall of gray stone, nothing else. But when I infiltrated this place just four hours ago, wasn't there something else there? A door...no, a square entrance. I seemed to recall seeing something I thought was strangely small.

"...There it is!" I said softly, racing down the passage.

Along the way, I recognized that one of the cells on the left wasn't just a tiny chamber but also the waiting room to load the next monster into the arena cage, but that wasn't a problem for now. I passed by it, rushing to the back wall and pressing my hands against the gray stone.

The stacked, seamless blocks were cold and hard and did not budge to any amount of pressure. But there had undoubtedly been a little doorway here. If it was a hidden door, then presumably one of these blocks functioned as a switch to open and close it. They were usually in the corner and usually had some physical marking as a hint.

First I looked at the wall on the right, then on the left. One of the stone blocks on the left edge was just barely shining, reflecting the light of the lamp, unlike the others. In a flash, I brushed the surface with my fingers and found that the surface in the middle was smooth and worn down, unlike the rough texture elsewhere. Certain now, I gave it a push.

With a heavy clicking sensation, the block went in about an inch.

I could feel faint vibrations through the soles of my shoes. The center part of the stone wall began to rumble, audibly sinking into the floor.

Within five seconds, there was an opening less than three feet tall and wide in the wall. It was pitch black inside, but I immediately detected complex smells in the air. Among them was a trace of that sharp, sweet spice. I felt fairly reassured that the Rubrabium Dye was in here.

Even if I hadn't been here before, I knew I would have found the hidden door within the two-hour limit, but I couldn't deny the possibility that I'd go into the monster cells first. In that sense, my unplanned sojourn into this stable earlier was the silver lining of the storm cloud...or a blessing in disguise...or...

I turned my back on the wall, thinking pointlessly about which idiom was the most apt for the situation, and waved at the others, standing in the middle of the hallway.

"There's a hidden storage area here!"

Promptly, both Nirrnir and Kio smiled. They hurried over, followed by Huazo and Lunnze.

I waited next to the wall opening, suppressing my urge to jump right into the storage room and look for the jar of dye. If I leaped first and made a mess of things, the consequences would be worse than just a scolding. I had to procure the evidence not just in front of Nirrnir and her people but in sight of Bardun Korloy, too.

Speaking of which—I stretched to look past the others and saw that Bardun's group was still in position at the other end of the hall. Their hidden storage had been spotted in no time, but they didn't seem to be worried. Was this an expected part of their plan? No...they didn't seem relaxed. They seemed to be *waiting* for something.

I frowned, squinting at the ceiling above. There were no falling traps up there, of course. If there were pits in the floor, I would have fallen into them first, and the only thing on either side was iron bars.

To my right, there was a large, goatlike monster lurking in the back of its cell. It did not react when I looked it in the eyes; its "Employment" was still effective.

On the left, it should have been empty, because that was where I'd broken the Rusty Lykaon free. I checked it just in case, but of course, there was…

Something there. Long and narrow, curled up in the darkness. A coiled rope, perhaps? I focused on the bundle, just in case—and no sooner had the red cursor appeared than the shadow zipped away, leaving it behind.

It slid along the floor in silence, bunched up briefly, then jumped like an uncoiling spring, emerging into the center hallway through the bars of the cell. The narrow body gleamed like silver in the lamplight.

It was a snake—the Something-or-Other Serpent I saw when I snuck in here the first time. But the last time, it was in the cell with the tighter mesh walls, one cell over. Why was it in a normal cell? And why did it stay still when I walked past it earlier—and waited until now to jump out?

I put my hand on the hilt of my sword without the answers to these questions. As I drew my weapon, I called out, "Kio, snake!"

Without waiting, I took a big step forward and sliced upward from left to right. The sharp end of the Sword of Eventide just managed to nick the snake's body. But the thin snake, barely an inch wide, just made a metallic *kching!* sound.

It's so tough! I gritted my teeth and pushed with all my strength. The sword slid along the snake, creating sparks, and finally caught it between the scales, cutting loose the back third of the creature.

But the snake's flight did not stop. It adjusted its course, writhing in the air, and fell toward Nirrnir.

"Hah!"

Kio unleashed a sharp cry, then thrust her estoc, free of its sheath, with phenomenal speed. The extremely narrow weapon was glowing with a pale white effect. That was the rapier sword skill Linear—no, wait, it was the high thrust Streak.

The estoc jutted forward just as fast as if thrust by Asuna, the expert, and pierced the center of the remaining two-thirds of the snake as it flew, undulating, through the air.

The extra force of the attack rippled through the room as a shock wave. That attack would have gone straight through heavy plate armor.

But it was too much power for this particular moment.

Rather than simply pinning the snake's body, the thrust split it right in two. The third of its body with the head was still alive somehow, falling upon Nirrnir.

"Hissss!"

In the real world, it could never have hissed so loudly, but this one did, its mouth open as wide as possible. Long, sharp fangs glinted ominously in the light.

Behind Nirrnir, Huazo and Lunnze leaped for their young master, faces stricken with desperation. They were not going to make it in time. The hooked fangs plunged onto the shoulder of the black cloak.

Abruptly, so quickly I almost couldn't see it, Nirrnir's right hand darted out and snatched the snake in midair—the eighteen inches left of it, at least.

Her reaction speed was incredible. It would be hard enough to fight off a snake flying at that speed with your sword, but to grab it with your bare hand? Neither I nor Asuna could do it.

"Lady Nirr, just—"

Hold on to it! I was about to shout. But the small remaining portion of its body that was movable, just four inches at best, curved as far as it could and sank its fangs deep into Nirrnir's wrist. A moment later, its HP bar dwindled to zero, and the shortened body of the snake burst into blue particles.

"Lady Nirrnir!!" Kio screamed. She cast her estoc to the floor and reached out for her master. Stunned, I watched Nirrnir's thin lips twist into an ironic smile. She whispered, her voice barely audible.

"...Well done, Bardun."

And then the young master of the Grand Casino, Nirrnir Nachtoy, collapsed into Kio's outstretched arms.

20

"A SNAKE...?!" ASUNA REPEATED, WIDE-EYED.

I nodded limply. "Yeah. I screwed up...I'd seen the snake when I snuck into the stables earlier and thought it was strange, but I didn't see its attack coming..."

I downed the glass of water in my hand, but it did nothing to wipe away the bitterness in my mouth.

"Strange how?" asked Argo, who had returned to Room 17 from the casino before we got back. She was trying to keep the conversation going, not because it was in her nature as an info agent, but because she could tell I was devastated. I appreciated her kindness and lifted my head.

"The snake was only an inch or so around. So in the stables, they kept it behind bars that were even smaller—more like a mesh fence, really. But you saw the golden cage they fight in for the arena, right? The bars are about four inches apart there. So it occurred to me when I first saw it that the snake would just slither right out into the audience..."

If only I'd held on to that suspicion and considered what it might mean, I lamented, getting down on myself all over again.

This time, it was Kizmel who said, "Meaning that the Korloy family was keeping that snake not as a combatant in the arena but for the sole purpose of allowing it to attack Lady Nirrnir...and they moved it from its special cage to a normal one before the inspection?"

I looked up, straight at the dark elf sitting across from me, and nodded. "It's the only answer I can understand. When she was bitten, Bardun Korloy and his butler, Menden, didn't seem surprised or bothered in the least..."

If anything, I thought I saw a thin smile on Bardun's lips.

Nirrnir's collapse put an end to the inspection, and I rushed after Kio, who carried her master back to the room on the third floor of the hotel. I assumed she was going to bring a doctor to the girl, but Kio instead took Nirrnir into the bedroom, and they had not emerged in nearly twenty minutes.

Huazo and Lunnze were outside the door for protection, while the other two members returned to the stable on Kio's orders. But there was no sign of being able to resume the inspection, so presumably whatever criminal evidence was hidden in that storage space had been moved elsewhere by now.

Was the development of the snake ambush a preordained event within the quest or a spontaneous happening caused by other factors? There was no way to know at this point. If the former, there should still be a way to save Nirrnir, but if the latter... perhaps we might see a repeat of what happened with Lord Cylon of Stachion......

I plunged into a swamp of unease and regret once again—but my left knee suddenly felt warm. I looked up and saw Asuna smiling next to me, her hand resting on my leg. She met my gaze and nodded with purpose.

"It's all right, Kirito. A little snake venom isn't going to take out Lady Nirrnir."

She didn't present any evidence for that claim, but I decided to agree with her and nodded slowly in return. "Yeah...you're right."

"That's right. We haven't gotten the quest reward, fer one thing!" added Argo, grinning wickedly. More seriously, she said, "Plus, there's still more we can do."

"Huh…? Like what?"

"There might be a cure for the snake venom. Kii-boy, what was the name of the snake that bit Lady Nirr?"

My mind went blank for a moment, and then I realized she was right. I'd read somewhere that only special antibodies called anti-venom, produced by humans and other animals, would counteract snake venom, but that was in the real world. A random antidote potion from a street seller probably wouldn't do the trick—Kio would have used one right away if that were true—but there could certainly be a medicinal item just for that particular snake.

I stared at the surface of the table, willing my memory to cough up the answer. I'd only seen the "Something-or-Other Serpent" on the color cursor for a moment, but if I couldn't recall it, I was a failure of a top player. I thought not of the word itself but the mental image of it, the visual snapshot I still contained in my memory, and read out the English letters.

"Uh, it started with an *A*…I think it was Argent Serpent? I don't know what the first word means…" I said.

Asuna and Argo glanced at each other and then spoke at the same time.

"It's silver."

"That's silver."

"Silver…? Why isn't it just 'silver,' then?" I asked.

It was a very straightforward question, but Asuna glanced at Kizmel with some concern before saying, "*Silver* comes from German. *Argent* comes from French."

"Ah, I see…" I murmured, then realized what Asuna's concern was about. To Kizmel, this world's language was, well, *Aincradese*. There was no distinction between Japanese, English, and German.

Fortunately, Kizmel didn't seem to be hung up on what she said. If anything, the pensive look on her face said she was hung up on something else, instead.

Before I could ask her what it was, the knight blinked and looked right at me. "You are certain that the snake that bit Lady Nirrnir was called an Argent Serpent?"

"Y-yeah. Are you familiar, Kizmel?"

"Only by name. But if true...this is no trifling matter. At the very least, you will not find the antidote in any town of human-kind," Kizmel claimed with certainty.

I stared at her, distraught, and asked faintly, "Why is that...?"

Now it was Kizmel's turn to hesitate. After a few moments, she said quietly, "In the old words, Lady Nirrnir is known as *Dominus Nocte*...a Lord of the Night."

"Lord of the Night?" the three of us repeated in unison. I'd never heard that phrase in Aincrad before, not even in the beta test.

Asuna, however, gasped after a moment. And Argo, who sat on the other side of Kizmel, murmured to herself. The two of them made eye contact, then Asuna whispered to Kizmel, "Are you saying...she's a...vampire?"

Whaaaaat?!

Only tensing my jaw could keep me from shouting the exclamation out loud.

Nirrnir? No way...

The thought struck me as ludicrous, but all the supporting evidence suddenly fell into place in my mind. The heavy curtains over the windows, even during the day. Her exclusive beverage of choice, red wine. The heavy cloak she wore before going to the stable. The wall Kio had us make before she crossed the light of the sunset. All these things gave credence to Asuna's suggestion.

Eventually, Kizmel nodded, almost imperceptibly. "That is another name...but you should not repeat it here. The lords of the night are not ghouls wandering the graveyard at night. They are a proud people. Some of them live far longer than even we elves, from what I hear."

"Wow..." I murmured. Then I recalled something and asked the knight, "Is that why you knelt when you greeted Nirrnir for the first time? Because you knew she was a Domi...Dominus Nocte?"

"That's right. I saw one of them at the castle when I was a child, just once, but I could tell from her airs."

"Ah…"

I exhaled, trying to recollect my stunned wits. I was shocked to learn that Nirrnir was a vampire, or a Lord of the Night, but that did not change the fact that she was my quest client or the fondness that I felt for her. And vampires were an RPG staple; it almost seemed strange that we hadn't come across one before now.

"And when you say this is *no trifling matter*, what did you…?"

But I realized the answer before I could finish the question. The classic vampire weaknesses were garlic, sunlight, and silver. In fact, the very first time we visited this room, Kio pulled my shortsword out of its sheath and said, "Plain steel." She had been checking to make sure it wasn't silver.

I didn't know if she was weak to garlic, but there was no question that walking in the late sun gave Nirrnir a kind of weakened status—in retrospect, the black circle with spikes in the icon was probably supposed to be the sun. So it couldn't have been a coincidence that the snake that bit her had the word for *silver* in its name.

"…So is the poison from the Argent Serpent only effective against a Dominus Nocte? And that's why it's not easy to find an antidote…?" I asked.

"I do not know for certain," Kizmel hedged, "but I know that the Argent Serpent lives in deep, deep caves and lives on silver ores. Its scales are made of fine silver and can be sold for a high price. And the silver venom that drips from its fangs, once smeared on a weapon, will provide extra power against ghouls and wraiths. Naturally, a Dominus Nocte is a rare and elite being…But silver is dreadfully poisonous to a Lord of the Night. It is similar to how dry lands sap the strength from elves…"

"…!"

I couldn't help but clench my jaw. A poison that could augment a weapon had been poured straight into Nirrnir's veins. If I had remembered the Argent Serpent's name properly and told Kio or Nirrnir before the inspection, it would not have come to this disaster.

There was a fury setting my blood to boiling, and it was not entirely at my own foolishness.

Bardun Korloy, his butler, Menden, and all their soldiers knew that Nirrnir was a Lord of the Night, not just a regular human. That was why they opened the loading bay door to flood the room with sunlight, just to inconvenience her. And not just that—it might have been to intentionally weaken her so her reflexes were slower. They moved the Argent Serpent to a normal cell and waited for Nirrnir to walk closer before setting it upon her. At the very moment that he demanded she be present for the inspection, Bardun intended to poison Nirrnir with silver.

Of course, this could have been the written scenario for this quest all along. But Bardun had stared down at Nirrnir, collapsed and weakened, and leered at her. He was saying, *This is what you deserve.*

"...Kizmel, is there any way to counteract the silver poison?" I asked, knowing it was a futile question. But I couldn't go without asking it.

Amid a pained silence, the knight just shook her head. But then a hard, tense voice spoke, filling the living room.

"There is one way."

I spun around to see that the door to the bedroom had opened at some point, revealing Kio, the battle maid.

Her face was just as pale as Nirrnir's had been when she fainted. For an instant, I thought that perhaps Kio was a vampire—or Dominus Nocte—too, but then I remembered that she had been perfectly fine in the midday sun when helping us with the decolorant for the Rusty Lykaon and the healing herbs.

For another thing, Nirrnir was the descendent of the long-dead

Falhari, and her parents were dead, too, for all I knew. As long as they didn't die from accidents or murder, that suggested that her family members were average humans. So did Nirrnir turn vampiric due to some experience in her life, or was she a foster child with no blood relation to her parents?

At this point in time, that was far from important. I stood up from the couch and took a few steps toward Kio. "You said there's a way...? Is there some medicine that will cure Lady Nirr? More importantly, is she all right now?"

"...Come this way," Kio said, beckoning with her hand before silently returning to the bedroom. We rushed after her.

The bedroom was almost entirely dark, with only a small lamp at her bedside, glowing a mysterious pale green. It was not a fire shining within the enclosed glass, but a bonfire shroom, like the ones in the hidden passage from the plaza.

In that cool light, Nirrnir was visible on the bed, her eyes closed.

Her eyelids and long flowing hair were absolutely still, which made me nervous that she was no longer alive, but the visible HP bar had about 30 percent left, where it was still. Below the bar were two icons, a silver snake on a black background—silver poisoning, I presumed—and a blue flower on a black background.

With some exceptions, status icons in *SAO* held to a general pattern: Debuffs had black backgrounds, and buffs were a different color. So it was highly probable that the blue flower icon was also a negative status.

It took all my willpower not to touch her little forehead to check her temperature. There was still a golden *?* floating over Nirrnir's head. As long as the sign of the questgiver remained present, our connection couldn't be severed, I decided.

"What is this state she's in?" I asked Kio.

The loyal maid bit her lip in frustration and whispered, "Lady Nirrnir is in a deep sleep induced by medicine...Did you explain to them about her, Lady Kizmel?"

The knight nodded gently. "I did, although I was not certain if it was right to do so of my own accord…"

"No, I thank you for saving me the time," said Kio, giving her a look of gratitude. She turned to me. "As you heard, Lady Nirrnir is an immortal Lord of the Night. Even I do not know her actual age, only that she has watched over the Nachtoy clan and the Grand Casino for over three hundred years."

"Three hun…"

I couldn't find the words.

The moment I'd heard she was a vampire, I had a suspicion she wasn't as young as she looked, but the truth was an entire digit greater than what I expected. Now it made much more sense that Kizmel had taken a knee. I motioned for her to continue.

"A Lord of the Night is said to have everlasting life, but things that are harmless to us, like sunlight and pure silver, are terrible poison to them. However, a brief moment of direct sunshine, or a small wound from a silver weapon, can be recovered from if treated appropriately. The Argent Serpent's silver venom, however, cannot be removed from the body once it is inside. If left unattended, it will take only a single night to…"

Kio could not finish that sentence. She reached out and brushed Nirrnir's golden hair with her fingertips, as though checking that the flame of her life was still burning. Satisfied, she pulled back, then lifted a small blue bottle from the side table. It seemed to be empty already.

"So I used this elixir…no, this poison of the lobelia flower, to put her to sleep."

"Poison of the lobelia…?!" Kizmel gasped. She looked from Kio to the blue bottle, shocked. "That is a poison that even the Ring of Purification Her Majesty gave to me cannot cure. A single drop of it can kill. You gave her that entire bottle?!"

"Lords of the Night have a powerful resistance to poison—all poison except for silver, that is. In any case, I could not put Lady Nirrnir to sleep without using this much of it."

"...I see," said Argo, breaking her silence at last. She looked quite pensive. "Fight poison with poison, eh? So Lady Nirr's not just sleeping, but she's in a kind of comatose state, I assume?"

"That is correct. This is how we can keep the effect of the silver poisoning to a minimum."

"And...if we keep her asleep until the effect of the silver poisoning wears off, Lady Nirrnir should survive...?" Asuna asked, clutching her hands together in prayer.

But Kio let out a long, heavy breath and shook her head. "No...the silver poisoning will not naturally go away. Even as we speak, it is slowly but surely eating away at her body, devouring her life. The sleep may slow it down, but even in this state, she will last two days at most."

Her voice was calm but tinged with deep anguish, lamentation, and anger. I could tell that the anger was directed at Bardun for setting up the trap and at herself for failing to stop it. I felt the same thing within myself. In fact, I now realized, I was biting my lip with frustration.

"Oh..." Asuna gasped. She opened her window and brought out a crystal colored a deep rose pink. Abruptly, I, too, murmured, "Oh..."

She took a step toward Kio and held out the eight-sided crystal. "Do you think...this could heal Lady Nirrnir?"

"......A crystal of healing? But it is so rare, so valuable..." Kio said, unable to hide her shock.

Asuna shook her head firmly. "No. I'd give this up in a second if it meant saving her life. Right, Kirito?"

I quickly nodded in response. "Yes. We can always get more of them."

"...Thank you. Your generosity is too kind," said Kio, bowing her head. But she did not reach out to accept the crystal Asuna was offering. She put her hands on it and pushed away. "But I'm afraid even this will not work. To cure the poison requires a crystal of purification, not a crystal of healing, and because Lords of the Night are so powerfully resistant to poison, they are also nearly immune to the medicines of humans and elves. Crystals are no exception."

"......No way..."

Asuna lowered her chin, clutching the healing crystal to her chest. I started to reach out for her, then drew my hand away in a hurry. There was a question I needed to ask again.

"But, Kio, you said there was just one way to cure silver poisoning. What is it?"

"...Dragon's blood."

"Dragon's blood...?" I repeated, waiting for her explanation.

But Kio was not in any rush to explain. She just stared at her sleeping master. After a long silence, at least ten seconds, she finally spoke in a hushed whisper.

"...Perhaps you are aware that the Lord of the Night must drink human blood to stay alive."

"......"

For a brief moment, I was taken aback—but it should have been obvious. She was a vampire. In fact, for all the times I had been in this room, I could not recall seeing Nirrnir drink anything but that red wine.

"Meaning...that red wine...was actually human blood...?" I asked, afraid to hear the answer.

Kio gave a frail smile and shook her head. "No, that is actual wine. Very fine wine...While it might contradict what I just said, in the ten years I have served her, and most likely long before it, Lady Nirrnir has never drank human blood. This is what she drinks instead."

She pulled a small black bottle out of the pouch she kept at her side. It was the object she'd offered Nirrnir outside the stable entrance, when Nirrnir walked across the sunset light and collapsed. But she refused to drink it.

"What is that...?"

"It is the one thing that a Lord of the Night can substitute for human blood...dragon's blood. According to legend, it provides far greater vitality than mere human blood, but it must be diluted by spirits in order to be stored for long periods of time, and it is treated with many kinds of medicinal herbs, so the effect is greatly weakened. Lady Nirrnir drinks one bottle every seven days, and that is how she has lived without human blood."

"……"

Asuna, Argo, Kizmel, and I were lost in silence once more. We stared at the sleeping girl's face.

I didn't know why Nirrnir refused to drink human blood, and I had a feeling I should not ask Kio for the answer. All I knew for certain was that Nirrnir was going to die within two days if we did nothing. I wanted to save her.

"So…if she drinks fresh dragon's blood that hasn't been diluted or preserved, Nirrnir can overcome the silver poisoning?"

"That's right."

Asuna said worriedly, "But where will we find a dragon? There hasn't been a single one on any floor thus far."

She was right. Ever since the early days of tabletop gaming, dragons and fantasy role-playing games had been inseparable. But in Aincrad, they were as rare as vampires. We'd heard of the dread dragon, Shmargor, and the water dragon, Zariegha, but as Asuna said, we'd never encountered a single one.

But that streak would end here on the seventh floor. I shared a look with Argo, and we spoke together. "At the labyrinth tower." "In the boss chamber."

"Huh?" Asuna was wide-eyed with surprise. She turned to look in the direction of the tower, blocked by thick stone walls, then swiveled back to me. Her surprise turned into unease. "You mean…the floor boss?" she whispered. "The boss of the seventh floor is a dragon?"

"Yes, finally. Or 'already,' if you want to see it that way…"

I was going to name-drop the boss dragon but reconsidered, thinking it wouldn't be good to present concrete details like that before Kio and Kizmel. We could fool them into thinking our inventories and instant messages were "adventurer's magical charms," but we couldn't explain away advance knowledge from the beta test.

Fortunately, Kio did not seem suspicious that Argo and I knew the floor boss was a dragon. She nodded seriously. "That's right. In the tower far to the west is a flame dragon known as Aghyellr. If you can defeat it, there should be more than enough blood to save Lady Nirrnir's life."

"Agiella..." I repeated, sounding the name out. It seemed off to me. The seventh-floor boss in the beta was definitely a fire dragon, but its full name was something like *Aghyellr the Igneous Wyrm* in English...

It was only once I mentally examined the letters that I realized "Agiella" *was* how you pronounced that name. During the beta test, the game did not feature any official guides for how to pronounce monster names—they were written entirely in English—so you either had to hear it out loud from an NPC or guess on your own. There weren't any NPCs in the beta who mentioned the boss's name, so mentally, I ended up calling it something like Ahjierre, like it was French. Apparently, I was dead wrong.

Thanking my lucky stars I hadn't proudly spoken it out loud to Kio, I said, "So the point is: We just need to beat Aghyellr and get its blood, right? We need to pass through that tower to get to the next floor anyway, so we'll have to fight it sooner or later..."

Belatedly, I realized that *later* wasn't an option.

"W-wait. Kio, you said two days?"

"...That's right," said the warrior maid. I stared closely at her face.

Volupta was located precisely between the main town, Lectio, and the labyrinth tower. And the difficulty level ahead was going to be much higher than the Tailwind Road that took us to this point. A highly motivated team would still take from morning until night just to get to the tower entrance. It would take another full day to reach the top floor. In other words, if we left as soon as possible—let's say tomorrow morning—it would be nearly impossible to beat the boss before the evening, two days from now.

Plus, even assuming Kizmel's assistance, it would be suicide for the four of us to tackle the boss on our own. While the beta team included a majority of the members who'd gone bankrupt—including me—defeating Ahjierre…er, Aghyellr, had required a huge raid party with over fifty members.

The help of the ALS and DKB would be necessary to tackle the floor boss. But neither seemed ready to leave this town before they got the Sword of Volupta. I leaned over to Argo and asked quietly, "Were they taking part in the daytime arena?"

"Of course. Both of 'em seemed ta have brand-new cheat sheets, and they won all five daytime matches."

"Uh-huh…"

That just meant they were even less likely to be interested in what I had to say before the night matches were finished. And if they lost all their chips at night, they'd probably just go through the same damn thing tomorrow, too.

I hurried back to Kio and tried to explain the situation as briefly and transparently as possible. We needed the cooperation of the adventurers staying in this town in order to defeat Aghyellr the Igneous Wyrm. But they were entranced by the Sword of Volupta, the grand prize at the casino, and they would continue gambling until they got it or were completely broke. I also brought up that there was a questionable cheat sheet they were using for their betting strategy…

When I was finished, Kio gave my tale careful consideration and exhaled heavily.

"…I see. The Grand Casino that the Korloy and Nachtoy founders built for their own enrichment is now ironically endangering Lady Nirrnir's life…"

"That's being too pessimistic," Asuna stated. She put the healing crystal back into item storage and stepped forward, clasping

Kio's hand in her own. "Those brothers who first built the casino might have been thinking of money, but Lady Nirrnir runs the casino fairly and faithfully, to provide a respite for those who come seeking entertainment, doesn't she? And all those visitors of Volupta provide business to the restaurants and hotels and other businesses here. Lady Nirrnir's been working hard for centuries for the sake of all the people who live in this town. It's not right to act like this is all fate..."

I was startled to see that there were tears forming in Asuna's eyes. I had just assumed she was against the casino's existence due to her dislike of gambling. She probably still hated it, but maybe she didn't think the casino was pure evil because it also served as a tourist attraction. It was the long, stable operation of the Grand Casino that brought this town its vitality and loveliness, and it was hard to argue that it wasn't due to Nirrnir's skill and nobility.

Asuna's so much more mature than me, I thought, adding my hand on top of where my partner held Kio's.

"I don't think the casino that Lady Nirrnir put so much of her love into would stab her in the back. I'm sure there will be a way for us to get the frontline group...the adventurers...to leave before the end of the night. The point is: We just need one of the two groups to earn a hundred thousand chips through the night arena," I said, considering this carefully. "I'm almost certain that their cheat sheets are a Korloy trap. Out of the ten matches, only the last one has false information, where they can make off with all the chips the bettors built up to that point. So if they bet the opposite of what the sheet says, they should win..."

Then I remembered we'd talked about the same thing yesterday.

"But that's working under the assumption that the Korloy family can only lose the match on purpose. Kio, in a match that's been set up with the intent to lose, do you suppose there's a way to flip the result into a win?" I asked.

For some reason, the armed maid just made a face and said

nothing. Belatedly, I realized I was indirectly holding Kio's hand through Asuna's and pulled back with haste. Asuna removed her hands next, and Kio cleared her throat to speak at last.

"It was our failure that we did not realize the Korloy family was distributing these 'cheat sheets,' as you call them. Now that I think of it, it seems that every time there is an especially big gambler present, the Korloy monster is more likely to lose in the final match. Lady Nirrnir and I are careful to watch for wrongdoing, but to think that they would *lose* on purpose..."

She paced around the bedside twice, stared at the sleeping Nirrnir again, then continued firmly, "It would not be too difficult to lose intentionally in a match between monsters of equivalent rank. Each family's monster trainers have hundreds of years of accumulated knowledge behind them in the area of monster health management. Just as there are medicines that cure wounds and illnesses, other herbs can excite monsters, or weaken them... or kill them. If given an herb—a poison—that slows the monster's reactions before the match in violation of the rules, that monster would be highly likely to lose. But in order to overturn that into a win, you would have to not only remove the poison's effect, you would need to give them a medicine that brings out strength. The chip payout rates are determined by numerical charm just before the match, which wouldn't leave enough time to feed the monster a number of different concoctions..."

"In other words, there's no way to overturn a match the Korloys are determined to lose?" I asked, feeling somewhat relieved, but I did not get an affirmative answer from Kio.

After a few seconds, she opened her pursed lips and said, "As you saw, Bardun Korloy is a crafty man. While he might be possessed by the fear of death, it has not dulled his wits. There is no way that a man like him would fail to take into account the possibility that his trapped cheat sheet might be discovered. I would assume he has some way of turning a loss into a win that doesn't involve medicines. I just cannot guess what that is."

"………I see…"

I thought back on what I'd seen in the monster arena, but with the cage surrounded on three sides by onlookers, I couldn't imagine any way of tampering with the monsters. At best, I came up with the possibility of shooting something small, like a dart, through the bars to hit the monster. But that was almost certain to be discovered.

So there's no way to ensure that the ALS and DKB win in the night arena? I thought, crestfallen. But then Asuna gasped.

I glanced at her. The fencer's hazel brown eyes blinked several times. Her face was slack as she murmured, "It's so simple. Just have the ALS and DKB bet on different monsters for the final match. Then one of them is guaranteed to win, and they'll have the hundred thousand chips, right?"

"Oh!" I gasped, too.

She was exactly right. Not even Bardun Korloy could manage to make *both* monsters win or lose. In fact, if Lind and Kibaou had just bet on different monsters last night, one of them would have the Sword of Volupta already, and they'd have spent the day slicing up the powerful monsters in the second half of this floor with its broken specs.

The problem was how to get them to agree to bet on different monsters…but there had to be a way to do that. I thought of some people who might be willing to hear us out and, just to be sure, asked Kio, "Listen, I'm not doubting it, but…is the stuff in the pamphlet about the sword worth a hundred thousand chips all true? About poison nullification, constant healing, and every attack being a critical hit? Because it's almost preposterous."

"That is exactly what 'doubting' is," she pointed out with a smirk before adopting a serious expression again. "The Sword of Volupta is indeed the sword of the hero Falhari, who defeated Zariegha the Water Wyrm, and there is no falsehood in the description, Lady Nirrnir said previously. But it is the treasure of the Nachtoy and Korloy clans and the symbol of the true heir of the family. So one wonders why Falhari's sons would turn it into a casino prize...and *that* was a question my lady would not answer..."

"Ahhh..."

That was indeed a good question. It seemed a little too hasty to turn around and use the dragonslayer's heroic sword, a memento of their ancestor, as a tool for pulling in crowds. But as long as the sword really did have the specs on the listing, that was enough. Aghyellr didn't have a poison attack, assuming no changes since the beta, but the HP regeneration would help against its flame breath, and a guaranteed critical hit would do wonders against its tough scales. I didn't know if it was the ALS's Kibaou or the DKB's Lind who would wield the sword, but neither was the kind to shrink in fear from the game's first real dragon boss. If he stood in as the main attacker and allowed the rest of us to focus on support, we'd be able to finish the boss in short order.

But that was assuming we broke through the labyrinth tower before sundown two days from now, the time limit to save Nirrnir's life. If we couldn't leave Volupta tonight, then we could go early in the morning and reach the final town of Pramio by night, spend the evening, then tackle the labyrinth the final day...But even that would be cutting it very close...

Then I realized something and gasped, sucking in a sharp breath.

It was impossible for us to match that schedule. Before noon tomorrow, we needed to stake out the shrine of the sacred key on the southwest edge of the floor, then follow the dark elf retrieval team coming to get the Ruby Key, fight off the Fallen Elves who were sure to stage an ambush, and pin down the location of their hideout.

If we missed that event tomorrow, there would likely never be another chance to take back the four sacred keys Kysarah stole. And then Kizmel would eternally be an exile from her own people, nothing more than an escaped convict from Harin Tree Palace and suspected spy.

If we saved Kizmel, we couldn't save Nirrnir—and vice versa.

It was a dilemma like none I'd ever faced before. I balled my hands into fists and found myself looking to my partner for help.

There was deep anguish in Asuna's eyes. She must have realized from the moment Kio said that only dragon blood could save Nirrnir, and the dragon was the boss of this floor, that there wasn't enough time to do both.

We couldn't bring ourselves to say a word. But Kizmel gently asked, "Asuna, Kirito, why are you hesitating?" She strode over to us and tapped our arms. "I will be fine. There will be plenty of chances to take back the sacred keys. But Lady Nirrnir's life is in danger now. Let us worry only about saving her. I will assist you in vanquishing the dragon, of course."

"......Kizmel..." Asuna whispered. She clutched Kizmel's hand.

Kio watched this interaction with great confusion. "What are you talking about?"

Back in the living room, we put on tea together and had a seat on the couches.

Kio refused to sit on Nirrnir's long sofa, so the five of us sat on the two smaller couches instead. They might have been subsize in comparison, but they were still three-seaters, so it wasn't uncomfortable at all.

After moistening my throat with warm tea, I explained to Kio the problem Kizmel was facing—with her permission, of course.

Kio scowled and considered the story for quite a while in silence, then glanced toward the door, as though her brother Huazo and the monster handler Lunnze, both standing guard in the hallway, were in danger of overhearing. She dropped her voice.

"Do any of you recognize the word *Neusian*?"

Before I could even react, Kizmel's head shot upward. "Miss Kio, where did you hear that?"

"I will explain in a moment, but first, could you tell me what it means?"

"......"

The knight seemed to hesitate for just a moment, then slowly began to speak.

"It is a very old word. It means 'One who is with neither'... Neither the Lyusulans nor the Kalessians. In other words, the Fallen Elves. But it is considered the greatest of slurs toward them, so no one uses that word anymore."

"...I see. As I suspected," said Kio, suggesting that she was anticipating this answer. She lifted her teacup to her lips for a sip, then looked at Asuna, Argo, and me. "Do you remember Lady Nirrnir saying that Bardun Korloy was gathering a huge sum of money in order to buy a brief extra bit of life?"

We nodded. I'd noticed that, and it bugged me. *SAO* had an orthodox fantasy aesthetic, but I'd never heard anything about a means to extend one's life span in exchange for money...yet.

In hushed tones, Kio continued, "I once asked Lady Nirrnir what this meant, exactly. The only thing she said was that it was a 'wicked Neusian plot,' and would not tell me anything more. After Lady Kizmel's explanation, however, it fell into place for me. The Fallen Elves have made contact with Bardun and offered him some kind of a deal."

"Speaking of which," Asuna said, throwing a glance my way, "the dark elf guards were saying something about us back at Harin Tree Palace. That they must have offered to extend our lives—and that humans always fell for that..."

"Ohhhh..."

It flooded back to me at last, but to be honest, the more vivid memory in my mind was of the snort of outrage Asuna had made when she heard them say it.

Argo's cheek twitched with a smirk, as though she were watching it happen before her eyes. She leaned back against the plush cushions. "Aha, I gotcha now. So this is a common trick the Fallen like to play. It *does* give us hope of a way forward, however."

"Huh...? What do you mean?" I asked, befuddled.

The info dealer waggled her eyebrows at me rather obnoxiously. "Listen. If the Fallen Elves brought old Bardun a deal, then it's a real good chance he's got a means to contact them, too. And with that in our pocket, we might have a way to get to the Fallen hideout without needin' your complex pursuit plan."

"Ah!" I cried. Asuna immediately brought her finger to her lips and shushed me, while Kizmel just smiled. She said to Argo, "Your suspicion is most likely correct. The Fallen have many eerie tools and charms, and one of them is the ability to send signals to far-off places. Perhaps they used such a thing to arrange a meeting at an agreed-upon location."

"Ahhh, wouldn't that be handy," murmured Argo enviously. I knew how she felt. We players could send entire messages, not just signals, but it wouldn't work if one of the two people was in a dungeon, and that was when you wanted communication the most. Even an item that just transmitted light and sound would allow for much better cooperative play.

But if Argo was correct, and the Fallen Elves had given Bardun some kind of item for communication...

"...The problem is how *we're* going to get our hands on it..." I murmured, only to be met by a lackadaisical voice from my left.

"We just gotta steal it, obviously."

"Huh?"

Argo was leaning back, hands behind her head and legs crossed. Her painted whiskers were perked upward in a confident smirk. "Bardun might be a greedy miser, but he wouldn't sell this thing for thousands upon thousands of col—he probably won't even admit he's got it. So we'll just hafta sneak into his room and steal it, eh?"

"Oh, come on..." I said. Kizmel was an honorable enough knight that she even hesitated to escape from prison in order to restore her unfairly ruined reputation, and Kio was a servant of Nachtoy who had sworn to uphold the order of the Grand Casino. It stood to reason, I thought, that neither would take kindly to a blithe suggestion of burglary under this roof.

But Kizmel just said, "Ah, I believe Argo is correct."

"Yes, that seems to be the only way to do it," agreed Kio.

".......R-right. Of course," I agreed, grimacing. Next to me, Asuna shifted; she was probably biting back a smile. I pretended I didn't notice and continued, "Still, it's going to be really hard to sneak into his chambers. We don't know when he leaves his place...and where does he live anyway?"

That question was for Kio. The battle maid glanced at the door, then looked back at me. "Just over there. In room seven of the Grand Casino Hotel...right across the building from room seventeen here."

"What?!" I yelped; I couldn't help myself. Asuna shushed me again. The enemy boss was living right under our noses this whole time? So why did it seem like I'd never seen any Korloys inside the hotel?

Kio could sense my skepticism and pulled a rolled parchment from the drawer of the coffee table. She spread it out on the flat surface.

"This is a layout of the hotel. As you can see, the facilities like the bath, kitchen, and storage area are in the center of the building, while all the guest rooms are on the northern or southern walls...but only the hotel entrance and hallway to the shared facilities offer passage between the north and south sides."

"Oh, so *that's* why there were no windows in the bath!" Asuna cried. I'd passed on the bath, but indeed, it was located on the western side of the center of the building, surrounded by hallways to the north, south, and west—and the wall of a different facility to the east. The hallways split north and south from the entrance, then turned ninety degrees to the west, traveling along the building until they hit dead ends. In other words, passing from one to the other required cutting through the bath or kitchen.

"I see...So the only things the Korloys and Nachtoys share are the entrance, the bath, and the kitchen," I murmured.

Kio quickly added, "As a matter of fact, only the hotel employees may enter the kitchen or storage room, and the bathing time for each family is strictly divided, so the only times they might come face-to-face are at the front lobby."

"Uh-huh…And when are the Korloy bathing hours?"

"From nine until midnight. And the Nachtoy hours are from noon until three. Three to nine is the slot for the hotel's guests to bathe."

"And what about midnight to noon?"

"Those hours are reserved for cleaning and water replacement."

"Ah, I see."

I thought the natural bath beneath Castle Galey had been open twenty-four hours a day, but that might have been the exception to the rule.

"In any case, if we're going to sneak into Bardun's room, our only chance will be while he's in the bath. After nine o'clock, though…That's a long wait ahead of us…"

It was currently 6:20 in the evening. If Bardun waited until eleven o'clock to take his bath, that was a wait of four and a half hours, and the night matches of the monster arena started at nine; we needed to get working on our plan for the ALS and DKB. It was going to be a tightrope walk.

Across from me, Kio murmured worriedly, "But…Bardun will have guards outside the bath entrance while he bathes. And the door of room seven is visible from there. It will be extremely difficult to sneak in without being noticed."

"Oh…"

Crestfallen, I let my eyes drop to the hotel layout on the table again. Indeed, the north-facing door of the great bath opened right into the hallway near Bardun's room. The two doors were not even fifty feet apart. If the guards standing watch so much as glanced to their right, they would have a perfect view of any trespasser. In this situation, the standard thing to do was make noise in the opposite direction to distract the guards, but there was no way to get to the opposite side of the hall. Someone could speak to the guards to occupy them, but they couldn't hold a conversation long enough for the infiltrator to find the item we needed and escape without seeming extremely unnatural.

I grumbled deep in my throat, deliberating on our quandary. Kio spoke up again.

"When going to the casino or stables downstairs, they don't put guards up in the hall, I believe…But unless something extreme happens, I doubt Bardun will be leaving this floor tonight."

"What would count as 'extreme'?"

"Well…if another phantom thief like you strikes, for example, or if there's a riot in the casino…"

"I see."

Maybe I need to slip back down into the Korloy stables again and make off with the Giant Pincer Rat this time, I thought desperately. But I ruled out the idea just as quickly. They'd clearly stepped up their security, and the Korloys had seen my face now, so if I got caught, it would be a total disaster. Perhaps causing a scene in the casino was the only option…

"By the way, what kind of stir would it have to be to get Bardun Korloy to bolt out of his room?" I asked, perhaps a little too innocently.

Kio considered it. "From what I can remember, Bardun has come down to resolve a situation when there was a disagreement between guests about cheating with cards that turned into a big fight, when some rich child saw a monster in the arena and had a screaming meltdown demanding to have it as a pet, and when a guest with astronomically good roulette luck placed a huge bet at the wheel."

"Aha," Argo proclaimed. "Kii-boy, A-chan, what if ya go down to the casino and get into a knockdown, drag-out fight on the floor?"

The scary thing was that I couldn't tell if she was joking or serious, so I replied with a straight-faced, "Maybe you should roll around on the ground in the arena and scream '*Buy me that monster, buy me that monster!*' instead."

The info dealer and I traded level gazes, each daring the other to blink. Asuna sighed and interjected, "Neither of those is a sure bet. As for the third possibility....Kio, the big win doesn't have to be at a roulette table, right?"

"Right. Bardun's only concern is the casino losing income...*his* income, I should say. Whether cards or dice or whatever, he is very uneasy about big rollers putting up thousands upon thousands of chips in wins."

"Uh-huh..."

Asuna looked to me. I quickly shook my head.

"You're dreaming if you think we can intentionally win big at any of those casino games. If that were possible, I wouldn't have..."

I had to catch myself before I started revealing what happened to me in the beta test. But Asuna caught my drift and picked up where I left off.

"I know, I know. But while roulette and card tables might be out of the question, there is *one* place where you can win up to a certain amount with a sure bet."

"Huh?" I gaped.

On Asuna's other side, Kizmel nodded wisely. "Ah, you mean the arena. According to what you said, the first four matches of the night will play out as the sheet said, yes? So if they shove all their money...pardon me, bet all their chips, they might be able to compile winnings alarming enough to bring Bardun out of his chamber."

"Oh...right..."

It seemed to me that Kizmel's AI was not just smarter than me with a better memory, but it was also surpassing me in imagination.

"True, that's a much more practical option than testing our luck at the roulette wheel," I admitted. "But the ALS and DKB won over fifty thousand chips through the fourth match last night, and Bardun didn't show up then. So he must be prepared for winnings that big. We'd need to win at least an extra fifty thousand to get him out of his room, I'm guessing…But it's already going to be hard enough to get Lind and Kibaou to bet on different monsters. How are we *also* going to get them to add more to the pot?"

Even with communication skills ten times better than my own, I didn't think my partner was capable of handling this one. But Asuna just shook her head and said, to my utter shock, "We're not going to force the ALS and DKB to bet more. *We're* going to do the betting. How many col do you have right now, Kirito?"

Whaaaat?!

It was all I could do not to scream. Instead, my mouth just hung open soundlessly for a few seconds.

"Er…well…if I sell all my excess items, I might be able to get a hundred thousand col…"

"Same for me, then. So we can combine that for two hundred thousand col, which would convert into two thousand chips, right? The odds in the arena are always between one-point-five and three to one, so if we take the average and assume two-point-three to one, winning four matches in a row betting everything, that should put us at over fifty thousand, just like the others. If there are three people putting huge bets on the final match, wouldn't you think that'd draw Bardun's attention?"

"Well, I suppose…"

But despite my agreement, there was no way to know who'd win the final match at this point. If everyone lost, then Lind-Kiba would only lose twentysomething thousand col in total between yesterday and today—but we would be losing all our assets. And even if we won, we'd only be able to buy casino prizes, and it was very unlikely we'd be able to sell those items to recoup the monetary value.

Of course, I didn't want to skimp out on whatever it cost to save Nirrnir, but if lack of funds made us unable to update our equipment or restock on consumable items, it might ultimately put Asuna's life in danger…

"I could pay fifty thousand col, too."

In shock, I turned to face the person who made the offer: Kio.

She mistook my expression, however, because the battle maid looked away and murmured, "I'm ashamed that it's the best I can do when my lady's life hangs in the balance…but that is the entirety of my assets, saved after ten years of work. Of course, there is an unimaginable amount locked away in the Nachtoy family's vault, but only Lady Nirrnir can open that."

"N-no, no, the opposite!" I insisted, trying to correct her mistake. "I wasn't thinking that fifty thousand is too little; I was worried that it might be too *much*…I mean, if we happen to guess wrong on the final battle, we'll lose everything, and even if we win, you won't be getting the original amount back…"

"Losing my money means nothing to me. Huazo and I could serve our entire lives for free and still not repay the obligation we owe to Lady Nirrnir."

I didn't really understand what she meant by this initially, but the expression on Kio's face told me she didn't want to answer any further questions on the subject, so I withdrew my curiosity.

Asuna gave me a little nod of agreement; it seemed ethically questionable to allow an NPC to entrust a player with fifty thousand col, but if we refused, Kio was only going to be more hurt, given that she was already blaming herself for not stopping the poison snake.

"…All right. Your fifty thousand col will be a tremendous help to us. Thank you."

Asuna and I bowed deeply to show our appreciation, but it seemed to unnerve Kio, who insisted, "Please, raise your heads. I am the one who should be thanking you."

"But…"

It was like a bowing competition over the coffee table.

"All right, enough already," said a third party, who tossed a clinking pouch onto the table the size of a fist. "I'll go in on yer gamble, Kii-boy. That's fifty thou, right there."

"Huh?"

She jabbed her finger right at my nose. "But you *better* win, got that? Then, not only will we lure Bardun out, we'll also get that sword. Two birds with one stone!"

It's not going to be that easy! I thought. But I couldn't say that now that we were all on the same page, so all I could do was nod without a word.

21

"I WILL SELL MY EQUIPMENT TO RAISE MONEY, TOO!" insisted Kizmel. It took all of our efforts to dissuade her from this plan of action, and after filling our stomachs with room service meals, we started on a full breakdown of our plans.

In the evening section of the monster arena, which started at nine, Asuna and I would bet using our war chest of two hundred thousand col as our starter money. That was fifty thousand each from me, Asuna, Argo, and Kio. After checking with her, I found out that it wasn't *all* of Argo's money, but if she came out of this with nothing to show for it, she'd be living on good old black bread for a while—no cream this time.

Asuna asked Liten for the latest favorites according to the cheat sheet, which she happily leaked to us. We knew we would win the first four matches, then. The problem was the final match, the outcome of which was entirely under the Korloys' control. In any case, when we, the ALS, and the DKB started betting with a total of a hundred and fifty thousand chips, Bardun should come racing down from the third floor, which would be when Argo and Kizmel, masters of infiltration, had a window to sneak into Room 7. Just in case Bardun sent assassins of his own, and given the possibility that her master might take a sudden turn for the worse, Kio would stay in the bedroom tending to Nirrnir.

While the final match was happening, hopefully Argo and Kizmel would find the means of contacting the Fallen Elves. If not, we were planning to bet on different monsters than Lind and Kibaou, so no matter what, at least one of the three groups would reach a hundred thousand chips. Once someone claimed the Sword of Volupta, which had shone as an unclaimed prize behind the counter for centuries, Bardun was sure to be away from his room for a while.

Preferably, *we* would get the legendary sword, use it to beat the boss, then sell it back to the casino so we could give Kio back her fifty thousand col. But this was the sort of plan where any kind of greedy overreach would endanger the entire scheme, so I told myself that if Lind or Kibaou got it, that would be perfectly fine. By eight o'clock, we had finished our briefing.

For the next twenty minutes, Asuna and I worked on our disguises to fool the Korloy family. In execution, this meant Asuna wearing Kio's personal black dress, and me in Nirrnir's dad's black tuxedo, both of us sporting masquerade masks.

The masks seemed like a bit much to me, but there were a number of NPCs dressed up in costumes as well; obviously, I couldn't show up with the tux and a burlap sack over my head again. The ALS and DKB would see us by our color cursors, and they'd probably wonder what the hell we were up to, but I chose to believe that they wouldn't mess with us until the matches at the arena were finished.

Lastly, we made sure there weren't any glaring holes in our plan, and right at eight thirty, we were all set to leave Room 17.

Except that Kio held us back for a moment. "Asuna, Kirito, I am so very grateful. On behalf of my master…and speaking of course for myself, you have my deepest thanks."

"Let's save all that for when she's feeling much better."

Asuna, wearing a black butterfly mask, gave Kio a quick hug. Of course, I couldn't do any such thing, so I just gave her a meaningful nod. After a brief glance toward Argo and Kizmel, we left the hotel room.

Huazo and Lunnze, who'd been standing guard by the door, already understood the gist of the plan. We gave them a quick nod and headed for the hotel entrance. As we passed the front counter and crossed the hall, I glanced at Asuna. Through the mask, I could tell she was just a bit miffed about something. I assumed at first that I'd done something wrong…then realized that the problem was that I hadn't done anything at *all*.

"Um…you look very nice in that dress, Miss Asuna…" I said, feeling awkward. She gave me a silent look, then suddenly reached out with her left hand. I tensed, expecting one of her usual punches to my side—but instead, she grabbed my wrist. After adjusting my arm so my palm was facing upward, she lined up next to me and placed her hand in mine.

We started walking down the spiral steps like that. I hastily slowed to match her pace and asked under my breath, "Um… what is this?"

"Shut up; this is just what you do."

That seemed like an unfair response, but I realized that arguing wasn't going to get me anywhere. All I could do was walk—and pray no other players witnessed us. I was already feeling strange enough in the shiny leather shoes, which I'd hardly ever worn in the real world, but I couldn't complain to Asuna, who was easily managing the preposterously delicate high heels on her feet.

Fortunately, I didn't trip and fall down the stairs or see anyone I knew. When we reached the first floor, I pulled loose the hand I'd been using to escort Asuna, exhaled silently so she wouldn't hear, then headed for the chip purchase counter in the gaming room.

There was no way to prevent my voice from cracking when I told the lady in the bow tie, "Two thousand chips." She smiled and replied, "Of course, sir," which brought up a payment window. I dispelled my hesitation and hit the OK button, instantly obliterating the two hundred thousand col in my inventory. Two large coins appeared on the counter, with 1,000 VC stamped on the front. I plucked them up and dropped them into the inside pocket of my tuxedo jacket.

The next two hours would determine whether these chips turned into one hundred thousand or simply vanished into nothing. It brought the nightmare of the beta test back into vivid memory—and a prickling sweat to my skin.

At the time, having my entire fortune riding on the last huge bet sent my pulse racing so fast that I thought I'd pass out. And now it wasn't just my fate riding on the line, but Nirrnir's life and Kizmel's honor.

There was no longer any possibility for me to cut them loose and say that whatever happened to mere game NPCs didn't matter in the end. Aincrad had a built-up history of centuries, possibly even a millennium, and Kizmel, Nirrnir, Kio—even the sword-fighter in Harin Tree Palace, Lavik, and Viscount Yofilis—were all true people who spent their lives in this world...

"Come on, let's go."

She pulled on my arm again, and I looked up, distracted from my thoughts. There was Asuna, looking at me just the way she always did.

Belatedly, I realized that although I was carrying a weight far heavier than anything I felt in the beta, I wasn't doing it alone anymore. I took a deep breath and said, "Yeah...I'm ready."

Tapping the two coins in my jacket pocket through the fabric, I started walking forward. Asuna took my side and naturally placed her hand on my arm.

"Um...is this what you do, too?"

"It is what you do," replied my temporary partner without missing a beat. I glanced sidelong at her face, which was now a few inches higher thanks to her heels, and thought I caught a hint of a mischievous smile on her lips below that butterfly mask.

I couldn't help but think, *Is it really...?*

The monster coliseum on the basement level of the Volupta Grand Casino, also known as the Battle Arena, was even louder and more enthusiastic than last night.

The spacious hall was packed with dressed-up NPCs, their

voices so excited that it drowned out the pleasant string accompaniment playing on the upper floors. After a quick examination of the scene, I found the DKB hanging out in the dining area on the left side of the hall, while the ALS were gathered on the right, talking excitedly around a table.

They were dressed in rough, ordinary clothes and clearly hadn't done anything more than remove their combat gear, but almost all the NPCs were dressed in formal wear, plenty of whom had masks on, so at a quick glance, most people probably wouldn't recognize us. We had fifteen minutes until the first match, so the first thing to do was head to the ticket counter next to the bar and get a list of the night's odds.

Which one should I pick? I wondered. Ultimately, I went for the dining area on the right, where the ALS sat. I guided Asuna to an open table in the corner, whispered, "Wait here," then headed for the ticket counter. The magical, automatically updating odds sheets were free to take, so I grabbed one and quickly made to return to my seat.

But then a voice said "Yo, ya finally made it, eh?" and a hand patted my shoulder. I jumped, froze, and awkwardly turned around.

It was a man with short brown hair with spiked bunches like a mace, a short, triangular beard on his chin, and scowling features that suggested an extremely stubborn personality—the leader of the Aincrad Liberation Squad, Kibaou. One of his eyebrows rose as he took in my appearance from head to toe.

"The hell you dressed like that for?" he said, at which point there was no way to play innocent. Plus, to his eyes, the name KIRITO would be emblazoned right over my head. I gave up on slipping away and returned the greeting.

"Heya, Kibaou."

"...Well, I don't got the time, and I don't care about yer clothes. Where's yer partner?"

"Uh...over there," I said, pointing at the table in the corner. He turned and started windmilling his hand toward us.

"C'mon, get on over here!" he roared, drawing disapproving looks from the nearby ladies and gentlemen in their finest garb. Asuna realized—as did I—that he could potentially ruin the whole plan by drawing the attention of any Korloy people in the room, so she quickly wove her way through the crowd and murmured, "Good evening, Kibaou."

"Yeah! Evenin'. Well, well…you look a lot better in those clothes than he does."

What the hell do you want anyway?! I had to bite my tongue to keep it in my mouth. "Listen, Kibaou, we don't have time, either…"

"I know, I know; I'll get to the point."

He took us to an empty table nearby, glanced at his fellow guildmates at their table, then said, "I heard from Liten about how the cheat sheets were a trap set up by the casino. I gotta thank you for that."

The sight of his spiky head actually dipping an inch in gratitude shocked me. Asuna had given Liten a warning that it was 99 percent likely to be a trap in exchange for learning the sheet's odds; I just didn't expect it would lead to a personal thank-you from Kibaou.

I guess people really can change, I thought.

But then he said, "The thing is: We already had our suspicions last night. I mean, followin' every last bet the paper says and winnin' every one? Seems a little too good ta be true, know what I mean?"

"But…you still bet according to the sheet in every match, right?" I pointed out.

Kibaou put on a bitter scowl. "Well, I mean, it *did* get nine outta ten matches dead-on. All five matches earlier today played out like it said, and I assume the first four tonight will, too. But we're gonna bet against the sheet on the last one. I just wanted ta tell you that," he said, then turned on his heel, gave us a quick good-bye, and started walking back to his people.

"H-hold on! Not so fast!" I exclaimed, grabbing his moss green shirt and turning him back around.

"What?"

"I mean…if you want to bet the opposite, that's your business, but did you talk with Lind about it?"

"Why would I?"

"Why? Because…if the ALS and DKB bet on different monsters in the final match, it ensures one side will win…"

"Listen, pal," he said, looking exasperated and jabbing an accusatory finger at my chest, "I know it ain't ideal to always be buttin' heads with them over every little thing. Like you said, if we bet on both monsters, one of the two of us is gonna win, guaranteed. But it ain't gonna work out like that this time. You saw the specs on that sword, didn'tcha? That's a balance breaker. It's even more broken than that guild flag. Neither Lind nor I is the big enough man to step aside and give our rival all the glory!"

He pulled back his finger and smacked his chest with his hand, then walked back to his companions. Three seconds of stunned silence later, I looked at Asuna.

"…I've never seen someone brag about not being a big enough man before," she noted.

"Well…I guess that's more trustworthy than someone who would claim they were the bigger man…" I murmured back.

The clock said we had just seven minutes until the start of the competition. I quickly laid out the odds paper on the table so we could examine it together. To my surprise, the paper already had altered entries for the first match, which was where the monster was due to be substituted. The Rusty Lykaon had been replaced with a Quad Scissors Crab, apparently.

According to Liten, who'd been feeding information to Asuna, the older man with the cheat sheets showed up out of nowhere just before the night matches began, handing out updated odds for the altered first match. If I didn't know what he was up to, I'd be amazed at his helpfulness. We used a brass pen attached to the table to mark the latest predictions next to the monsters on the list.

Match One: Scaly Badger (○) vs. Quad Scissors Crab (×)
Match Two: Studded Stag Beetle (×) vs. Squiddy Vine (○)
Match Three: Lightning Squirrel (△) vs. Rocket Gopher (○)
Match Four: Bestial Hand (○) vs. Ferocious Hand (×)
Match Five: Tiny Glyptodont (△) vs. Verdian Bighorn (○)

"...Interesting that there are no rockets in this world, but it's there on a monster's name," I remarked, spinning the heavy brass pen after I'd checked all the names.

Once again, Asuna exhibited a shocking depth of knowledge. "From what I recall, the word *rocket* comes from a spool of thread around a stick. Surely they have those in Aincrad."

"Oh...I see."

"Also, there's a family of rodents from North America known as pocket gophers, so I would assume that Rocket Gopher is a pun on that."

"Oh...I see," I repeated, feeling like an automated chat bot, so I added, "so it's just like the *melibe viridis* and hematomelibe, huh?"

"Please don't bring that up," Asuna said, glaring at me through her mask. She slid her finger down the list of odds. "It seems like they've got the Nachtoy monsters on the left side and the Korloy monsters on the right."

"Huh...? Oh, you're right."

I hadn't noticed yesterday, but now that she mentioned it, all the Nachtoy family's monsters were listed on the left side of the sheet. So the cheat sheet suggested that the Nachtoy side would win the first and fourth matches, while the Korloys would win the second, third, and fifth matches.

But if the final match was the only one that would run counter to expectations, like yesterday, then it would be the Nachtoys'

Tiny Glyptodont that won. Kibaou said he was betting on that one, and perhaps Lind's group would do the same.

If so, then the Glyptodont's odds were going to be much lower. Depending on how much was won through the first four matches, it was possible that winning the final match might still leave us short of the required hundred thousand chips. But that wasn't my concern...

"So who are we betting on in the last match?" Asuna asked.

I shrugged. "Depends on how Lind-Kiba play things, but if they both bet on the Nachtoy monster, we'll probably end up betting on the Korloy monster."

"Hmmm...If the Korloys are able to manipulate victory and defeat however they want, wouldn't they want to make their monster win, because they'll make more on the losing bets?"

"That would be the rational decision, yes."

"......I have a feeling that this is going to make your popularity drop among the Linds and Kibaous of the game even more than the guild flag incident did..."

"Can't get any lower than zero, so I'm not that concerned..."

At that moment, the hall was suddenly filled with the sound of a tremendous gong crash. Spotlights shone down from the walls at a booth toward the center of the floor.

"Ladiiiies and gentlemeeeeen! *Wel*-come...to the crown jewel of the Volupta Grand Casino, the Battle Arenaaaa!"

It was the same stylish NPC with the white shirt and red tie who had emceed the event last night, bellowing from the spotlights. It was literally the exact same speech, even.

"The first match of our night schedule will be starting shortly! Ticket sales are ending in just five minutes, so get those wagers in now, while you have the chance!"

The rumbling murmur in the crowd rose in pitch and volume, and a dozen or two NPCs moved toward the counter. I had to summon my courage before joining them, converting chips worth two hundred thousand col into a single ticket.

"…Well, here goes. I'm about to bet on the Scaly Badger in the first match," I announced, feeling sweat slicken my palms.

"Right," said Asuna. "I'm going to buy some drinks and get us seats up front."

"…Thanks."

For being so terrified of ghosts, she sure is fearless when it comes to situations like this, I thought, hurrying off to the ticket counter.

The Scaly Badger was, as the name suggested, a large badger-like monster covered in hard scales, while the Quad Scissors Crab had four huge claws rather than two. The crab nimbly caught the badger many times, but it could not break the metallic scales; the badger crushed an arm and a leg with its sharp teeth to finish off the crab. The cheat sheet was right on this one: We now had 4,320 chips.

The Studded Stag Beetle in the second match was an insect whose black carapace featured tack-like silver protuberances along its length. Its enemy, the Squiddy Vine, was a plant monster with ten long, wriggling, squid-like limbs. The stag beetle attempted to sever the vines with its jaw, but the vines bent and stretched like rubber and were surprisingly hard to cut. It wrapped up the hapless stag beetle and crushed it. We had 8,424 chips now.

In match three, the Lightning Squirrel measured about sixteen inches, tail included. Its fur was pure blue, and its front teeth were long and sharp. The Rocket Gopher, like Asuna said, was a short, squat rodent, colored a dull gray. The squirrel, in keeping with its moniker, was blindingly fast, leaping all over the cage, and it tore at the gopher with its teeth and claws. I started to worry that we'd made the wrong choice, but right after the gopher's HP bar turned red, it shot fire from its tail and shot through the air just like a rocket, obliterating the squirrel. Twenty-one thousand, eight hundred and eighteen chips.

In the fourth match, the Bestial Hand and Ferocious Hand were disgusting-looking crustaceans that resembled human hands—only three times the size. The Bestial Hand was the base species, while the Ferocious Hand was a color alternate. The Bestial mainly attempted to grab the other, and the Ferocious had a special stunning ability. At first, I thought this one might go against the expectations again, but the stun didn't seem to work against its own kind; the Bestial's superior gripping strength helped it crush the Ferocious Hand.

In the end, all four matches turned out the way the cheat sheet said they would. We would have lost everything if any of them had gone the other way; it made me sick to my stomach that I didn't know how they were manipulating victory and defeat. Was there a monster dyed a different color like the Rusty Lykaon? Was one of them given a stimulant or tranquilizer to alter its nature? Yesterday I assumed that the latter would be a dead giveaway thanks to a buff or debuff icon, but I wasn't the one fighting them, and you couldn't assume that an event battle would act like ordinary game play.

In any case, we had no other choice than to bet all 62,013 chips on the final match.

As she stared rapt at the six ten-thousand-VC chips, the two one-thousand-VC chips, the single ten-VC chip, and the three one-VC chips, Asuna murmured, "I see now."

"You see what?"

"If it's this exciting when you already know who's going to win and lose, I suppose I understand just a tiny bit of what you felt like when you went bankrupt in the beta."

"That's good to hear...I mean, it's probably not good," I commented, taking a sip of the champagne gifted to high rollers—though the official item name was just Sparkling Wine. "At any rate, our winnings are over sixty thousand now, so even if we lose it all, we should be able to earn passes to the beach for the two of us."

Behind the butterfly mask, Asuna's eyes went wide, blinking with surprise. Then she blurted out, "Oh! That's right. It's what I wanted in the first place from all of this. I completely forgot."

"Even if we get the passes, it'll probably be a while before we can actually enjoy the beach, unfortunately. Plus…"

I didn't finish that sentence, but I trusted that Asuna understood. If we weren't able to save either Nirrnir or Kizmel, we weren't going to be in the mood for the beach anytime soon. Step one to fully enjoying the white sand and crystal-blue water was getting that dragon blood and the four sacred keys.

Whether that succeeded depended on if we, Lind, or Kibaou reached a hundred thousand chips after the final match—and if it lured Bardun out to the arena, like we hoped.

"Ladiiies and gentlemeeennn!" boomed the announcer NPC again, accompanied by the gong. "It's time for this evening's grand finale! The pitched battle between our two last combatants will be starting momentarily!! Ticket sales will be halted in five minutes! Bet large and bet often!!"

The furor inside the hall rose yet again, and many visitors pressed toward the counter, Lind and Kibaou surely among them. I wanted to get it over with, too, but I couldn't make my move until I knew which one Lind-Kiba were betting on.

After ten agonizingly slow seconds, Asuna opened her player window just above her lap. She glanced at her messages, then leaned closer to me and whispered, "Both the ALS and DKB bet on the Tiny Glyptodont."

That information was coming from the ALS's Liten and her boyfriend, the DKB's Shivata. Both understood that the cheat sheet was coming from a fishy source and agreed to help inform us of their guilds' choice. Only because they liked Asuna so much, of course.

"I see…So they're both betting against the sheet," I muttered, checking the odds table. The Nachtoy clan's Tiny Glyptodont had a triangle symbol next to it, while the Korloy clan's Verdian Bighorn had a circle. If the sheet was as accurate as it had been so far, the bighorn would win, but both Lind and Kibaou suspected the sheet was a trap laid by the casino, and they intended to take advantage of it by betting on the opposite.

That *should* be the right choice. We knew the sheets were a trap, and if I had a simple choice between the two, I would bet against the monster listed on the paper. Kio claimed she could not imagine Bardun Korloy failing to envision someone breaking his pattern, but whether the trickery employed in the final match was color-changing or chemical agents, it was hard to imagine any means of reversing that in the less than ten seconds between the end of the betting and the start of the match.

In any case...

"If Lind-Kiba bet on the Nachtoy monster, then we'll just have to bet on the Korloy monster, as much as it pains me. That way, we're still covered if they've set up an extra layer of cheating," I said, tapping the Verdian Bighorn's name on the sheet.

Asuna nodded. "Right...but even still..."

She didn't elaborate, so I glanced at her through the mask. She just shook her head.

"Sorry, it's nothing. Go and get the ticket...and another champagne, if you don't mind."

"Got it."

I stood, clasping the coin in my palm, and hurried to the purchase counter.

Sixty-two thousand and thirteen chips—equivalent to 6,201,300 col—were exchanged for a single slip of paper. Now Lind-Kiba and I were wagering over a hundred and fifty thousand chips alone, and with all the other visitors added, the total had to be over two hundred thousand.

Next, I got two glasses of champagne from the bar counter nearby and returned to our seats. Asuna sent her message, which she'd composed in advance, to Argo on the third floor. Lastly, we just had to see if Bardun Korloy would come down to monitor the situation...

"Threeee minutes remaining to make your wagers! It's the last and biggest bout of the night, so make sure you join the fun!!" roared the NPC announcer from the spotlight. The odds list was changing rapidly as the bets poured in. For now, the Nachtoys'

Tiny Glyptodont had a payout of about one-point-seven. The Korloys' Verdian Bighorn was at two-point-three. The Glyptodont, which the ALS and DKB were riding high on, was under a double payout at this point.

"I wonder if they'll be able to reach a hundred thousand chips," murmured Asuna.

I did a quick mental calculation. "Um...if they've made at least sixty thousand, like us, then they should just clear that total. And if we win, we'll be over a hundred and forty thousand chips..."

"How are you so fast at calculating the winning amounts?" she asked.

"Huh? Uh, it's just simple multiplication, so..."

Asuna performed a quick operation on her window, which was still open. She raised her head and whispered, "Bardun's on the move."

"Finally!"

The warning had come back from Argo, who was lurking in the hotel's hallway, watching the front desk. That was one hurdle to the plan cleared.

But the difficult part was only just beginning. Our luck was up to the heavens now—in the form of those two monsters—but for Argo and Kizmel, they had to sneak into Room 7 and find the item Bardun Korloy was using to make contact with the Fallen Elves before he and his armed guards returned. And we had no idea what kind of item it might be.

"It'll be fine. It'll work out," Asuna whispered. She reached for the hand resting on my knee and squeezed it.

Yes, our present course of action was just to trust that our companions would be up to the task. We had our own job: to do everything needed to delay Bardun returning to his room, if it should come to that.

"One minute left to buy your tickets, folks!" the NPC announced. I thought I heard a faint swell of strings and looked over my shoulder.

Through the open doors to the arena, an elderly gentleman was entering the room, guarded by four men in black clothing. His slender frame was clad in an elegant three-piece suit, and he had a finely kept mustache and beard—it was unmistakably Bardun, patriarch of the Korloy family. The squat form of his butler, Menden, was visible behind him.

"There he is." Asuna sent Argo another message of confirmation, then closed the window resolutely.

Bardun's group proceeded straight through the crowds of NPCs in the hall, until they marched into the VIP box seats just behind the announcer's booth. Asuna and I were in place at the front line where we had a good view of the cage, so we couldn't see Bardun's face unless we looked over our shoulders. But I didn't want to stand up and draw any attention with the match beginning in less than a minute, so moving seats wasn't an option.

I faced ahead once again. The gong crashed louder than ever.

The many lamps placed high on the walls automatically focused their light—however it was that it worked—creating four spotlights that split the darkened hall. They illuminated the golden battle cage, which shone even brighter, drawing the eye.

The rectangular cage, separated into two parts by its partition gate, was about twelve feet across on the short side—and thirty on the long side. But the two monsters that were about to make their appearance would surely make this seem cramped. Kio had told us that the only monsters listed on the ranked chart were the right size to fight within the cage and did not possess any special attacks that might harm the audience or structure. These two, I presumed, would represent the very limits of those bounds.

A heavy rumbling left ripples in our champagne. Two spots on the stone wall lining one side of the cage pulled back, then began to rise.

"Now starting the final Battle Arena match of the evening!" the bow-tied NPC announced enthusiastically as two spotlights focused on the right gateway—the passage leading to the Korloys' underground monster stable.

"Our first combatant...hailing from the Verdian Plains to the

east of Volupta, the two-horned beast that scattered travelers and smashed carriages! The Verdiaaaàn...Bighooooorn!!"

A scraping of hooves—*clok! clok!*—issued from the passage, and a black-and-brown quadruped appeared, featuring curved, twisting horns. It looked somewhat like a goat or cow, but it was nearly six feet long, and there were sharp fangs lining its jaw.

New spotlights alighted on the left doorway, which led to the Nachtoy stable.

"Next! From far to the west of Volupta, ruling over the bleached white plains, the bizarre creature that smashes through all comers with a head as hard as steel! The Tinyyyy Glyptodonnnnt!!"

Thudding heavily into the cage was something that looked like a real-world armadillo, with a mountain of a shell on top. Its head was much bigger than an armadillo's, however, and it had a jutting, hammer-like forehead. It was just as large as the giant goat on the right side.

"The bighorn I get, but what's a glyptodont...?" Asuna muttered. I already knew the answer, because I'd looked it up out of curiosity during the beta period.

"An ancestor of the armadillo that died out thousands and thousands of years ago in the real world," I whispered. "I guess they're still alive in Aincrad."

"You're right. It looks exactly like an armadillo," she replied, ignoring the second half of my comment. "But what's supposed to make this one 'tiny'...?"

"I'm guessing there's a non-tiny glyptodont out there somewhere. I didn't see one in the beta, at least."

"I hope we never come across it," she said, making a face.

The announcer NPC shouted, louder than ever, "Beast against beast! Whose mighty head will give way first?! Let the match...*begin*!!"

The gong smashed, and the fence partition inside the cage began lowering into the ground.

The bighorn lowered its impressively protected head and

scraped at the floor of the cage with its hooves again. The glypto-dont jutted out its hammer-like head from its armored body, tensing its limbs.

When the fence was completely out of the way, the two crea-tures roared, the combination ugly and discordant. They charged from opposite ends of the cage with great ferocity. While large, each was only three feet wide at the most, and there was twelve feet of lateral space in the cage, giving them plenty of room to pass each other—but they had no intention of doing that.

Even I wouldn't want to defend against these monsters' attacks. They hurtled directly along two ends of the same line and smashed head against head with vicious force.

They were only normal attacks, but a light effect appeared on impact, white with red streaks, followed by a fierce shock wave. The marble floor shook, and it even caused some of my leftover champagne to spill.

Both bighorn and glyptodont merely stumbled briefly before regaining their balance and taking distance again. The HP bars of both were about 20 percent down.

"Th-the entire *arena* just shook! What a powerful collision!!" the announcer called out, prompting a wave of applause and cheers from the crowd. But I wasn't in such an excitable mood. I knew I didn't have the right to pity the monsters who'd been captured and forced to fight, but if I was able to compartmental-ize my feelings that strictly, I wouldn't have let emotion take over and freed the Rusty Lykaon from the stable in the first place.

At the very least, I had to keep my feelings level and watch out for any signs of wrongdoing in the match. If my guess was correct, the Korloys would attempt to maximize their profits by flipping the outcome back around so that the Verdian Bighorn won, matching the cheat sheet. I just had no idea how they were going to do it.

Neither of the two monsters seemed to be in anything less than fine condition, and presumably there were no color variant species on this floor, so dye-based cheating was out. It seemed like the best method would be to throw something in from outside the cage, but not a single person watching was up close to the cage due to the shock wave of the monsters' impact. If you'd been close enough, you would have easily suffered splash damage.

The bighorn and glyptodont backed away to their respective corners, then lowered their heads. Under the glare of the spotlights, I could see each enter the charging motion—the bighorn pawed at the floor, while the glyptodont spread its limbs and tensed. A moment later, the second charge was on.

Neither monster was anything more than standard fare, but the impact that shook the room seemed worthy of a boss monster's strongest attack. I could only imagine the sight of stacked chips falling and roulette balls escaping in the first-first casino, and my mounting concern made me sneak a glance at the VIP seats behind us.

The seating area was in the dark, but the VIP seats were close enough to the announcer's booth that the proximity to the light made them barely visible. Bardun Korloy was seated in the center of a sofa with his legs crossed, drinking champagne. The serene look on his face betrayed no hint that he was concerned about damage to the casino or the exposure of his cheat sheet ruse.

"Don't look too hard, or he'll notice," Asuna whispered, so I quickly straightened my neck again.

The second clash of bighorn and glyptodont did another 20 percent of damage to each, but it seemed that the bighorn's HP loss was just slightly higher. I remembered the two being about as tough as the other during the beta, but the bighorn's habitat was in the front half of the floor, while the glyptodont could be found in the back half. It would make sense, therefore, that the glyptodont would have a slight statistical edge.

"At this rate, it seems like the glyptodont is going to win," I whispered, tilting my head to the right.

Asuna leaned in likewise. "I was thinking the same thing... Does that mean the Korloys weren't able to cancel their trick before the match started?"

"Probably. Or maybe they never assumed their trick would work a hundred percent of the time from the start."

"Uh-huh…"

She sounded uncertain, however. I could sense that frustration, too. The trap with the Argent Serpent was extremely clever. Anyone who could devise and carry out such a plan would *have* to have a backup in case the target audience saw through the cheat sheet. After just a single loss, both Kibaou and Lind suspected foul play, and they were betting accordingly tonight.

If the glyptodont won, Lind-Kiba would each win over a hundred thousand chips and take the grand prize of the Sword of Volupta away from the casino. Would a man as crafty as Bardun Korloy simply say "Oh well" and let it happen?

There had to be something more, I knew. I kept my eyes peeled on the cage.

But there was nothing I could see wrong with the walls, the floor, or the ceiling. There was no betting gentleman ready with a poison dart or a fine lady about to sprinkle medicinal herbs.

"Again?! Are they going to do it again?!" shouted the NPC as the spotlights blazed down on the two monsters.

"Hmm," Asuna murmured. I noticed that her eyes were wide and blinking rapidly.

"What's wrong?"

"Nothing…I'm fine. I think my eyes are getting tired from staring so hard."

"Huh…"

I was marveling that this phenomenon could happen in the virtual world, too, when the monsters charged for a third time.

The vibrations rattled through the floor. Instantly, I was struck by a strange sensation. The supposedly superior glyptodont was just a bit slower than the previous two times.

That wasn't an illusion. When the two collided, it was about three feet to the left of the cage's center. The impact was still as fierce as ever. The champagne glass that had withstood the shaking so far tilted over, and I had to use both hands to catch it.

All of the light and smoke effects inside the cage faded. The bighorn's curled horns were raised high in the air, and the glyptodont shook its low head back and forth. It seemed that the slower speed of its charge was making a difference, because now the bighorn's HP bar seemed to be better off.

"But why did its speed drop out of nowhere…?" I muttered.

Asuna shook her head. "I don't know…There wasn't any exterior interference…"

"Exactly," I agreed, searching carefully. But there were no foreign objects sticking into the glyptodont's massive body and no sign of any liquid splashed onto it.

The bighorn had a little over 40 percent of its health left, while the glyptodont was at about 38. Two more charges would probably do it. If the glyptodont continued to fall further behind, the bighorn was going to emerge victorious.

Was this change an effect of Korloy manipulation? And if so, how…?

"Ah, there it is again…" Asuna mumbled, blinking.

"What's happening to you?"

"I don't know…Something's wrong with my eyes. It felt like the monster's color just changed a little bit…"

"Huh…? The glyptodont's?"

"Before, yes. But this one was the bighorn's."

I quickly looked at the cage again, but I couldn't sense any change in color. The glyptodont's gray shell and the bighorn's blackish-brown pelt were exactly the same as when the match started…

No.

It wasn't the monsters. It was the stones they were standing on. There was just a slight difference in color between the two, I thought. Under the glyptodont's feet, the stones were a neutral gray, while the spot beneath the bighorn's hooves was just the slightest bit green…

"Huh…?!"

I sank down a bit and turned around without drawing

attention to myself. I wasn't looking at the VIP seats, but much farther back, at the four spotlights near the top of the stone walls of the casino. The illumination from the large lamps up there was reflected through concave lenses before being focused into tight beams of light. From my perspective, the two on the right were the color of natural flame, but the two on the left were just a little bit greenish. Asuna's keen senses picked up on the difference in the monsters' colors, but I could only tell the difference on the floor tiles.

There was no way that such a subtle difference in color was intended to be part of the ambience. Most likely, there was some kind of debuff effect in the green-tinted light.

They were using it so the bighorn would win by surprise…But wait, that didn't make sense. According to Asuna, the green spotlights were shining on the glyptodont earlier, but now they were over the bighorn.

If the Korloys were the ones operating the lights, it would mean they were inflicting damage on both monsters.

"……!!"

Suddenly, one possibility leaped to mind. I straightened up and reached to open my window—only to stop myself. Argo was sneaking into Bardun's chamber now, so I couldn't ask her to relay any messages to Kio.

Instead, I pulled the odds sheet out of the pocket of my tuxedo. At the very bottom in tiny script was a list of arena rules and regulations.

Penalties for interfering with the monsters inside the cage…

Nullification of one's claim if the ticket is lost or destroyed…

Payout of winning tickets have a deadline of midnight on the day of the event…

And then, hidden among the fine print, I found it.

If both monsters should become unable to fight for a period of at least three minutes, or if both monsters should die simultaneously, there will be no declared winner, and no chips will be paid out.

"…That's it…!"

"What?" Asuna asked, looking confused. I pointed out the item near the bottom of the list. Two seconds later, she tensed up and froze, her black dress twitching briefly.

"In a tie...all wagers are forfeited to the house?!"

"This is what they're going for. That green light is slowing down whatever monster it shines on. They're using it to fine-tune the damage amounts, so that their final collision ends up knocking them both out."

"But...surely it's not *that* easy to force a tie..."

Asuna had a point. If animals in the real world continued bleeding in a near-death state, they would eventually perish, but as long as a monster in *SAO* had one hit point left, it wouldn't die. And while the attacks might seem to happen simultaneously, in almost every case, the system registered a time difference of less than a tenth of a second, with the first hit given precedence. In order to cause a tie in PvP, the person who took the first attack and lost all HP had to either inflict some kind of exceptional damage via a skill or item—or manifest some kind of actual miracle to keep their avatar moving until it counted as a tie.

The same was presumably true of battles between monsters, but it had a much higher probability of turning into a draw in this particular matchup. The bighorn and glyptodont both used head-butt attacks exclusively, meaning their attacks and the damage suffered would happen simultaneously. If Bardun Korloy had chosen to pit a bighorn against the Nachtoys' glyptodont specifically for this reason, then his slyness and cunning were the real deal. Although I had no proof, I suspected this was not a preprogrammed part of the quest but the work of Bardun's excellent AI planning and preparation for any outcome.

Inside the cage, the two large beasts were readying their fourth charging attack. The bighorn scraped the floor with its front-right hoof, and the glyptodont tensed its thick limbs against the ground.

The creatures raised their heads high, then bellowed with such volume that the quaking of the air was practically visible.

That was bad. It was a special attack—a finisher. It would still be a head-butt but with twice the power. If they collided directly with full force again, the bighorn might survive with its hit points advantage, but it was also under the debuff lights. The fine-tuning of the damage amounts could easily succeed at killing them both, fulfilling the requirements to cause a tie.

The two creatures growled, waiting for their chance to charge. We had to do something about the debuff light within the next ten seconds, or we, the ALS, and the DKB would lose all our chips together.

Could we block the light with a cloth of some kind? No, that was impossible. The spotlights were shining down from high up on the wall behind us, and no amount of stretching would allow us to reach the angle of the beams. A smoke screen? No, we had no way of creating enough smoke at once to block the light. If we couldn't block it, we'd have to do something about the lights themselves, but they were well over a hundred feet away. Even an instantaneous dash would never reach them in time.

Within half a second, I had brought up and rejected three different ideas. *If only I had magic spells!* But even if I *could* shoot a fireball across the arena, it would only cause a riot. I'd be accused of interfering with the match and penalized, possibly even imprisoned.

No magic, no bow and arrows; I could probably throw a knife or pick the needed distance, but there was no time to find them in my inventory. If only I had something to throw, preferably heavy, hard, and long…

There was a champagne glass in my hands. I looked down at the floor, then at the mini table affixed to the back of the seat in front of me.

There was a cup-shaped holder in the corner of the table that contained a number of items for the guests' use—a hemp napkin, a small fork and spoon, and a brass pen, the same kind found at the table in the dining area.

I set down the champagne glass and grabbed the pen. It wasn't as fancy as a fountain pen from the real world, just a hollow container of ink with a hole at the end for it to ooze out of, but that made it tough and reasonably heavy.

There was another brass pen on the table before Asuna, which I picked up and handed to her, making a pointed glance at the spotlights behind us. My partner took my meaning and nodded back.

Inside the cage, the glyptodont and bighorn stopped growling and lowered their heads.

Asuna and I turned around, using the backs of our seats as cover. The audience area was totally darkened, and everyone else was enraptured by the combat. If I used a sword skill, it would draw some attention, but neither Asuna nor I had the Throwing Knives skill. That meant we'd have to hit spotlights a hundred feet away, without any kind of assistance from the system.

The targets were light condensers about eight inches across. Striking them with the pen wasn't going to extinguish the flames that were the source of light, but if the lenses cracked, the light would scatter, which should disable the debuffing effect.

"There are pens on other tables, too; don't hold back, just throw!" I whispered, right into Asuna's ear.

But in truth, we didn't have time to try again if our first throws missed. Behind my back, I could practically sense the monsters in the cage starting their charges. Ducking behind the back of the chair, I pulled back my hand as far as it could go. Asuna did the exact same thing at the exact same moment.

System assistance or not, Asuna and I had level-20-plus stats, concentration forged by many deadly situations, and (probably) the protection of the Holy Tree's priestess.

We can hit it!! I thought, willing victory into the brass pen as we hurled our missiles.

As the two pens sailed through the darkness, they flickered just once, reflecting the light.

Behind us, the two monsters began to charge.

Then the two distant spotlights shattered, both concave lenses and reflective mirrors breaking to pieces. The roar of the crowd was so great that it was impossible to hear the shattering.

The debuffing light refracted in all directions. I turned back around and saw the bighorn and glyptodont, glowing blue and red, respectively, charging toward each other.

The bighorn seemed to be just a bit slower to start, but it straightened up and accelerated again. The curled horns and jutting shell slammed into each other right at the center of the cage.

I gritted my teeth, bracing against a shock wave twice as powerful as the previous. The crowd screamed as champagne glasses shook off of tables, shattering into blue shards. The light effects the two monsters created were so strong that nobody seemed to notice that the spotlights were only half as bright as before.

If anyone *would* notice the difference it would be Bardun Korloy...But right now there was something more pressing.

In the center of the cage, the light and smoke of the impact were still swirling viciously. I couldn't make out the monsters very well, but the two HP bars visible in the air were dropping at exactly the same speed.

They were under 30 percent, 20 percent...10 percent.

Was our incredible pen toss wasted? Were the bighorn and glyptodont going to fall in unison, leading to a draw and earning the house all the incredible number of chips bet on this final match?

Asuna's left hand reached out and grabbed my right. I squeezed it without thinking, and she clutched for all that she was worth.

At last, the visual effects were waning, revealing the forms of the two huge beasts. The bighorn and glyptodont were standing motionless in the center of the cage, heads pressed against one another. Their HP bars were still draining: 7 percent, 5 percent, 3...

Then the bighorn's HP stopped dropping.

The glyptodont's HP continued, however, and fell to 0.

The stout strength went out of its limbs, and the small mountain of a beast sank with a rumble to the floor of the cage. Blue light surrounded its body, which momentarily compressed before exploding into countless pieces.

In the shocked silence that followed, the bighorn slowly lifted its head.

"Wha...wha...what a collision!!" raved the NPC announcer as the crowd erupted into jubilance and anguish. "The winner of this ferocious bout, one of the greatest and most intense in the history of this Battle Arena is...Verdian Bighooooorn!!"

The victorious bighorn tossed back its horned head and bellowed triumphantly.

I let out the breath I'd been holding and glanced over at Asuna, who returned the look. She might not have realized she was still holding my hand—or maybe she did.

Either way, she murmured, "So...who were we betting on, again?"

"I think it was the bighorn."

"So we won the bet? How many chips does that make?"

"Um..."

In my head, I tried to multiply the roughly sixty-two thousand chips we'd won before this by the odds on the bighorn, only to feel a sudden prickling on the back of my scalp.

I stopped calculating and peered between the chairbacks behind us. Bardun Korloy was standing up from his spot in the VIP area, pointing boldly in our general direction, his eyes smoldering with fury. He didn't miss the sight of the pens flying through the darkness, it seemed. Four men in black suits left the VIP area, heading our way.

"Uh-oh..."

I hunched my neck and tugged on Asuna's hand. We stayed crouched, passing between the legs of the other audience members and the backs of the chairs ahead of us as we made our way left down the row. Once we reached the steps at the end, we turned and hurried upward into the dining bar area, then toward the exit.

"Wh-where are we going?"

"Let's go back to the third floor to change. I'm worried about the others, too."

"Good point..."

Beneath her butterfly mask, Asuna's lips pursed. We were slipping through the crowd at the dining bar, keeping our heads down, when a recognizable voice bellowed with rage and agony off to the left somewhere.

"How'd it come ta this?!"

22

"MY GOODNESS..."

Kio's eyes narrowed when she saw the green fragment I held out to her. She plucked it from my palm, gave it a whiff, then held it before the lamplight. About a third of the rectangular shard was charred, but the rest still held a dull gleam.

I'd picked up this bit among the pieces of the spotlight lens and mirror on the ground before we left the arena. As we climbed the stairs, I tapped it to discover the name KERUMILA INCENSE, along with a simple description: INCENSE CREATED FROM DRIED AND GROUND KERUMILA FLOWERS. That didn't explain much.

Kio examined the piece for a few seconds before lowering her hand. "This is called kerumila incense. It exudes a scent like nothing else in this world when held above flames, but it also causes the flames to emit a poisonous light. It's an assassin's tool that slowly weakens one's target over time."

"Ugh, what a nasty concept." I grimaced. At my side, Asuna had taken off her mask but was still in the black evening dress.

"But now we've identified the Korloys' final trick," she said coldly. "They had this incense burning over the lamps for the spotlights, and that's how they were inflicting its weakening light on only the monster they wanted, right?"

"The crafty old man really thought of everything," I said in admiration, despite myself.

Kio looked away; she was clearly chagrined. "I inspected the arena at regular intervals. To think that I failed to spot such a significant mechanism…I'm not fit to serve Lady Nirrnir…"

"L-look, you can't be blamed for not noticing. There was nothing special attached to the lights themselves. They just brought out this kerumila incense to put over the lamps when they wanted to weaken the monsters," I pointed out, but Kio was not heartened by this argument.

"When the Argent Serpent attacked her, I could have dispatched it with a simple thrust rather than a sword technique. Then the snake might not have torn itself loose. In fact, I should have confirmed the contents of all the cages before we started our inspection. Especially after Lady Kizmel pointed out that Bardun's insistence that Lady Nirrnir be present was likely a trap…"

I'd assumed that she was significantly older than me, but the way Kio was so crestfallen made her look much younger than before. But now wasn't the time to get distracted with such matters. I had to get her esteem back up again so we could discuss what came next.

"Listen, Kiocchi, the plan worked out in the end, so let's focus on the plus side, yeah?" said another voice. Over on the sofa, a glass of wine in her hand, was Argo.

By the time Asuna and I had rushed back to Room 17 on the third floor of the Grand Casino as quickly as we could, Argo and Kizmel had already returned from Bardun's room. The infiltration mission was a success, apparently, but the only thing on the table was an old map, and they hadn't shown us anything that looked like a means of remote communication.

Kio nodded in response to the curiously relaxing quality of Argo's voice and lifted her head. She brushed the edges of her eyes with a finger and put on a smile.

"Yes, of course. Asuna and Kirito's betting plan worked out well, and Argo and Lady Kizmel found the charming tool of the Neusians…er, Fallen Elves. We have all the things we need to save Lady Nirrnir's life. I shouldn't be lamenting what could have been."

She stretched and walked over to the table, picking up the open wine bottle and a fresh glass. She poured it half full of wine and downed the liquid all at once, exhaling heavily.

Relieved that she seemed to have recovered her mood, I took a quick glance at the time readout. It was 10:55 at night—ten minutes after the Verdian Bighorn won the final bout at the arena. Just like last night, Lind and Kibaou lost over fifty thousand chips in one go. Presumably, they were with their guildmates in the basement bar or some nearby tavern, commiserating their loss, before they returned to their inns for the night. We needed to make contact before then, explain the reason the cheat sheet was *right* this time, and ask for their help in defeating Aghyellr the Igneous Wyrm, boss of this floor.

The big question was: When would Bardun Korloy detect that his communication item was gone? After his debuffing light in the arena had been destroyed, after he'd lost a hundred thousand chips—technically, 142,629—and after he'd lost the means of speaking with the Fallen Elves who promised to extend his life span, there was no telling what he'd do next. Of course, he didn't have a single bit of evidence that the ones who destroyed his spotlights, won big in the final match, and burglarized his unoccupied room were the four of us—or anyone related to the Nachtoy family. Still, if that was enough for them to back down, they wouldn't have arranged a rare poisonous snake in an attempt to kill Nirrnir.

Huazo was supposed to warn us when Bardun returned to his room from the arena. There was something we needed to discuss before that happened.

Kio gave back the partially burned piece of kerumila incense, which I returned to my inventory, just in case. I walked over to Argo and asked, "So…what kind of tool was he using to contact the Fallen Elves?"

"It's right in front of ya."

"Huh?"

I blinked and looked down at the table. The only things on top of it were the open wine bottle, four glasses, and a parchment map. The map showed the entirety of the seventh floor, which might be useful for a strategy session, but there was no tool in sight—unless...

"Wait, this? The map?"

"Correct." She smirked, and I gave her a piercing gaze.

"But...how did you know this was the way Bardun was communicating as you searched? I would have passed over it, a hundred percent."

"You forget, I had Kizucchi on my side," Argo said, raising her wineglass toward the dark elf knight on the other couch.

Kizmel gave us a proud grin and directed our attention to the bottom-left portion of the map. "Look at this."

"Um..."

We leaned in closely enough that our heads touched. In the corner of the parchment map, there was a strange mark drawn in dark red ink. It was two interlocking zigzag lines. I thought I'd seen them somewhere before.

"Oh! It's ice and lightning! The symbol of the Fallen!" Asuna cried. "Ohhh," I exclaimed. It was indeed the same insignia carved into the Fallen Elf dagger dropped by the PKer on the sixth floor, the Dirk of Agony.

"Where in the room was this?" I asked Argo. She replied, "In the third drawer from the top in a huge desk." If it wasn't already placed out in the open, then maybe he wouldn't notice it was gone right away, but either way, we couldn't allow any time to go to waste.

"How do you use this, Kizmel?" I asked promptly, but the knight just gave me a brief, knowing smile.

"I understand you're in a hurry, but I suggest you sit down first."

"Oh...um, sure."

I sat down next to Kizmel, and Asuna took the spot next to

Argo, with Kio on the other side. The knight cleared her throat and brushed the map with her fingertips.

"This might look like parchment, but it is not. It is created from very rare monsters that appear in abandoned manors and castles named Scyia, which are killed in a particular way, then dried and used like paper."

"Scyia…"

I'd never encountered such a monster in the beta test, and I didn't know if the name meant anything. Asuna and Argo looked confused, too, and it would probably take some time to figure out, so I let her continue the explanation without interrupting.

"Scyia always appear in pairs. When you defeat them both and create paper with them, the pieces are bound by a mysterious power. When blood is dripped onto one, the spattering will appear in the same place on the other."

It still wasn't making much sense to me, but at that comment, Asuna cried, "Oh! So they drew the exact same map on both pieces of paper, and if the owner of one map drips blood onto the map, they can indicate those coordinates to the owner of the other map!"

"Aha…" I said.

"Very interesting," murmured Argo.

A moment later, Kio chimed in with, "So if he drips blood somewhere on this map, the stain will appear on the map's partner, and Fallen Elves will show up at that location…?"

"That would seem to be the case. However," Kizmel said, frowning, "that would not indicate a time to meet. Perhaps they go to the place and simply wait until the other side appears…"

That did feel like a rather inefficient way of doing things. Would the Fallen Elves, as busy as they were with their various tricks and schemes, really wait around all hours of the day?

"So, if you write on this map in blood, it'll show up on the other map, Kizmel?" I asked.

The knight shook her head. "No, I have heard that only freshly dropped stains of blood direct from the finger will transfer. Of course, you might be able to write large letters if you spill enough drops…but I believe the stains will fade after some time…"

"Ya don't say," I commented, mimicking Argo without realizing it and earning a snort from the girl herself.

"Kii-boy, if you don't show Big Sis some respect, she won't teach ya how to tell time with this thing," she snapped.

"What? You figured it out, Argo?!" asked Asuna, wide-eyed. She slapped her hands together in prayer. "Please! Tell us how! We'll make Kirito stand out in the hallway for punishment if you want!"

"Awww, come on," I whined. Kizmel and Kio giggled in unison. If it was what it took to get the maid in better spirits, standing out in the hallway didn't seem so bad—if it weren't for the fact that I was curious, too. "Sorry, sorry. I'll buy you a baked sweet potato to make up for it. Just fill me in on the secret."

"Why a sweet potato?" Argo replied, pursing her lips with dissatisfaction. She got over it right away, however, and pointed to the right half of the map. It was not on the map itself that she was pointing, actually, but the aperture of Aincrad itself. I suddenly noticed that there were very small dots placed at regular intervals all the way around the perfectly circular floor.

"See how there's twenty-four of these? I bet they use 'em to indicate the time."

"Oh…!" Asuna and I exclaimed together. I almost cried out "It's a clock!" but held myself back because I wasn't sure if Kio or Kizmel knew what a clock was. It wasn't that there weren't any mechanical clocks in Aincrad whatsoever—there was a huge clock tower on the Town of Beginnings on the first floor—but I couldn't recall seeing any analog clocks in the elven castles.

Kio and Kizmel understood what Argo meant immediately, however.

"I see. Each dot is one hour; is that it?"

"So the daytime hours would be on the right, and the night hours on the left," they said respectively, at which point I realized that the map's clock was not a traditional twelve-hour type but a twenty-four-hour clock. That meant the dot at the very top was midnight, and the dot at the very bottom was noon.

"Ah, so they drop blood in two places for location and time," said Asuna with understanding. She looked up from the map at the rest of us. "So...when and where do we summon the Fallen Elves?"

"Not so fast, A-chan," said Argo, wincing. She glanced down to her right at the game clock. "If you indicate an hour from now, the Fallen ain't gonna show up in time, I assume. Plus, we've got stuff to take care of first, don't we?"

"Oh, right...We need to negotiate with the DKB and ALS to convince them to leave first thing in the morning. Kirito, you mentioned you had a plan for that—how are you going to get those guys in line?"

Four pairs of eyes landed on me. I shrugged.

"Should be easy. I'll just say that if we beat the floor boss by the evening of the day after tomorrow—on second thought, let's make that by noon of the day after tomorrow—I'll sell the Sword of Volupta to whoever fought harder, for two hundred thousand col."

"*Huh?!*" squawked Argo, the first to react. She swirled the remnants of her wineglass around as she yelled, "Are you serious?! That's not a bit?! That broken-ass sword's worth a hundred thousand chips! Ten million col! And you're just gonna sell it off for two hundred thousand?!"

"Lind-Kiba aren't going to budge unless I sweeten the pot that much. Besides, two hundred thousand col is the seed money we put into winning the sword in the first place, so it'll mean we've gotten our investment back."

"Still...you could at *least* ask fer three...or four hundred thousand..." she insisted, sounding more like the Argo I remembered.

Just then, Kio lifted her hand, which brought us to silence. There was a deep furrow between her brows, despite the fact that she had just looked like she'd overcome her misgivings.

"Asuna, Kirito, Argo, Lady Kizmel. The truth is...there is one thing I should explain to you about that sword..."

Once again, however, she was interrupted. There was a quick, quiet knock on the door, and without waiting for her to respond, the person on the other side opened it a crack, revealing that it was Huazo.

"Bardun's returned to his room, Sister!"

"Finally!" I said, seething at the long-awaited news. I rose from the sofa and said, "We'll hear what you have to say later. We've got to exchange this first," as I patted the chest pocket of the tuxedo I was still wearing.

Asuna got to her feet as well. "I'll join you. We should stock up on food and things anyway."

Five minutes later, I was placing a shining golden chip worth a hundred thousand VC on the counter. The NPC guests around me broke into hushed murmurs—or so I imagined.

The lady behind the counter seemed to freeze for a moment but regained her bright smile just as quickly.

"Exchanging for a prize? Which item would you like?"

"That one!!" I cried, pointing at the very top of the list on the board, while Asuna yanked on the back of my collar. Through the holes of the butterfly mask, her eyes had the look of an elder sister scolding her foolish little brother. She pulled me back and took my spot at the counter. She opened up the prize pamphlet she was holding, pointing daintily at an illustration of a sword.

"We would like the Sword of Volupta."

"Of course," said the woman with a perfect smile, before turning on her heel. The prize display was affixed to the side of the massive pillar at the center of the space behind the four-sided counter, and the hundred-thousand-chip sword shone at the very top, out of reach without a stepladder—or so I assumed.

Instead, she pressed a button or some other contraption hidden on the bottom of the display, causing the entire thing to descend with a heavy rumble. In five seconds, the bottom edge made contact with the floor and came to a stop.

Still, there was nearly seven feet to the sword, and the woman had to stretch for all she was worth, removing the black leather sheath just below the sword first. She handed that to another NPC waiting beside her, then reached for the Sword of Volupta at last.

In my imagination, it was going to be very heavy; fortunately, she removed it from the rack without dropping it, then slid the platinum-and-gold longsword into the sheath her companion was holding. It clicked in at the hilt, at which point she took the sheath and lifted the entire thing.

Then she returned to the counter and held it out. "This is the Sword of Volupta. Please accept your prize."

Before either of us moved, Asuna shot me a look. Apparently, she was giving me the honors. I hurried forward, slipping my hands under the sheath and carefully putting my strength into them. The sword left her fingers.

It was…not heavy.

Not that it was light, either. But it was hardly any different from the Sword of Eventide +3, my current weapon. According to the crusty blacksmith of the dark elf camp on the third floor, Landeren, it was especially sharp, even among the masterpieces of Lyusula, which meant it was also delicate. I'd put all the points into sharpness, which made it lighter than average among swords of its class.

If anything, the Sword of Volupta was wide and thick, so the fact that it felt nearly the same weight as the Eventide probably meant…

I cut off that troubling train of thought before I could reach a conclusion and took a step back. "Thank you. I accept this item."

The lady with the bow tie deftly plucked the chip off the counter, and she and her coworker lowered their heads deeply. That was the end of our mission, I assumed—but no sooner had the thought entered my mind than the lady produced a number of black cards from behind the counter and held them out with both hands.

"These are passes to the private beach the casino operates. Please do enjoy."

I wanted to shout *Yessss!* but I had a feeling Asuna would grab me by the back of the neck again, so I held it to a gentlemanly smile as I took the cards. They weren't made of plastic, of course, but it was a rough material that didn't feel like wood, paper, or metal, either. The black surface was decorated with a logo combining a flower and dragon, which was presumably the symbol of the casino. I counted four of them; we'd earned a hundred and forty thousand chips, so the math checked out.

I slid the cards into my chest pocket and thanked them again. The women bowed once more and replied, in perfect unison, "We look forward to your next visit to the Volupta Grand Casino."

A huge round of applause rose from around us, catching me by surprise. There were rows of casino guests surrounding the exchange counter, clapping and beaming at us.

Ordinarily, I might get carried away and wave to the crowd, but by now, the Korloys would be receiving word that the Sword of Volupta, the prize that had shone unclaimed at the top rack of the Grand Casino's prize board for centuries, was now gone. It wasn't clear if Bardun would be descending from the third floor again, but I certainly didn't want to encounter him.

"Thanks, thanks," I said, lifting my right hand to clear the way through the crowd with the sword tucked under my other arm. We headed out to the staircase hall, where I slipped behind a pillar to open my inventory and toss the Sword of Volupta inside.

We'd cleared the most difficult of the night's series of missions: winning the needed chips to acquire the sword. Part of me wanted to check the properties immediately and see if they were truly as broken as the description said, but there was one more job to do first.

"Where are they now, Asuna?" I asked, looking up.

My partner's bare shoulders rose and fell. "The ALS and DKB

are commiserating at a restaurant a bit to the east of the casino square, they said. Liten and Shivata succeeded at luring them both to the same place."

"I see. We really owe those two…We'll need to treat them to dinner at some point."

"I'd suggest Menon's, then," Asuna offered, a smile teasing at the corner of her mouth—surely at the thought of Shivata being forced to carry a great number of plates by the cook. I wanted to see that, too, of course. But in order to see that, we needed to finish an even harder mission: beating the floor boss and taking back the sacred keys.

"All right…let's go," I said, mentally preparing myself for the next step, when Asuna tugged on my tuxedo to hold me back.

"I'd like to change clothes."

"Oh…right."

Numerically and visually, her dress offered little defense; it made sense that she wouldn't want to head outside in it. And if I was being honest, I didn't want those ruffians in the frontline group to see my partner looking like this, either. But it would take too much time to return to the third floor, change outfits, then come back down again.

"Well, uh…I guess I could hide you like this…"

I motioned Asuna over to the wall and blocked her with my body, opening the tuxedo jacket wide to offer a tiny bit more cover.

Behind the butterfly mask, Asuna blinked a few times, then lifted her hand in a most elegant way and clenched it into a fist.

"But then *you'll* be able to see me up close!"

It was as the impact of her fist rumbled through the system's barrier and into my right side that I belatedly realized, *Oh, right…*

23

IT WAS EIGHT IN THE MORNING ON JANUARY 7, NINE hours after our great gamble at the Grand Casino.

Asuna, Argo, Kizmel, Kio, Nirrnir, and I made up a party of six, heading quickly across the Field of Bones on the west side of the seventh floor of Aincrad.

While it was a six-person party, only four of us could really fight. Nirrnir was still in a coma, wrapped in a heavy cloak and a cape to shut out the sunlight, and Kio had her master secured tightly to her back with leather straps.

The Field of Bones, meanwhile, was a desolate wasteland, with dead trees that stuck out of the ground like bones; there was virtually no green plant life to be seen. As an elf, Kizmel would normally be hit with a weakness debuff in less than a minute here, but fortunately for us, she still had the Greenleaf Cape she'd borrowed from the treasury of Castle Galey, which kept her from suffering in the arid landscape.

According to her, when leaving Castle Galey for Harin Tree Palace, she'd been given the treasured cape to use by Bouhroum, the older man in charge of the treasury at the castle. Surely he hadn't anticipated that Kizmel would need it after escaping prison and going off to reclaim the keys, but the ancient steak eater was a man of many mysteries. One day I wanted to return to the castle to grill him about the Meditation skill—and maybe get a chance to eat the hamburg steak I missed out on (what had he called it, a fricatelle?), too. But we couldn't even approach the dark elf territories until we recovered the stolen keys.

Frankly, it had felt like we were grasping at straws in the quest to get the keys back, but now we had finally found the thread we could follow to victory. And it was leading us toward two small figures flickering on the far end of the bleached wasteland.

Seven hours ago, Asuna and I returned to the third-floor hotel room after negotiating with the two guilds. We gave our report to the group and decided at last to make use of the item for contacting the Fallen Elves: the map of Scyia.

The location we indicated was a pair of aspen trees that stood on the path from Volupta to Looserock Forest. The time was three o'clock in the morning.

I accepted the job of dripping the blood. Kizmel was very insistent that she should do it, but Bardun was a human being, and if elf blood just so happened to cause a different reaction in the map, the Fallen would know it was a trap.

Somehow, I managed to convince Kizmel of this, and so she stood back while I attempted to prick my finger with a thin knife from Kio. This was when Asuna, Argo, and I belatedly realized a major problem. Nirrnir's room—and the rest of Volupta, of course—was inside the anti-criminal code zone, where players could not harm other players. That included oneself, of course. Jabbing at my finger with a knife just brought up a purple system wall in the air.

Kizmel rolled her eyes at the overprotective nature of "humankind's magic" and tried to take the knife from me, but Argo fortunately came up with a solution. There was one way to temporarily cancel the safety code within the safe zone of town: with the dueling system.

I challenged Asuna to a first-strike duel, which she accepted with a suspicious look, making a huge countdown window appear over the table. The sixty seconds passed as agonizingly slowly as I remembered them doing before, and once the duel had begun, I was able to prick the tip of my finger with the knife. The blood in this case was not realistic liquid but shining red bits of light. I dripped the first one over the aspen trees on the map. Next, I added a second drop over the mark on the edge of the map corresponding to three in the morning. A sharp little needle of red light extended about two inches from that spot and began to tick down each second. In a minute, the light was gone, and there was nothing to do but trust in the map and wait.

Three minutes later, a blue pillar appeared over the map this time. It was not indicating the same place and time, however.

The location was an especially large, dead tree standing in the middle of the Field of Bones, far to the northwest of Volupta. And the time was seven in the morning.

Clearly, the Fallen Elves had indicated a new time and place, as though to say, "We're not following *your* instructions." We couldn't just spurn this counteroffer, so I was going to approve when I came up short. Where was I supposed to drip the blood to indicate acceptance?

The group erupted into suggestions and arguments, until Kio spotted two oddly shaped letters for *Y* and *N* in the corner of the map. Two minutes had already passed since the Fallen's response by then, so I quickly added a new drop on the *Y*. We waited five more minutes, just in case, but another pillar of light did not appear, so we allowed the duel to end as a draw.

We left the map out on the table and took a late dinner with some light food Asuna bought out in town. It was a waste of time to travel back to the Ambermoon Inn, so we just chose to sleep in the hotel. Then we got up at four o'clock, took thirty minutes to get ready, left the casino through that hidden passage again, and exited the town from the north gate, hurrying northwest. There were monsters along the way, of course, but we had Kizmel the elite-level NPC.

In the town, she kept her broken saber on hand, but out in the wilderness, Kizmel had to give up and switch to the Elven Stout Sword I gave her. The utter power she exhibited made it clear that unfamiliarity with the weapon was no issue. After how helpless Kizmel had been against Kysarah the Ransacker, thinking about the eventual second confrontation with that foe made my legs turn to jelly. At least Kysarah wasn't going to gain any levels in the meantime, though. We just had to make the most of our time to power up before then.

With this thought and more passing through my mind, I gained a level on the trip, as did Asuna, putting us at 23 and 22, respectively. Argo had been busy leveling up on her own time, but as usual, she declined to tell us her number or skill selection. Her claw attacks were even faster than Kizmel's, and although the damage itself was low, she wreaked havoc on the monsters and kept them distracted while we unleashed big attacks.

And even with Nirrnir strapped to her back, unable to move in any violent fashion, Kio managed to shatter many foes with precise, high-powered thrusts from her estoc, if they were foolish enough to stand in her way. The party crossed the grassland that surrounded Volupta without stopping, Looserock Forest distant on the right-hand side as we continued northwest, until the sky began to grow light just as we reached the Field of Bones.

As the most dangerous outdoor region on the seventh floor, the monsters were definitely a rank higher than elsewhere, but not enough to give us serious trouble. The only struggle was against a pack of Rusty Lykaons—real ones this time. Kio sprinkled a strange-smelling liquid, however, which dulled the movement of the lykaons and made it much easier to defeat them.

It was occurring to me now that between the Rubrabium Flower Dye that started this whole incident, the lobelia flower poison we used to put Nirrnir to sleep and slow the silver poison in her veins, the kerumila incense used to create the spotlight debuff, and the strange liquid Kio used on the pack of Rusty Lykaons, there was certainly a lot of poison and powder going around right now. That was probably because the Korloys and Nachtoys were adept with medicines and mixtures. But perhaps there was some connection to the fact that Nirrnir was a vampire—er, a Lord of the Night.

In the meantime, we crossed the Field of Bones and arrived at a hill with a good view of the huge dead tree—the Dragon Bone— thirty minutes before the meeting time the elves demanded.

There were a number of perfectly serviceable rocks atop the hill that offered us a hiding spot. We took turns watching the huge tree and took the time to rest and refuel. The morning sun was already shining through the outer aperture of Aincrad, which made me worry that Nirrnir would start taking damage despite the cloak and cape, but according to Kio, she would be fine during her coma as long as she was not exposed to direct sunlight. I thought back on her walk through the setting sun before the stables and recalled that she had weakened but not lost any HP.

Still, the silver poisoning was bringing Nirrnir closer to death, bit by bit. Our time limit was tomorrow evening. We had to find the Fallen Elf hideout *and* defeat the floor boss before then; there wasn't a moment to waste. I watched and waited impatiently, and around 6:55, Argo spotted two figures approaching from the opposite side of the wasteland.

Our hiding spot was over three hundred yards from the Dragon Bone, so the figures were just black dots in the distance. But that was all Kizmel needed to say: "They're Fallen."

The Fallen Elves were still elves, so ordinarily they wouldn't be able to cross the Field of Bones without using something akin to the Greenleaf Cape. But like the soldiers who attacked Castle Galey on the sixth floor, they were surely equipped with the taboo branches. Perhaps they had selected the Field of Bones assuming that no dark elves from Harin Tree Palace could get anywhere close.

I watched the two Fallen Elves reach the Dragon Bone. Of course, we couldn't leave our hiding spot. If we snuck up from the opposite side of the tree and performed an ambush, we could probably beat them, assuming they weren't Kysarah and General N'ltzahh. But they weren't going to give up the location of their hideout even under torture, and more importantly, Asuna wouldn't approve of that.

So we stayed crouched behind the rocks, prepared to wait as long as it took for the Fallen to move—or so we thought. But as soon as it turned 7:05, the pair began walking in the direction they'd come. For a brief moment, I thought, *You wanted people to meet you in the middle of the wasteland, you gotta give 'em a bit longer than that!* But then I remembered we were the ones who'd called them, not Bardun Korloy, and the sooner they went back home, the better for us.

So now it was eight o'clock, and we were hurrying to follow the Fallen Elves as they presumably returned to their hideout. I was worried because there were few objects we could hide behind, but we had the sun at our backs, so the light shining off the bleached ground offered a kind of natural camouflage, I hoped.

Either because we were in the midst of a special event or because the Fallen had used some kind of magical charm several hundred yards ahead, there were no monster attacks, despite the fact that we'd been walking for an hour since leaving the Dragon Bone behind. At some point, the sharp mountain peaks beyond the wasteland and the labyrinth tower looming behind them had become much clearer.

I adjusted my walking speed so I lined up with Kio, who was behind me.

"You've been carrying Lady Nirr this whole time. Are you okay? I'll switch with you if you're getting tired," I whispered.

The ever-loyal battle maid gave me an exquisite glare. "It is not a problem. I am not so weak that I would become 'tired' by carrying Lady Nirrnir on my own."

"Oh. Of course. Sorry," I said quickly. Her expression softened a bit.

"...But I thank you for thinking of me. I must not forget that the job I hired you to do ended with the investigation of the stable. There is no way for me to express my gratitude that you have done so much to save Lady Nirrnir's life, beyond the point your mission was done."

"Uh, gosh..."

I scratched behind my ear awkwardly, then cast a glance at Nirrnir, who was strapped to Kio's back. Her face was hidden by the hood of her cloak, plus the cape over it, but there was a golden *?* rotating slowly over her head. It was the indicator that Nirrnir was my current questgiver and would not disappear until I finished, failed, or abandoned the quest. I wasn't going to choose the third option, that was for sure.

"...Asuna and I didn't come to the casino to gamble. We came to Volupta to enjoy the beach," I said, looking back at Kio. For a moment, Asuna looked over her shoulder from where she walked with Kizmel ahead of us. She wasn't scolding me for talking about it, so I continued the story.

"To get into the beach, you have to win thirty thousand chips at the casino per person and get a pass, right? We'd never make that much playing normally at the card tables, roulette wheels...or the monster coliseum, of course. But we won a hundred and forty thousand yesterday, enough for me, Asuna, Argo, and Kizmel to get our own passes, and that was only because Lady Nirr hired us to do that job..."

At some point, I started losing track of what I was trying to say. A subtle smirk crossed Kio's lips.

"If you had simply asked, we could have arranged beach passes at any moment."

"Huh? R-really?"

"The staircase pass we lent to Argo has essentially the same privileges. They can be given indefinitely to anyone hired by the hotel owners."

"Oh...I didn't know..."

In that case, theoretically, we could have borrowed the pass directly after meeting Nirrnir, then gone straight to the beach, gotten our fill of sun and sand, and abandoned the quest before heading right to the next town.

But that would have left Argo to continue the quest on her own, so Nirrnir would presumably have been bitten by the Argent Serpent anyway. In that sense, I was glad that we hadn't gotten any unscrupulous ideas—but I wasn't sure if I wanted to express that to her.

"*Even if my brother, Huazo, and I serve Lady Nirrnir for all our lives,*" Kio continued quietly, "*we could never make up the debt we owe her.* Do you recall that I said this before?"

"Y-yes, of course."

I'd been wondering what she meant by that. Up ahead, Asuna and Kizmel were listening in careful silence, as was Argo behind us.

"Our father was a swordsman originally in the Korloy family's employ."

It took all my willpower to stop myself from screaming, *What?!* I managed to hold it to a simple nod, prompting Kio to continue.

"He worked in dangerous conditions every day on their monster-capturing team. But when I was six, and Huazo was four, the team was ordered to capture a monster in the northern mountains called an Amphicyon...They were successful at their mission, but there was one casualty: our father."

"......"

Amphicyon was the name of an extinct type of large carnivore that lived twenty million years ago in the real world, and they were some of the toughest monsters on the seventh-floor map. It was tough enough just to kill them; capturing them had to be significantly more dangerous. I wanted to close my eyes and offer a silent prayer to his memory, but I couldn't lose track of the shifting figures on the horizon. So I just nodded again.

"At the time, our mother had already died of a plague, so the family was just the three of us. Now our father was dead, and because we lived in the Korloys' quarters, Huazo and I were driven out with nothing but the clothes on our backs."

I didn't fail to notice the way Asuna's hands balled into fists. I felt a flare of anger in my gut, too, but held it back and focused on the horizon.

Kio gently adjusted Nirrnir on her back and resumed quietly, "We had nowhere to go and nothing to eat—my brother and I would have surely joined our parents soon if we were left on the street. But Lady Nirrnir was aware of our plight, and she sought us out in the backstreets of Volupta and took us under the Nachtoy family's wing. Although she was much taller than I was when we first met, I eventually outgrew her...But for the thirteen years since, I have never wavered in my loyalty and gratitude to her. No matter what happens, I must always do everything I can to save her."

She let her left hand drop to the pommel of her estoc, then lifted it up to hold the straps again.

It was a struggle to hold down the smoldering anger toward Bardun Korloy that rested in the pit of my stomach. But there was a question I'd repeated to myself many times that was rising to my mind once again.

Were the events Kio described *actual* things that happened thirteen years ago in this world—before *SAO*'s official launch? Or were they all just story points that had been programmed into her memory to serve as background?

But this was a pointless question. Asuna, Argo, and I were real human beings who were born and raised in the real world, and I knew we'd all been trapped in Aincrad due to Akihiko Kayaba's sick criminal scheme, but there was no evidence that any of this was the truth. It could be that we were AIs just like Kio, Kizmel, and Nirrnir—and that I was only being convinced that I was a player in a game by the name of Kirito or Kazuto Kirigaya.

"Thanks for telling us," said Asuna, the first to break the silence. Despite the fact that she was facing forward and speaking quietly, her voice carried strangely clear back to Kio. "I love Lady Nirrnir, too. I don't want to have to say good-bye to her. Just let us help you defeat this dragon."

It was clear that Asuna was delivering her answer to Kio's earlier statement: "Nothing can express my gratitude that you have already done so much to save Lady Nirrnir's life."

If I was, in fact, an AI, that would make Asuna one, too. But even in that case, the love she felt for the people of this world was still deep and true. It was with this thought in mind that I opened my mouth to say, "I'll help, too."

"Ya got me on yer side as well," added Argo.

"And me, of course," Kizmel finished.

Kio fell silent for a while. Eventually, she spoke, her voice very quiet.

"......Thank you."

It was the first time I'd ever heard her say those words—no, the second, after Asuna tried to use the healing crystal. But it was this thank-you that reached deep into my heart, resonating with me and leaving a lasting glow.

Whatever happens, we have to defeat Aghyellr and get that dragon's blood, I told myself. This, however, was not something we could achieve on our own, no matter how well we played. Defeating the game's first dragon-type floor boss would never happen without the help of the two big guilds.

Speaking of the DKB and ALS, they were traveling along the road south of the Field of Bones toward Pramio, the final town of the seventh floor. It always took more time when traveling in a big group, but they'd surely reach the town by this evening. They would stay the night, then head toward the labyrinth tower early in the morning. If they could reach the boss chamber before noon somehow, we *could* defeat the boss before Nirrnir's HP was gone for good.

That was an extreme pace compared to the usual speed, but as a matter of fact, we'd finished the fifth and sixth floors on a similar schedule, and both guilds had to have high motivation at the moment. That was because, last night, I'd offered Kibaou and Lind not just the Sword of Volupta as a reward, which they'd been desperate to acquire at the casino, but the equally broken Flag of Valor, the wildly valuable guild flag.

After we beat the fifth-floor boss, and I had earned the flag, I had relayed to the ALS two possible conditions under which I would give them the flag.

One was if another floor boss ahead dropped the same item. If that happened, I would ensure that both the ALS and DKB each had one flag.

The other condition was if the ALS and DKB merged. In that situation, I would immediately give their unified guild the flag.

These conditions were necessary to ensure that the power balance between the guilds wasn't broken, throwing the state of our best group of players into chaos, but even I knew that either of these conditions was going to prove very unlikely. Now we had another item, not the same as the guild flag, but a weapon with specs and potential on par with it.

The Flag of Valor had tremendous support ability but almost no attack value as a weapon; the Sword of Volupta had no benefit to allies but offered overwhelming strength to the equipper. If I was forced to choose between the two, it would definitely take me hours.

I told Lind and Kibaou that whichever guild helped more in the fight against the seventh-floor boss would be given the right to buy either the flag or the sword at a price of a hundred thousand col. Of course, the item that wasn't chosen would be offered to the other guild for the same price. Both men listened in stunned silence, surely because they couldn't believe the bargain they were getting.

If we sold both flag and sword at a hundred thousand each, then we'd be getting back the two hundred thousand col that Asuna, Argo, Kio, and I put in. But considering that Lind offered three hundred thousand for the guild flag on the sixth floor, I knew that either of them would have paid that much. Still, considering how we got the items, I didn't want to use them as a moneymaking scheme, and there was that matter of Kio, claiming that there was something she needed to explain to us about the Sword of Volupta…

I was about to ask Kio what she'd meant by that, but an instant sooner, Kizmel muttered tensely, "The Fallen have entered the valley."

Up ahead, the two figures had left the edge of the Field of Bones, walking into a canyon area beyond it. It was a place called Ant Tunnel Valley, with cramped ravines and tunnels in a complex three-dimensional arrangement that would get you lost, even with the help of a map.

And like the name said, there were monstrous ants living there, each one not too difficult but very quick to summon more of their kind. If you weren't careful, you'd find yourself surrounded by a huge swarm without an escape route.

"I'm guessin' their hideout's in that valley somewhere," Argo murmured ominously.

My brow furrowed. "There are tons of dead-end tunnels in there, too. It's the perfect place for a secret hideout. And it's dry, if not as dry as out here, so no dark elves or forest elves would ever waste their time there…"

"Even the monster-capturing teams at the Grand Casino hardly ever venture into the valley to capture ants," Kio commented. This was starting to feel as ominous as the commute to school late on a Monday morning.

But Asuna, who knew no fear as long as there weren't ghosts in the area, said crisply, "It's almost showtime. Let's get ready to rumble."

She was right: This wasn't the time to be feeling sorry for myself. There was no guarantee the four sacred keys would be at the Fallen Elves' hideout, but even if that was true, we'd surely find a clue. For Kizmel and for Nirrnir, I had to give this challenge my very best.

"Let's try to get closer without drawing attention. The ground is soft in the valley, so we should be able to follow their tracks, but if we lose sight of them, it could be a disaster for us."

Asuna, Kizmel, Kio, and Argo nodded with determination.

As soon as the two figures reached the entrance to the valley far ahead, we began to run, keeping our footsteps light.

24

"*NGUK...*"

The sound of my own choked snore woke me up, and I opened my right eye just a tiny bit. I checked the time, confirmed I had another thirty minutes until my personal alarm went off, and closed my eyes again.

A snore was the sound of the windpipe near the throat vibrating with the passage of air from the lungs, so it seemed a bit unfair that my avatar would snore when it was only pretending to breathe actual air. It was probably just some particular fixation of Akihiko Kayaba's, like the game's sneezes and yawns. I bet the man had also tested out a battle system where getting slashed with a sword brought terrible pain, gouts of fresh blood, and internal organs that fell out of the cut. The reason he didn't was probably because no one would want to challenge his death game anymore...or perhaps because it was beyond the ability of current full-dive tech to simulate.

This gruesome thought dispelled the sleepiness from my mind, so I gave up on falling back into slumber and rose to a sitting position.

The room was small, with reddish-brown stone walls. The floor was about thirteen feet to a side, which was a decent size for a real-world apartment room, but inside a tower that was over a hundred and fifty feet wide and three hundred feet tall, it was fairly cramped.

"…Are you awake, Kirito?" came a whisper.

To my left, with her back resting against the wall, the dark elf knight was smiling cryptically at me. I hunched my shoulders, thinking she heard my snoring, then crawled over to sit next to her.

"Did you even get any sleep, Kizmel?" I asked, just as quietly.

She blinked slowly in confirmation. "Yes. I just woke up a minute ago as well. Not that I slept deeply in the first place; I have never rested in a Pillar of the Heavens before…"

"I see. It's not my first time, but I'm always nervous inside a labyrinth," I replied. But this room was a safe shelter. No monsters would spawn within it or come inside, so the reason for my shallow sleep was something else.

After following the two Fallen Elves into Ant Tunnel Valley, we never found their hideout. We didn't lose sight of them or get spotted ourselves. They passed straight through the valley, in fact, then the plateau after that, and walked right into the labyrinth tower at the western edge of the floor.

This was not an outcome I expected, but we had no choice other than to follow them. We set foot in the tower before the ALS and DKB and pursued the Fallen as best we could, but there was no ignoring the monsters that attacked us in the dungeon. After a few battles, we lost sight of the elves and continued to explore, trusting that their hideout was somewhere in the tower, but here we were now, close to the very top floor.

It was already late at night by that point, so we used a nearby safe room to eat and catch some sleep, which was where we were now.

It was four in the morning on January 8, the fourth morning since we started on the seventh floor—and about twelve hours until Nirrnir's life ran out.

It hurt that we'd failed to recover the keys within the previous day, but at the very least, it seemed certain that the Fallen Elves' base was somewhere within this tower. As long as we meticulously searched through the map, we should reach it eventually. Once we beat the floor boss and saved Nirrnir, we could put our focus on finding them.

There were only one or two floors to go to the boss chamber, so once we resumed, we should find the hideout right away. But the main brunt of the player base, the DKB and ALS, were scheduled to arrive around midday. Whether we waited here or ground some experience nearby, eight hours was a painful length of time to wait with so much on the line.

I wanted to prod and push them to move faster, but not to the point of causing a careless accident. Besides, there was no way to send or receive instant messages while inside a dungeon. The only option was to wait it out, I lamented.

On the other side of the room, Asuna, Argo, and Kio, who was cradling Nirrnir, were sharing one giant blanket, fast asleep. Kio's consternation was painful to see once her master's HP dropped under 20 percent last night, so I wanted to let her sleep until she awoke on her own, but once the other girls' internal alarms woke them up, she would probably wake up, too.

At the very least, it would be nice to offer her some hot tea as she woke, I thought, and decided to get out the camping cook set from my inventory.

But just then, Kizmel leaned forward off the wall, and I soon heard it as well. Multiple sets of footsteps were approaching the safe room.

The heavy footfalls did not belong to any monster. But it was too early for the DKB and ALS to be arriving. The Fallen Elves made almost no sound when they walked, and the PKers were balanced for PvP combat and wouldn't have the gear and skill sets to fight in the farthest part of the labyrinth tower like this.

"Wake them up, Kizmel," I whispered to the knight, getting to my feet. There was just one entrance to the room, which was blocked by a door. If the group approaching us was hostile, I didn't want our only escape route to get blocked. I had to go outside before they came in, whether they saw me or not.

I grabbed my sword, which I'd taken off my back and rested against the wall, and rushed to the door. After a moment of careful listening, I quietly opened the door and slipped through it into the corridor.

The hallway went both left and right, and the footsteps were coming from the left. There were already multiple lantern lights wavering through the gloom.

Even when dealing with friendly players, contact in dungeons had to be undertaken carefully. There were many stories of players instinctively drawing weapons and attacking the other party in a rush for initiative, only to realize after the fact that it was someone you knew.

In order to avoid such accidents, it was best to first confirm the color of the other side's cursor, then make your presence known firmly and from a distance. I backed against the wall and activated the Hiding skill, then squinted down the hallway.

My eyes caught the vague figures behind the flickering lantern light, bringing up their cursors. The color was green. I exhaled with relief, then checked the name.

"Huh?" I blurted out, leaning away from the wall to stand in the middle of the corridor. The group noticed me then and came to a stop. A rich, baritone voice called out, "Hey, there. I shouldn't be surprised that you work fast, Kirito."

Three minutes later, I was back in the safe room, sipping tea against the back wall and grumbling about how cramped it was.

There were only four new players in the room, but they added a new level of sardine-packed pressure—because all four were large, burly men who used huge, two-handed weapons.

There was Agil, the bald, ax-wielding leader; Wolfgang, the swordsman with the wolflike long hair and beard; the hammer user Naijan, who was cool and macho; and Lowbacca, the scruffy ax wielder. *SAO*'s avatars were based on the appearance and build of the original player, so every time I saw the group, I was impressed that so many burly guys managed to find each other. I privately called this group the Bro Squad, and whenever they got around to making it an official guild, I hoped they took my suggestion and made it official.

The Bro Squad took up spots in the front half of the room and started a fire in a portable stove, cooked up some sausages, popped them in buns, and ate them loudly. Our group was all awake now and eating breakfast in a circle, too, but our menu was only tea and biscuits. I felt like I was as big an eater as anyone, but even I couldn't handle hot dogs this early in the day. But maybe my lack of hunger had more to do with the pressure of the boss fight we simply *had* to win coming up.

I finished the dark, strong tea, then turned to Agil and asked, "You know, I didn't see you at all in Volupta; when did you get to the labyrinth?"

The giant lifted his shoulders and an eyebrow at the same time. "Well, of course you didn't. We took the north route."

"What? You went on the Headwind Road?! Why?"

"Why not? If you have an easy route and a hard route, isn't any gamer gonna go with the hard one?"

"I said I was for the easy route, for the record," Wolfgang interjected. Naijan and Lowbacca both chimed in. "Yeah, that's right."

It was classic game design, of course, that if you chose a higher difficulty, there would be rewards to match. I was going to ask if they'd gotten good weapons from the trip, but Agil was a split second faster.

"So, Kirito...what's up with that girl? She's totally knocked out and barely has any HP left."

I glanced at the far wall, understanding why he'd be curious. There wasn't a single window in the seventh-floor labyrinth tower, so Kio took the light-blocked cape off of Nirrnir and had pulled back her cloak's hood. Her face was shockingly pale in the torchlight, and there wasn't a hint of life to her.

I rushed over to Kio to reassure her that Agil and his team were trustworthy, and she gave me permission to explain the situation to them. With her blessing secured, I returned to Agil and told them that Nirrnir was the head of a powerful house in Volupta, she'd been poisoned by a rival and her life would end by tonight, and only the blood of a dragon could neutralize the poison. The only thing I didn't mention was that Nirrnir was a vampiric Lord of the Night, but Agil's team didn't seem to sense any holes in my story, and I had a feeling it was the one thing Nirrnir should have the right to explain for herself, if she chose to.

The Bro Squad looked concerned about the state of affairs. They offered Kio their condolences and reassurances.

"That sounds like a tough card to draw. We'll help slay that dragon, of course."

"And we'll pound flat whoever poisoned her, you can be sure of that."

"Just tell us if there's anything else you need."

"Want a hot dog?"

Kio let her wariness of the large men subside enough to reveal her shock at the offer of so much help.

"Thank you," she said, "but I don't need anything to eat."

After our meal was done, we quickly packed up the stoves and utensils, then huddled in the center of the safe room.

When they were lined up this close, it was shocking just how *large* the Bro Squad was. In keeping with their appearance, they all focused on strength as their main stat. When combined with their imposing two-handed weapons, they easily had the best instantaneous damage potential of any group in the frontline population.

If the floor boss was a simple physical-damage-only kind of enemy, I might be tempted to try out the battle just with this group, but unfortunately, we were going to need shield-bearing tanks to counteract Aghyellr the fire dragon. It was going to blow fire breath on us, and our weapons wouldn't be enough to block it.

"I'm guessing the boss chamber is right above this room. I'd love to go right in there now, but we don't have enough people," I prefaced, before checking the time. "It's five AM now, and the ALS and DKB are scheduled to get here around noon. Which means we have to wait around this area for another seven hours. If anyone has any ideas about how to spend this time productively..."

Agil raised a large hand, so I pointed at him like a teacher would. "Yes, Agil?"

"We don't have to wait that long."

"...Huh?" I didn't grasp his meaning, so I stared up at the menacing—but also quite handsome—warrior. "What do you mean?"

"We just passed them around the fifth floor. They joined together into a thirty-person team, so they're on the slower side, but it's not going to take them *that* long. They should be right along."

"Huh?" both Asuna and I stammered. Argo, however, just grinned in silence from within her cloak's hood. I stared at her and asked, "Was this your doing?"

"Well, don't make it sound so sinister, Kii-boy." The Rat smirked. She put her hands on her hips and announced, "When we took a break at the entrance to the tower, I just gave Li-chan a little itty-bitty message: *We're already at the tower, so sorry if we beat the boss first.*"

No sooner had the sentence left her mouth than more sounds came from outside the door.

This time, there was no concern about groups of monsters or PK gangs. It was the sound of a stampede of footsteps—well, more than just ten or twenty.

25

DRAGON.

The word came from the Ancient Greek *drakon*, for *serpent*, a word that itself came from even further back in the Indo-European family, where it held meanings such as "to see," "bright," and "light."

As for why the word for "to see" evolved into *dragon*, it was apparently because dragon meant "something with a deadly gaze." It didn't make much sense to me when I read this on the internet in elementary school, but now, years later, I finally had the chance to experience what it was those ancients were so afraid of.

"Here comes the gaze! Everyone under level twenty, look down!" I shouted.

Two bloodred eyes flashed at the other end of the huge hall.

It was just light, neither hot nor cold. But an unpleasant freezing sensation raced up my back and prickled my skin all over. A number of players who ignored my warning and looked into the light froze up, affected by a stun effect.

The sources of light were two eyes with crimson irises and vertical slit pupils—the eyes of the seventh-floor boss of Aincrad, Aghyellr the Igneous Wyrm.

As I'd expected, Aghyellr was greatly strengthened since the beta test. One of the new features was the menacing gaze it emitted. It started by widening its wings, then flashing its eyes. If you looked into the light, any player under level 20 was immediately stunned. Asuna and I cleared that hurdle, but the recommended level for the seventh floor, if you accounted for a healthy safety margin, was only level 17, and most of the group was around there. Aside from us, the only 20s were probably Lind, Kibaou, Agil, Argo, and then Kizmel and Kio. If *SAO* wasn't a deadly game, you'd probably be able to finish the seventh floor at around level 10 with a lot of luck and ingenuity—and a good five to ten deaths—so it was asking a lot to expect people to be level 20 already.

But of course, the boss wasn't going to go easy on us.

In the back of the chamber, the massive dragon curved its long neck into an S shape, wings folded. Sparks began to spill from the edges of its closed jaw.

"Here comes the breath! Tanks, prioritize whoever's stunned!" I shouted again, and the six parties that made up our raid—teams A, B, and C, made up of the DKB, and D, E, and F from the ALS—gathered together, with the shield-bearing players taking positions up front. I was the leader of team G, and Agil was the head of team H, but because neither of our two teams had any shield users, we quickly retreated and hid behind the other parties.

Aghyellr's neck shot forward like a whip, and it opened its mouth wide.

Fwoom! The air trembled. The orange flames that emerged fanned outward, covering the long and narrow chamber.

As the flame breath hit the tank shields, there was an explosive roar, and the fire billowed upward, causing the experienced and talented frontrunners to shriek. Aghyellr wasn't the first boss to use a breath attack, but there was something about dragon fire that stirred primeval fears.

And unlike direct attacks, fire could still snake around the sides of the shield blocking it. If a six-person party bunched together as close as possible, they could all just barely fit behind a greatshield, but standing farther back, we still had to deal with the secondary wave of flames.

"Let's go...right here!"

Asuna, Argo, and I had Kio and Nirrnir surrounded, and on Kizmel's instruction, we used single-hit sword skills to the left and right against empty air. Four different attack vectors cut through the onrushing flames, neutralizing it. There was still a major cloud of sparks, however, and I couldn't help but swear, "*Ouch!*"

The reason that swearing was the worst I had to deal with was thanks to an icon below my HP bar featuring a shield and flames. A flame-resistance buff was extremely valuable in *SAO*—and we had that thanks to Argo, who pulled out all the Snow Tree Buds in her inventory and sprinkled the entire raid party with their ice water. If not for that, each bout of flame breath, even if blocked by shield and sword, would have taken a good 10 percent of our HP. To our right, the Bro Squad was utilizing a similar tactic, except that it was one person using a wider Two-Handed Sword skill, with the other three ducking behind him to escape the brunt of the fire.

Watching them almost made me want to try out the Two-Handed Sword skill. The rolling wave of flames passed by us and died out. Up front, a voice barked out sharp orders.

"A and C, move up and strike its left leg! D and F, take the right! B and E, pull back and heal! G and H, strike from the sides!"

At those words from Lind, the scimitar-brandishing leader of DKB, a few dozen players roared and charged. He'd been elected primary leader of the raid on a coin toss, and it was perhaps a sign of how crucial this fight was that the ALS's Kibaou was following those orders without comment.

Asuna and I were usually treated as "miscellaneous" members

during boss battles, but since we were offering special rewards this time, we were allowed to give orders to the raid as special supervisors. I'd told them I would give the guild flag or Sword of Volupta to whichever guild "helped more"—which was intentionally vague and undefined because I wanted to avoid a simple competition to inflict more damage—and that instruction had brought us this unexpected bonus honor.

But for now, I was only speaking up to warn about the boss's special moves. Lind was doing fine ordering the group's attacks. And honestly, when it came to keeping tabs on the HP levels of each party and moving them forward and back, he was a better leader than I was. Despite their bickering, Lind and Kibaou were both proving themselves to be good learners.

The attackers surged toward Aghyellr's front feet and began to hack at the beast while it was slowed after the breath attack. Aghyellr was over thirty feet long, and its head was twelve feet off the ground in a normal stance, so the usual strategy against monsters of this size was to attack their feet and get them to lower their heads. That was how we'd beaten Aghyellr in the beta, in fact.

Our teams weren't just standing around, either. We followed the leader's orders, the four of us aside from Kio (carrying Nirrnir) racing at full speed toward the left side of Aghyellr from our perspective and slamming our sword skills into the beast's unguarded flank.

Two or three seconds later, the Bro Squad's giant axes and hammers were smashing at the right side of the boss. In our second group attack, we eliminated the first of Aghyellr's six HP bars.

The Irrational Cube from the sixth floor only had a single bar, so six seemed like an endless slog, but this boss didn't have any complex puzzle gimmicks like that cube did, and the dragon's defense wasn't boosted up as high as I feared. If we could take out one whole HP bar in two rounds of offense, that meant ten more attack chances to finish the other five bars. *Not that it's going to be that simple*, I thought, just as Aghyellr recovered from its sluggishness and emitted a metallic roar.

"Arm attack...left!"

The DKB attackers around the left-front leg—the right leg, from Aghyellr's perspective—quickly retreated. The arm lifted high into the air and slammed into the ground like a piece of heavy demolition equipment, creating huge cracks in the ground. Nobody was hit directly, but three or four of them were swallowed up by shock waves that were impossible to avoid, losing about 20 percent HP.

"Now comes the right!" I continued, and it was the ALS's turn to back away. A ferocious rumble shook the entire boss chamber. The hit could be fatal if inflicted directly, but it was such a slow and obvious attack that nobody talented and dedicated enough to be a raid party melee fighter could fail to dodge it.

While it swung its arms, teams G and H continued to attack its sides, grinding down over a third of the second HP bar. The DPS numbers for Asuna, Argo, and the Bro Squad were top of the class among the group, but it was Kizmel's attack power that was truly outrageous. Even with a replacement weapon, her single-attack sword skills inflicted as much damage as two-part, two-handed skills.

But it's too dangerous to get greedy, I reminded myself, right as Lind cried, "Everyone withdraw!!"

He must have caught some lead-in movement of the dragon's head, which I couldn't see from my position. We rushed straight for the rear of the chamber, the sound of myriad scales sliding and scraping behind us. I glanced over my shoulder as I ran and caught sight of Aghyellr's huge body curled into a C shape.

Then a tail like a tree trunk swung forth and pulverized the stone walls to the left and right. Dust clouded the area, hiding the dragon's body. An omnidirectional tail attack was something new since the beta. The first time it used it in the fight, it caught three people, taking 70 percent of their health in one hit.

With everyone safely out of range, Lind gave the order for

the damaged parties to switch with the parties who had been staying back and recovering with potions. Next would be another menacing gaze, followed by another breath attack, I guessed. As long as we avoided the gaze, we could deal with the flame breath.

"At this rate, we might not even need to use that sword," Asuna whispered. I glanced over at the Sword of Eventide in my right hand.

She was referring to the Sword of Volupta, the weapon we'd gone to such lengths to gain in order to motivate the DKB and ALS—and to use as an ace up our sleeve against Aghyellr—but it was still in my inventory. It was registered to my quick-change setting, but I didn't want to equip it if possible. That was because, earlier in the labyrinth, Kio had explained the downside behind those broken specs, and they were worse than I could have imagined.

As for Kio, she was still carrying Nirrnir strapped to her back with those leather cords. We tried to convince her to wait outside the boss chamber with her mistress, but she insisted, and we had to give in and allow her to come with us. But with the boss's attacks demanding more dynamic forward-and-backward movement, and her burden leaving her unable to sprint, Kio was having trouble taking part in any of the offense.

She recognized her struggle, too, and gripped her estoc with obvious frustration. "I'm sorry...I was hoping I would prove to be useful..."

"Don't worry. Your job is to protect Lady Nirr," I replied at once, patting the maid's arm. "If you waited outside the chamber, there was a possibility that several powerful monsters could have spawned all at once. As long as you stay near the door, none of the attacks will reach you aside from the flame breath, and we'll be there to protect you from that. Our goal isn't to defeat the dragon but to save Nirrnir's life with its blood, right?" I said, speaking as fast as I could to save time. Kio looked me in the face and bobbed her head.

Up ahead, Lind shouted, "Here comes the gaze!"

Through the clearing haze of dust, I could see Aghyellr's wings stretching wide.

It seemed that the boss's attack pattern was fixed: gaze, flame breath, front leg attacks, tail attack. As long as you dealt with the gaze and the tail attack properly, we could push all the way through the fifth HP bar. It might change up its style on the last bar, like some previous bosses, but as long as we kept everyone's HP up, we should be able to withstand its near-death frantic mode.

I squeezed the hilt of my trusty sword and glared back into the crimson glow of Aghyellr's eyes. *Do your worst, you scaly bastard!*

From that point forward, the battle played out largely as I expected.

When we reached the fourth HP bar, meaning we'd finished off half of its health reserve, Aghyellr threw in a curveball by blowing fire three times consecutively, causing the majority of the frontline fighters to lose over 30 percent HP, but Lind and Kibaou deftly worked the groups into a healing rotation, and we were able to recover.

From that point on, the regular pattern resumed, and we took down the fourth bar, then the fifth. Forty minutes after the battle began, we reached the sixth and final HP bar of Aghyellr the Igneous Wyrm.

"Watch out for different attack patterns! Focus on guarding until you receive the order to attack!" Lind called out. The raid party turtled up on defense, with the tanks at the front. Agil's team and ours held weapons up to block whatever unknown attack came next.

"*Gwurrrrl...*"

Aghyellr growled in the very back of the chamber, low and long. It was deeper than its previous utterances, which put me in mind of a rage like oil threatening to ignite and explode.

The walls and floor were shattered all over from dozens of impacts from arms and tail, and pieces of rubble littered the ground. In fact, the buildup of obstacles had made it harder to approach the dragon's flanks, but pretty soon, I suspected, we'd be able to disable its legs. If its head fell down to the floor, we should be able to press a full attack that would take out the last bar.

Suddenly, Aghyellr's growling stopped. The wings spread to the sides.

"The gaze! It might be powered up! Everyone, look down, including level twenty and up!" Lind shouted. I recognized his logic and gave up on staring it back, looking at my feet instead. Asuna and Kizmel did the same on either side of me. The gaze effect activated about three seconds after the wings moved; I counted down the seconds in my head.

One, two...

"No! It's not!" shouted Argo, the first to notice. There was a flapping sound now.

"...?!"

I looked up to see Aghyellr floating toward the ceiling, beating its wings powerfully.

Even in the beta, Aghyellr had never flown—no boss monster had, in fact. Fuscus the Vacant Colossus from the fifth floor had its face stuck to the ceiling of the chamber, and the Irrational Cube from the sixth floor had floated ten feet high above the ground, but neither of them were really "flying."

Neither I nor anyone else in the raid knew what to do in the moment, so we froze.

"H-hey...he's flyin'! What's the plan, Lind?!" Kibaou demanded at last, but Lind was still stuck in place. Even I couldn't tell what the best course of action would be yet.

Aghyellr rose nearly forty feet to the ceiling in a blink, and then its eyes flashed red.

The gaze attack!

"Aaaah!"

"Aieeee!"

Screams erupted from all over the chamber. Everyone in the raid party looked the dragon full in the eyes. Everyone under level 20—which was 90 percent of the group—was going to fall to the floor, stunned.

A stun was different from paralysis. It only lasted about three seconds, but three seconds was an agonizing lifetime right now, because Aghyellr was most likely about to...

"It's going to breathe fire!!" Kizmel shouted, just as it opened its massive jaw and belched a mass of solid flames.

Unlike the previous breath attack, which fanned outward, this was a fireball about three feet across. A curtain of sparks sprayed from the sphere as it hurtled toward the center of the chamber. That was no simple ball-shaped mass of fire.

"Protect Nirrnir!" I shouted, covering Kio from behind where she stood in shock. Kizmel, Asuna, and Argo followed me, pressing in.

Just get through this, everyone! I willed to my fellow raid members, preparing for the shock.

Half a second later, the ball made contact with the floor—and caused a mammoth explosion.

First came the shock wave, then a wall of red flames a split second later. Clumped up together, we did our best to hold our ground, but it was impossible to withstand. We were tossed backward as though slapped by a giant hand and flew directly into the wall.

"Urgh..."

It felt like my body was going to be shattered to pieces. I willed my eyes to stay open so I could focus on not my HP bar, but Nirrnir's.

There had been only 10 percent left, and the damage of the impact instantly gouged away more, putting her under 5 percent. We'd avoided instant death, but that was only because Kio was able to turn her body to take the brunt of the impact herself just before hitting the wall. In fact, she'd taken so much damage that she went all the way down to 30 percent, and an unconscious icon appeared.

Asuna's HP was at 60 percent. Argo was at 50. Kizmel and I were at 70.

A heavy rumble passed through the floor. Aghyellr had concluded its hovering and landed in the center of the floor. The shock wave of the explosion slammed nearly every stunned raid member against the walls, where they collapsed atop each other. After a quick check of our HP list on the left side of my vision, I could see that no one had died instantly, but everyone was wounded. Many of them had only 20 or 30 percent remaining.

"*Goaaahhhh!*" Aghyellr roared triumphantly in the center of the room. It curved its neck to look at where Lind and team A were collapsed. All of them were deeply wounded; a single swipe from the dragon's claws would finish them off.

"Urgh…" I groaned, trying to get to my feet, when I heard a faint voice.

"Kirito, stand me up."

I looked to my right, feeling the breath catch in my throat.

Behind Kio's back, where she slumped unconscious against the wall, Nirrnir's eyes were open, just slightly, and staring at me. Up close, the crimson irises pierced my own.

"Hurry."

Her voice was a barely audible rasp, but there was a stately command to it that was impossible to refuse.

I nodded, then used my sword to cut the straps holding her down, circling my free hand around her tiny body so we could stand together. The others were recovering from the shock of the impact and were looking at us in stunned silence.

Nirrnir left my arm to stand on her own, faltering slightly. She undid the clasp of the cloak and let it fall to the floor. Her long golden hair danced in the gusting, swirling aftermath the explosion had left behind.

In the distance, the fire dragon was taking step after step toward Lind's group. It was barely ten yards away from them.

"Kirito, give me Falhari's sword," Nirrnir said, reaching toward me.

Deep in my heart, I knew this was coming. There was no other way out of this harrowing disaster in the making.

But Nirrnir only had 5 percent of her HP remaining...and because she had awoken from the comatose state the lobelia flower poison caused, the continual damage of the silver poisoning had resumed. She surely had less than a minute before it was all over.

Feeling like my insides were being torn to pieces, I opened my window and pressed the QUICK CHANGE button. The Sword of Eventide was wreathed in a white effect and vanished, replaced by the Sword of Volupta, a longsword of platinum and gold.

I held it out by the hilt and set the handle in Nirrnir's hand.

Her little fingers curled around the red leather of the grip.

Immediately, the white jewel set into the pommel shone crimson. An invisible energy pushed back against my hand, causing me to stumble a few steps back. Nirrnir's blond hair and black summer dress began to swell and swirl in the sudden gust of wind that rose, spiraling, from the floor.

The crimson light moved up the golden ridge on the flat of the blade and lit it up just as brightly.

The blade, which looked like platinum silver, turned a partially translucent black, like gilt melting and evaporating.

Yet the sword could not possibly have been made of silver. Only a Lord of the Night could draw out its true power—it was a vampire's weapon.

The moment the sword's tip took on its true color, the crimson flashed even brighter on the pommel and ridge. Aghyellr, sensing something was happening, stopped moving forward and swiveled its head around to look this way.

Nirrnir promptly pulled back the shining red sword with both hands and swung it forward with a piercing cry.

"Haaaaaa!!"

The scarlet blade of energy cut through the stone floor ahead of her and flew onward with shocking speed toward Aghyellr. But just before it split the beast's scaly snout, the fire dragon leaped sideways with uncommon agility for its size. The slash passed it with a heavy *zrunn!* but severed Aghyellr's left arm and wing at the root.

The sixth HP bar drained. It hit 70 percent, 60, 50—and then stopped.

"...I failed," Nirrnir whispered. The Sword of Volupta slid from her hands and made a strange sound as it fell to the floor.

Her little body slumped over like a puppet with no one controlling its strings; I held out my hands to support her. She had 3 percent of her HP remaining.

"Nirrnir!!"

I went down to a knee and cradled her head. Her closed lids fluttered and opened very slightly.

"Please, Kirito. Take Kio and run."

"Nirrnir..."

"Don't bother with me. At least save Kio..." the girl rasped, the light in her crimson eyes wavering, flickering, then pooling in small droplets.

Her remaining HP was 2 percent.

In the distance, Aghyellr was roaring with fury. But I paid the dragon no heed—my mind was busy racing.

How to save Nirrnir, Kio, the girls, and all the other players here? There had to be a way. Had to, had to, had to...

"Please..."

Nirrnir's voice was nothing but exhaled air now. Behind her thin lips gleamed white teeth...no, fangs.

Suddenly, I realized the only option I could take.

"Nirrnir, drink my blood!!"

"......"

The dying girl's eyes opened just a bit more. Her HP amount was down to 1 percent.

"...No. If I do that, you will—"

"I don't care! It's the only way! I'm not going to regret it! So please...take my blood!!"

I stared into her eyes from just inches away, pleading with her, then lifted her head and pressed her mouth to the left side of my neck.

Her lips trembled against my skin with deep hesitation and distress.

But then they opened wider, and two sharp fangs pierced deep into my neck.

There was no sense of pain in *SAO*. A sword could chop off one of your hands or feet, and all you'd feel was an unpleasant numbness. But strangely enough, just this once, I felt a sensation of pain, purely honed, colder than ice, and yet somehow sweet, all over my body.

Nirrnir's mouth and throat worked furiously, drinking all the blood flowing from my neck without missing a drop. When I dripped blood on the Scyia map from my finger, it was only a visual effect without physical form, but I could *feel* hot, thick liquid passing through my skin.

The girl's HP bar, with its 1 percent remaining, began to quiver. The continual damage of the silver poisoning was battling the recovery effect of her vampirism. Without the actual dragon blood, I couldn't purify the poison in her veins, but as long as this overpowered the damage, I could buy Nirrnir a few more minutes—or perhaps even longer.

Please...please work! I prayed, glancing briefly at my own HP bar, which was already under halfway. Obviously, there was no point if I died, so if I couldn't neutralize Nirrnir's poison by the

time I reached 10 percent, Asuna or Argo would have to take my place. I hoped it wouldn't come to that.

The floor trembled irregularly. Aghyellr was approaching. With the loss of its left wing and arm, it couldn't run normally, but it would surely reach us within thirty seconds...no, twenty.

I'm not going to make it in time, I lamented.

"Draw its attention! Hold it back!" shouted a rich baritone that filled the hall. I saw Agil and his companions charging toward Aghyellr from the right side. They'd all lost more than 30 percent HP, but there was no hint of fear in the way they brandished their two-handed weapons and struck at the dragon's leg.

They must have volunteered to buy time, trusting that I had some miraculous, do-or-die plan in mind. I couldn't leave them out there to die—but Nirrnir's HP bar still wasn't showing any signs of increasing.

My HP sank under 30 percent, approaching twenty. Was the gain from my blood perfectly equivalent to the continual damage of the poison? Even still, I couldn't just give up...

At that very moment, someone grabbed my right shoulder and called out a command in a loud, determined voice.

"*Heal!!*"

A pink glow surrounded my body. My HP bar, which had been close to 10 percent, instantly shot back to full, all the way to the right.

After a brief instant of shock, I realized what had happened. Asuna used our one healing crystal, the one we'd picked up from the Verdian Lancer Beetle, on me.

Healing crystals had no effect on a Lord of the Night. But even still, the healing power that melted into my blood seemed to confer some kind of effect to her...

Rather than jittering in place back and forth, Nirrnir's HP bar finally, just barely, began to increase instead.

Her mouth let go of my neck, and her hoarse voice sounded in my ear. "Thank you. I will be fine now."

Nirrnir had recovered a bit of color in her cheeks, and she gave me a brave smile, clearly withstanding a lot of pain.

"The dragon, Kirito. You can do it now."

I nodded and stood up straight, still holding Nirrnir around the side. Beneath my full HP bar, there was an icon I'd never seen before.

It was an image of crimson fangs over a black background. I didn't need to look at my status window to know what it signified.

All of a sudden, I was overcome with a strange sensation.

The warmth was draining from my skin—from my insides. I wasn't chilly. It was like my body temperature itself had gone cold. Although I couldn't see it myself, I was sure my skin must have gone extremely pale.

There was a strange, tickling sensation inside my mouth, and my upper canines suddenly sharpened. My vision was oddly clear and crisp, allowing me a very sharp view all the way to the far end of the previously gloomy chamber.

Fortunately, I wasn't struck with any sudden thoughts like, *I must have blood!* That was obvious, of course; the Nerve-Gear could control my bodily senses, but it couldn't control my thoughts. Still, I couldn't help but be a bit relieved.

I spun on my heel and handed Nirrnir over to Asuna. My partner gave me a piercing upward gaze but took the little girl anyway and stepped back. I sent her a look of apology, then picked the Sword of Volupta up off the ground.

It seemed to stick to my palm, fitting right in. I squeezed hard, and the blade glowed red again. Beneath my HP bar, three new icons appeared. My guess was that they represented poison nullification, HP regeneration, and increased critical hit rate.

The true name of the semitranslucent, obsidian-like sword was Doleful Nocturne, according to Kio; Asuna filled me in on the meaning of the words, which was something like "mournful night song." As the pamphlet at the casino claimed, it gave the wielder three extremely powerful buffs, but at the penalty of your soul power—meaning that it absorbed your accumulated experience points. Most likely, the real name and appearance had been hidden to conceal the fact that it was a terrifyingly wicked sword.

Only one kind of person could wield this sword without the downsides: a Dominus Nocte, or Lord of the Night. I opened my window just to check and did not notice my experience points going down. In other words, by allowing Nirrnir to suck my blood, I had also become a Lord of the Night—just like the ancient hero Falhari, who used this sword to slay the water dragon, Zariegha.

Was there a way for me to turn human again, or would I be like this forever? That was a question I didn't need to answer at the moment. As I told Nirrnir, this was the only way to save everyone. I didn't have an ounce of regret over my choice.

I gave the sword a light swing. Now that it was taking its true form, the feeling of flimsiness I got the first time I held the weapon was gone, replaced by a hefty strength that reminded me of my old friend, the Anneal Blade.

With both hands on the long grip, I hoisted the weapon high overhead. I wouldn't be able to activate any One-Handed Sword skills, but instead...

"Agil, get back!" I shouted, drawing the attention of the Bro Squad from where they stood keeping Aghyellr occupied. They gaped at the sight of me and quickly retreated.

With all my strength, I swung the sword straight down and promptly flipped my wrists to continue sideways. The brilliant red slash formed a cross-shaped shock wave that flew forward.

Dodge that one, if you can! I taunted the dragon. Aghyellr's right wing extended in another attempt to slide out of the way.

But the cross slash hit it right at the base of its neck, easily cutting it loose from the torso. Its long neck writhed like a great snake in the air, body and arm spinning backward with the force of the blow.

An explosion of blue flames erupted all the way to the ceiling, and Aghyellr the Igneous Wyrm's body split into pieces.

26

THE SOUND OF THE WAVES EBBED AND FLOWED.

Sea breezes carried the scent of flowers with it.

Fine white sand caressed my bare feet.

At last, our relaxing vacation time on the beach had arrived. We were only missing one thing: skin-burning sunshine pouring down out of the blue sky.

But I couldn't have that, or else I would burn up into ash.

It was nine PM on January 8.

I was standing in the simple kitchen on the private beach owned by the Volupta Grand Casino, peeling fruit with a knife.

The large basket on the work table was piled high with various kinds of fruit. I grabbed one, stuck in the knife at a suitable angle, and spun the fruit along it at a suitable speed. The peel slipped right off in a highly satisfying manner.

I handed the fruit to Kio, who deftly cubed it with a kitchen knife and tossed the pieces into a tremendous crystal bowl. The bowl was already full of a one-to-one mix of sweet sparkling wine and red wine. With each handful of fruit pieces tossed inside, the mixture wafted out more sweet, floral scents.

The only light to guide us was the lamp hanging from the ceiling and the moon's rays coming through the doorless entryway, but it wasn't a problem for me at all; I just focused on a place, and my eyesight would adjust in brightness automatically. The Search skill gave me fairly decent night vision already, but the vampiric version of it was on a different level entirely. The drawback, of course, was that just the sight of daylight through the window would make me scream and clutch at my eyes.

It wasn't just my night vision that was strengthened, however. I could feel that the proficiency level of various skills I hadn't learned yet had already been raised without my effort. Ordinarily, peeling this fruit wouldn't be as easy as it was proving to be without some levels in the Cooking skill and Daggers skill.

That made me curious about what other skills might be boosted by the effect, but I couldn't get carried away. With every great power comes...well, you know. Things I hadn't had to worry about before—mainly, sunlight and silver—were now a fatal weakness to me. In terms of everyday problems, the most frequent issue would be hundred-col silver coins, which would fizzle and burn my skin just by touching them.

Asuna, ever diligent, suggested we go through all our belongings and throw away anything made of silver, but I didn't think we needed to go that far...Though, maybe we *should*. If I turned to ash from silver weapons or sunlight, my biological brain was going to be fried by the NerveGear's powerful microwaves.

What to do, what to do, I wondered, rapidly peeling the fruit. *Shwik-shwik-toss, shwik-shwik-toss.*

Suddenly, Kio stopped slicing fruit and asked quietly, "Do you feel like rethinking this yet?"

"Huh? Oh...you mean *that*."

I stopped peeling and looked straight ahead. It was difficult for me to stare directly at Kio because she was no longer wearing her usual armored maid outfit—but a black one-piece swimsuit with a white apron over it. And she still had the estoc equipped.

Instead, I stared down at the mango-like fruit in my hand and cleared my throat. "Well...Asuna and I are adventurers. We have to go to the very top of Aincrad..."

"What will you find there?"

"I—I don't know…I couldn't say…" I mumbled, but the truth was that I *did* know.

On the first day of *SAO*'s official launch, Akihiko Kayaba took the form of game master in a red robe and told us, "There is only one condition through which you can be freed from this game. Simply reach the hundredth floor at the pinnacle of Aincrad and defeat the final boss that awaits you there. In that instant, all surviving players will be able to safely log out once again."

I couldn't imagine that boss's name or what it looked like, but one thing was certain: There was a final boss waiting for us on the top floor. If we beat it, all surviving players would be freed from this death game and wake up in the real world—and most likely, Aincrad and all the NPCs who lived inside it would disappear.

She sensed the sudden spike of pain in my chest. "Why do you pursue something that may not exist?" she asked, staring at the half-cut fruit on the board. "I have built a lifelong debt not just to my master but to you as well. In Volupta, you can lead a pleasant life without exposing yourself to the sun. There are plenty of medicines and tools for the people of the night, and we now have a full stock of dragon's blood, so you can survive without needing human blood. You should have accepted Lady Nirrnir's offer. Stay and live here with Asuna."

I'd be lying if I said I didn't consider it—if just for a brief instant.

But I couldn't take that option. If I gave up on beating this deadly game here, I would be betraying all the players who died up to this point, all the players waiting on the first floor for the game to be finished, all my fellow players advancing our progress, and of course, Argo and Asuna.

"…I have to go. I have to," I said simply, resuming peeling.

After a while, the sound of the knife chopping continued. Muffled by the sound, I heard her murmur, "I see."

We continued our work in silence, and in three minutes, all the fruit had been peeled and chopped into the bowl. I lifted the large fruit punch container and left the simple kitchen in the corner of the beach, which consisted of not much more than a water faucet and a prep table.

Immediately, I was met by a sight that could only be described as stunning.

The white sands covered an area that was easily five hundred yards across. Beyond that, the sea was a deep, dark blue, with the light of the moon shining brilliantly off its surface. There were dozens of torches standing along the beach at equal intervals, providing a perfect orange contrast to the blue of the night sky and water.

And at the water's edge, frolicking and laughing, were four women.

"It's all ready!" I called out as the two of us walked over. The four of them looked our way and waved.

Asuna, Argo, Kizmel, and Nirrnir were all wearing swimsuits Asuna had crafted with the Tailoring skill. It was a difficult sight for a middle-school boy like me to stare at, but I managed to keep my gaze steady by claiming to myself "I'm a vampire now!" as if that explained anything.

Just before the water's edge was a white table lined with ten beach chairs painted the same white color. I placed the crystal bowl on the table while Kio pulled out large glasses from the basket she carried in her other hand, setting them in a line.

Asuna and Argo left footprints in the wet sand as they ran over and exclaimed with wonder at the massive, fanciful presentation of fruit punch. Kizmel added an impressed "Oooh," and Nirrnir opined, "A very impressive display."

I was doing my best not to stare *directly* at their swimsuits with my keen night vision when a baritone voice said, "Wow, look at that!"

Four burly men were standing up from the seats on the left side of the table. Agil, Wolfgang, Naijan, and Lowbacca chose not to take the spiral staircase to the eighth floor, escorting us back to Volupta from the labyrinth tower. As thanks, Nirrnir invited them to enjoy the beach with us.

That was all fine and good, but why had they all chosen not to wear ordinary swim trunks like me, but revealing thong swimsuits instead? Their musculature was already bursting outward when they were fully geared up; now all that physical pressure had nothing to contain it.

Fortunately, neither Nirrnir, Kio, nor Kizmel seemed to mind. The fact that Asuna and Argo both seemed to be avoiding looking at them told me that, somewhat to my surprise, the Rat was still modest on the inside.

I was picking up the crystal ladle to start serving punch when Argo said "Not so fast" and opened her window. She removed five pale blue orbs: Snow Tree Buds. This was after she'd handed out buds to nearly fifty raid members. I asked her, "How many of those things do you *have*?" but Argo just smirked and tossed the five buds into the bowl.

"That's all of 'em. I'll hafta go pick more," she said. The buds were all cracking and opening, revealing petals that looked just like ice crystals. Nirrnir, who'd been sleeping during the exhibition before the boss battle, exclaimed, "Wowww..." with a look of innocent wonder that suited her features.

At the end of the early-morning battle against the floor boss, after I'd unleashed that cross-shaped slash from the Doleful Nocturne that defeated Aghyellr the fire dragon, and its huge form burst into a million shards like all the other bosses, there was one thought on my mind that precluded any celebration: "He blew up! What about the dragon blood?!"

I momentarily panicked, wondering if we were supposed to capture the dragon without killing it and use some kind of tool to extract the blood. Thankfully, *SAO* was not that cruel. Among the gobs of items that the boss dropped, there were seventeen jars of Fire Dragon Blood.

Asuna and Argo got close to ten jars themselves, but the Bro Squad didn't get any, which suggested to me that only players who'd been involved in Nirrnir's quest were set up to receive them. I tossed the sword into my inventory, materialized one of the jars, and rushed over to Nirrnir's side.

Close to 30 percent of her health had returned from drinking my blood, but the silver poisoning wasn't gone. Kio came to again and dipped her finger into the jar of blood, allowing Nirrnir to feed that way. By the fifth dripping, the debuff icon for silver poisoning went away. The relief that I felt in that moment rivaled the way I felt on the fifth floor, when I reunited with Asuna after she fell through the trapdoor in the catacombs.

Leaving Kio and Asuna to tend to Nirrnir, I turned to engage in other post-battle wrap-ups. This time, I couldn't sit back and watch the ALS and DKB lock horns. I needed to decide which of the two "helped out more" and offer that guild either the guild flag or the Sword of Volupta (Doleful Nocturne).

Or so I'd thought.

While I'd been busy, Kibaou and Lind had already spoken about the matter, apparently. The spiky-haired Kibaou scowled and said, "You can decide which guild ya wanna sell the flag or sword to at the next boss."

My mouth fell open. Lind shrugged and added, "After the sorry mess we made of things this time, it seems more than impertinent to argue that either of us really 'helped.'"

The guilds went to the staircase that appeared in the back of the chamber and ascended to the eighth floor.

Honestly, this came partially as a major relief to me; I didn't think I could have picked a winner between the ALS and DKB. But it was only kicking the can down the road a little. I hadn't yet explained to them about the terrible cost of using the Doleful Nocturne: its experience point drain.

If the draining effect absorbed one's accumulated experience but nothing more than that, it was something you might work around. But if it drained until you hit zero and leveled your avatar down, nobody was going to want to use it. The only solution was to become a vampire like I did, but that presented a new problem.

According to Nirrnir, when a Dominus Nocte sucked your blood, you didn't get all the power of your new master. Your actual title would be Civis Nocte, or Citizen of the Night, and your battle power was inferior across the board—although, with the increase I'd gotten, I couldn't begin to imagine how powerful a Lord of the Night would be—and the biggest difference was that you couldn't create followers of your own. I had fangs, so I could suck blood, and sucking human blood would restore some HP, but whatever player or NPC I feasted upon would not become a Citizen of the Night.

In other words, if anyone in the DKB or ALS wanted to become a vampire to use the Doleful Nocturne without penalty, they would have to be preyed upon by the Lord of the Night, Nirrnir, and she was very unlikely to say yes. She had gone for at least ten years—probably much longer—without once drinking human blood, and even as her life was hanging in the balance, she resisted drinking from me for so long.

In any case...

The big decision had been delayed until the eighth floor, and I returned to the others still holding both "broken" items. My partner looked like she had several things to say about what I'd done, but for now, she let me off with nothing more than a pat on the shoulder.

I wanted to return to Volupta at once, but we couldn't rush out into the outdoors with the light of the morning blazing all around. Over ten hours remained until sundown, which presented a decision to make. To my surprise, however, Nirrnir suggested we continue exploring the unmapped parts of the tower to search for the Fallen Elf hideout.

None of us protested, and the Bro Squad even offered to help out, so we continued filling out the map with a huge party of ten, slicing and dicing monsters as we went. After about three hours of this, Nirrnir's accentuated Lord of the Night senses kicked in, and she spotted a hidden door at the end of a cramped side hallway that even Argo couldn't spot.

This is it! I thought. Once everyone was fully ready for battle, we opened the secret door, but the small room beyond it was empty, containing nothing more than what looked like an old-fashioned altar. Neither Asuna, Argo, nor even Kizmel knew what it was, but after a careful examination, Nirrnir had the answer.

"This is an ancient teleportation device," she said.

As I reclined in the beach chair, enjoying a glass of fruit punch chilled with icy snow tree flowers, I gazed up at the night sky to the west. With the aid of my night vision, I could even see the faint outline of the distant labyrinth tower.

If we could figure out how to use that teleportation device, we should be able to reach the Fallen Elf hideout, once and for all. But most likely, that hideout was on the eighth floor, not the seventh. There was no other reason for them to place the device all the way at the top of the tower.

Nirrnir said she would look up how to use the device in some old books, once we got back to the hotel. After we received that information, we'd probably leave this floor behind.

On the eighth floor, I'd be forced to only move around at night. Asuna was the type of person who liked to get her sleep at night, so our activity time would no longer be aligned. If she brought that up as a reason for us to split up, I certainly couldn't blame her.

If I could turn from a Citizen of the Night back into a human, that would be best, but even Nirrnir didn't know how to do that, sadly. *Maybe the king of the forest elves or the queen of the dark elves would know,* she suggested, but if we set foot in the forest elf capital on the eighth floor, the guards would probably attack us en masse.

After running through various ideas in my head, I found my gaze drawn back to the distant tower.

This time, I noticed my temporary partner, sitting in the beach chair just to my right. She had her own glass of fruit punch in hand and was staring out at the sea with clouded eyes. She was wearing a simple white swimsuit, but combined with her clear skin and long brown hair under the moonlight, it seemed like her entire body was glowing. That couldn't *all* be due to my increased night vision.

The guys chugged their punch before returning to the inn, and Argo had simply fallen asleep in her chair, so there was no one left to tease me. I took advantage of the opportunity to gaze at my partner for at least a good ten seconds.

"...How long are you going to stare?" she said, which caught me so much by surprise that I nearly toppled out of my chair onto the sand. Thankfully, I recovered my balance and stammered, "I—I was j-just thinking that you look beautiful..."

Oh, shoot. That was just adding fuel to the fire. Or rubbing salt in the wound. Or whatever other idioms there are...

But my careless comment had an unexpected effect on Asuna. She was briefly stunned, then recovered and hissed, "A-are you really that stupid?" Then she turned in the other direction.

On her right side was Nirrnir, followed by Kio, Kizmel, and the sleeping Argo, but none of them seemed to have heard us. On second glance, the three who were awake might have been smirking to some degree, but I could pretend I didn't see that.

Asuna was silent for a while after that. Eventually, she said to Nirrnir, "Listen, Lady Nirr. If I wanted to be a Lord of the...er, a Citizen of the Night, would you drink my blood?"

"...!"

I sucked in a sharp breath and opened my mouth, intending to speak.

But Nirrnir just shook her head. "Don't bother. You are traveling with Kirito, aren't you? If both of you are Citizens of the Night, who will protect you during the day?"

"...But..."

Nirrnir held up a hand to silence Asuna. She sat up in the beach chair. Her slender body was clad in a two-piece black swimsuit of Asuna's design. Her luxurious blond hair shone like platinum in the pale moonlight.

She held up her right hand, exposing the skin around the wrist to the reflected rays of the moon. There were two very faint marks there: the wound from where the Argent Serpent bit her.

"There are more than a few who would dare to capture or kill a Lord of the Night. To most humans, we are closer to monsters than other people."

She lowered her hand and picked up her fruit punch from the table at her side, taking a sip. The ruby-colored liquid caught the moonlight and swayed with the movement of the glass.

"My grandfather, Falhari, was also a Lord of the Night. He defeated the water dragon, Zariegha, not to save the girl who was meant to be sacrificed but in order to gain the dragon's blood that would give him greater strength. You've come from the lower floors, I presume; did you not think it was strange you never ran across any dragons?"

Both Asuna and I nodded. Nirrnir did the same, then glanced over at us.

"That is because Falhari hunted them all down. He was living in a large town on the first floor but was banished for some reason I'm not aware of, then went up to the second and then third floor, slaying dragons as he went. Here on the seventh floor, he slew Zariegha the water dragon and was going to continue on his way, as he always did. Only the people whose village he saved hailed him as a hero, even knowing he was a Lord of the Night. I suppose he must have found that pleasing, because Falhari stayed in the village, wed the girl who was offered as a sacrifice to the dragon, and they had twin sons."

That much matched the story we heard from Kio earlier. I swallowed and listened, rapt, to the girl's story of the distant past.

"...But when a child is born to a Lord of the Night and a human, their chances of becoming another Lord of the Night are very low. Falhari's blood rose to the surface in me, his granddaughter, but my father and his elder twin brother were both human. After decades, their mother grew old and died, but Falhari didn't seem to age at all. When his sons began to grow old, too, they feared and despised their father. They couldn't accept that they might die before him, without ever receiving an inheritance. They became bitter, not like the bright and dandy young men of their youth...So one sunny day, they snuck into their father's bedroom. The elder brother tore down the nailed shutters over the windows, and the younger brother drove a silver blade through Falhari's chest. They killed him with the dual powers of sunlight and silver."

"What?!" I gasped, unable to stop myself. Asuna and Kio were wide-eyed with surprise. Even the longtime servant of the Nachtoy clan hadn't heard this part of the story.

"B...but then...that whole story about Falhari in his old age, pitting the rival sons against each other in a series of five monster battles to determine the true heir..."

"They made it up."

"Wha......?"

I was speechless.

From the farthest beach chair came the voice of Argo, whom I'd assumed was still fast asleep.

"Uh-huh. So the 'secret art of commanding monsters' that Falhari supposedly learned was a special ability of a Dominus Nocte, eh? His sons were human, but they did inherit that ability at least, I suppose."

"That is correct, Argo. The direct descendants of the Korloy and Nachtoy clans, even if born as humans, can at the very least use the art of Employment. So his sons used that ability to control monsters that would fight in their stead, in a competition to see who would inherit the hero's fortune. And the townsfolk, unaware that Falhari had been murdered, enjoyed the fights. Everything after that is as you know already."

"......"

I had an intuition from the moment I held the Dominus Nocturne that Falhari was a Lord of the Night, too, but I had no idea that such a gruesome, bloody secret was at the center of the Grand Casino's fanciful backstory.

With some hesitation, I asked her in hushed tones, "Is that the same reason that Bardun Korloy is trying to kill you? Because he resents that you will live longer than him...?"

The girl pondered this and took another sip of her punch. "You might say that, but it's not the only reason. For a long time, the Grand Casino has been operated by the Nachtoy and Korloy families together, but in a sense, it is only that way because I wish it to be."

"Meaning?"

"It's very simple. As the head of the Nachtoy clan, I do not perish, but the Korloy head changes every few decades. Bardun was late to have children, and his only heir is just ten. He cannot yet use the art of Employment well, so if Bardun dies, I will be in charge of the Korloys' monsters for a time. It would be very easy for me to effectively control the Grand Casino all on my own at that point. Bardun is afraid of that outcome."

"B-but," Asuna protested, sitting upright, "if you are gone, the coliseum itself will no longer function, will it? Surely Bardun understands that."

"Maybe he's thinking that if Nachtoy is going to control the whole thing after his death, it might as well crumble to dust altogether," Nirrnir said, shaking her head. She had recovered all of her beauty prior to the silver poisoning, but there was something in her manner that seemed exhausted, hollowed out. It caused me to hold my breath.

Bardun Korloy was likely to continue keeping Nirrnir in his sights. He would use whatever means he could to assassinate her, for as long as he lived. There was no guarantee he wouldn't have another trap as clever as the Argent Serpent that would ensnare her.

"Hey...Nirrnir," I said, leaning over the side of the beach chair to speak directly to the Lord of the Night—to *my* lord, in fact. "Would you and Kio come with us? I'm sure you'll have your hands full with the casino for a while, and it'll be difficult to avoid the sunlight, but there won't be constant attempts made on your life. There might be easier places to live on the floors above, and you might meet other Dominus Nocte...Besides, traveling is fun. The world is full of things you've never seen, beautiful things and wondrous sights."

She did not answer for quite a while. Kizmel and Argo just smirked with exasperation, and Kio was simply agape. Asuna had her back to me, so I couldn't see her face, but I knew that she would approve of the idea.

"Ha...ha...ha-ha-ha..."

Eventually, Nirrnir's tiny shoulders began to shake with mirth. It developed into open, delighted laughter, even more forceful than the way she reacted to the sight of me breaking narsos fruit with my bare hands.

"Ah-ha-ha-ha, ah-ha-ha-ha-ha-ha..."

She continued to laugh, spilling bits of punch at times. At last, the moment subsided, and she exhaled. Then she looked up at Asuna and me.

"Thank you. I'm sure it's the most tempting offer I've received in all my life...But I cannot go with you."

She didn't explain why, but I had a feeling I shouldn't press her.

"...Okay," I said, leaning back against the chair. There was a bit of fruit punch left, so I finished it off and chewed the mystery fruit at the bottom.

A slightly chilly night breeze blew past, whipping the beachside torches into action, one after the other. The ebb and flow of the waves mingled with the distant bustle of Volupta.

Just then, an animal howled, over to the west. *Awooooooo...*

I turned and saw, on top of a boulder at the very edge of the beach, a small silhouette. The skinny body and roundish ears identified it as a canine-type monster, but it was too far away for its cursor to appear for me. On a closer look, however, I could see a short chain hanging from a metal ring around its neck.

The monster lifted its snout toward the bottom of the floor above us and bayed proudly once again.

Another, slightly smaller monster of the same kind appeared, sitting down next to it. The moonlight coming from outside the edge of Aincrad lit the two, creating a dazzling silver sheen around their fur.

We said nothing but merely watched the two creatures until they left the top of the rock for a destination unknown.

(The End)

AFTERWORD

Thank you for reading *Sword Art Online Progressive 8*, "Rhapsody of Crimson Heat (Part Two)."

(The following will touch heavily upon the content of the book, so beware if you flipped to the afterword first!)

First, to address the subtitle of the seventh-floor story, "Rhapsody" is a word that refers (among other things) to a free-flowing musical composition that is unbound by most traditional forms. My initial plan was for the seventh floor to consist of a number of independent events happening in succession, but the casino plot turned out to carry most of the weight on its own. The "Heat" referred to the casino excitement that consumed Kirito, Lind, and Kibaou, and the "Crimson" looked like the blazing sun hanging over this floor of eternal summer—or so you'd think—but actually was the color of blood. Thankfully, Kirito didn't get *that* absorbed in the lures of gambling (*laughs*).

But while Kirito might have kept his cool in the casino, he was unsurprisingly driven to extreme measures and made a very impactful choice...Will he be able to conquer the eighth floor doing a "nights-only" run? How will he stay safe during the day? Will he be able to eat any delicious, garlic-heavy dishes again? There are many questions and concerns, but you'll have to wait for the next volume to find out the answers!

Speaking of which, I plan for that volume to get into the climactic part of the "Elf War" campaign questline. It started on the third floor, so the idea that we're finally to the forest elf castle on the eighth floor is rather fulfilling, isn't it? Still, there are a number of mysteries left about the Volupta Grand Casino (What's on the locked fourth floor? What will Falhari the Founder's judgment be? Where did the Korloys tame the Storm Lykaon? Why does it cost money to do the taming? Why were there bonfire shrooms in the hidden passage to the casino? And so on…), so I think Kirito and friends will go back to the seventh floor again. Something tells me old Bardun isn't going to give up after this setback. Look forward to that, too!

Moving on. I wouldn't want to take up more of your time (and this afterword) writing about COVID-19 each volume, so let's talk about something more enjoyable.

There's an *SAO Progressive* movie out! It should be out in Japan! The subtitle will be the same as the first-floor story of the series: "Aria of a Starless Night." But there will be new characters and a greatly beefed-up narrative, so I really hope you get the chance to see it on a big theater screen. And you better believe that everyone's favorite will be there: Diavel!

Like the sixth floor, the seventh took two books to tell, which made a lot of work for my illustrator, abec, and my editors, Miki, Adachi, and Hirai. But thanks to them, I'm very happy with how this story turned out. Thank you so much! I hope to see you all in the next volume!

Reki Kawahara—April 2021

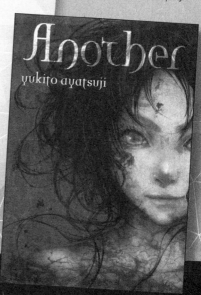